Linda Smolkin

Among
the
Branded

A NOVEL

ISBN 978-0-9986171-1-4 (paperback)

Cover design: AS Designs
Cover photo: Shutterstock
Book formatting: Ebook Launch

This is a work of fiction. Names, characters, businesses, places, organizations, events, and incidents portrayed in this novel are either a product of the author's imagination or used fictitiously, and they are not to be construed as real. Any resemblance to actual persons, living or dead, events or locales is entirely coincidental.

Chapter 1

It all started with the Moo Shoo Chicken, wreaking havoc on one of the moms in the upstairs bathroom. I felt for Jane, but had no desire to wear the shaggy costume meant for her. Svetlana stood next to me while the kids ran around, some playing tag, others spilling punch on the kitchen floor.

"Hey, guys," she said, "put down the juice boxes, or somebody's going to get hurt."

She grabbed a sponge and bent down to clean up the mess.

"Rockin' party," I joked.

"More like raucous. Put a bunch of four-year-olds together, and I'm having a love fest with the linoleum."

Sveta, as I'd called her for years, stood up and gave me a mischievous look, as if she was about to share some juicy gossip about a neighbor on her cul-de-sac. Instead, she asked me to take Jane's place and dress up as Ripsie the Retriever. She asked twice then begged. It brought me back to when we first met, and she insisted I tag along for a Thursday-night Happy Hour.

"Why can't you wear it?"

"Because I'm reading the book. And you're taller—it'll fit better."

I washed my hands and reached for some pretzels. "Uh-huh, great excuse."

There wasn't enough birthday cake to make me agree. *I'm claustrophobic*, I could say. *I'm allergic to dogs*, crossed my mind, even though I had my own version at home, a German Shepherd named Ginger. But the more I thought about it, I couldn't disappoint Sveta's grandson, Evan, on his fourth birthday. So on a Sunday afternoon, I became Ripsie.

I went to a spare bedroom overflowing with Evan's toys—a half-built spaceship near the door, coloring books and markers on the desk, an unfinished puzzle on the floor. I stepped over a train set, slipped my legs into the costume, and pulled it up and over. I looked pretty cute as a retriever, I admitted to myself in the mirror, even if I was bright yellow and already sweaty.

I took one last look then stepped over the train set again and waited in the hallway for Sveta's cue. First, she read *Ripsie Goes to the Bakery* then *Ripsie Makes a New Friend*. After finishing *Here Comes Ripsie,* Sveta said, "Well, kids, does anyone see Ripsie? Where could she be?"

From around the corner, I came out on all twos, waddling along as I waved both hands and wiggled my tail. A kid stood up and stopped in front of me.

He stayed there for a moment then shouted, "That's not Ripsie! That's some guy in a costume."

It was Evan.

He shouted some more. "Take off your head and show us your face!"

I was horrified and couldn't move.

Sveta walked over to whisper something to him. He sat down while a few kids came up to hug me and sit on my lap. "I love you, Ripsie," said a sweet girl. "You're so soft and fluffy," said another.

After a few more sweaty minutes and several waves good-bye, I walked back to the bedroom and changed out of the costume. I opened the door, startled to see Evan waiting there.

"Ha! I knew it!" he roared with laughter.

"Knew what?" I brushed the top of his hair then pushed softly on his nose. Evan reminded me of Jack when he was that age—so clever, so opinionated.

"You were Ripsie!"

"No, I wasn't!" I bent down to get a better look at his brown eyes then tickled him so he'd laugh a little harder.

"Yes, you were!" he shouted and took off with a mad dash when Sveta yelled, "Pizza's here. Come and get it."

As I put Ripsie back in the closet, it dawned on me that our little Evan could not be fooled. A few months earlier, he figured out his dad was the tooth fairy by comparing the fairy's letter to a grocery list on the fridge. When Evan was three, he knew Sveta was Santa after recognizing her ring accidentally left next to the glass of milk for hardworking Claus.

And because he couldn't be fooled, it crossed my mind to borrow Evan, to bring him home with me to see if Greg, the love of my life, was being honest or diplomatic. First, I'd ask Greg the not-too-serious questions, while Evan stood on the sidelines to give me a sign, a nod for yes, a cough for no.

Does my butt look big in these jeans?

Is my cooking really better than your mother's?

If that went well, we could move to some more serious questions.

Will you love me the same way in twenty years? Or, more pressing, *Will I be able to hold it together when Jeremy leaves for college?*

"Mom, I can't believe you dressed up," Jack said as I closed the closet door.

"Did I embarrass you?"

He gave me that what-do-you-think look.

"Who knows, maybe I found my calling," I said.

He picked up the half-started spaceship and looked through pieces on the floor to add to it, pushing aside rejected colors. "All the kids keep following me around."

"That's because they like hanging out with older kids. You did, too, when you were that age."

"Yeah, when I was young."

I laughed hard. That was one of Jack's favorite phrases, as if he were a seventy-year-old man remembering the days of his youth. The laughter stopped, but my smile remained. How and when did my twelve-year-old grow up so fast? Was it the time I blinked to let him win our staring contest over winter break?

My phone pinged, and I grabbed it from my pocket. These days, I had to put all my reminders in the phone or I'd forget to take care of them. Everything was in there. Change the sheets. Take Jack to taekwondo. Pay the bills. Water the plants. This time it was a more interesting reminder about our getaway.

We decided to take a short trip after dropping Jeremy off at college, and Jack would choose the place, within reason. For the past few months, we'd been so busy finalizing college plans, shopping for supplies, stockpiling food for Jeremy, and now it was Jack's turn for attention. I cleared the reminder from my phone and asked if he'd made a decision.

"Let's go to the Bahamas, to that resort in the commercials."

"Sweetie, it's hurricane season, and I can't take that much time off work. What if we hit a few theme parks?"

"That's boring."

Sveta walked in, overhearing our conversation. "Since you like costumes so much, why don't you go to Valor of the '40s?"

"What do costumes have to do with it?" I asked.

"You were so good as Ripsie. Maybe you'll want to reenact a war."

I rolled my eyes. "You're joking, right?"

"Only about dressing up. Jack would love it. They have World War II planes, tanks, all that cool stuff. And it's near Jeremy's college."

"Mom, can we go?"

"Sounds interesting. But maybe something more relaxing?"

"You just said theme parks. How's that relaxing?"

Jack had a point. He always had a point. He was twelve after all, and he was onto me like my expression lines.

"Okay, I'll talk it over with Dad. But learn more about it so you can teach me something new." I wasn't much of a history buff but could be convinced. Besides, the trip had to be Jack's choice, as we'd promised.

We followed Sveta back into the kitchen. Evan blew out his candles, and we passed cake around the table. Some asked for seconds, and I thought, *Why the heck not? You're only four once.* I handed out more slices, scooped out more ice cream, and began to imagine Valor of the '40s. Did I really want to go to some World War II event to see a bunch of guys pretend-shoot at each other or planes take off and hope they wouldn't crash down because of their age? Hell, I was hoping I wouldn't crash down because of my age, and I was only forty-three.

Jack sat in front of Sveta's computer and scanned the event's website while reading the schedule of activities out loud. Maybe it would be interesting and at the same time take my mind off Jeremy's departure. I took a piece of cake and loaded ice cream on top.

"How come she gets three scoops? I only got two," whined one of the little girls who loved me for my soft and fluffy exterior a few minutes ago.

I ignored her, giving my ice cream the excessive attention it deserved. *I'm allowed to have three scoops,* my cute little friend with blonde pigtails. I'm sending my first kid off to college in just a few weeks.

Chapter 2

On the way to Pennsylvania's Freymont College, Jeremy drove while Greg sat in the front giving unwanted driving advice. Jack and I claimed the back and kept a close eye on snacks for the three-hour trip.

"Jeremy, don't forget to check your blind spot," Greg said while holding on to the handle. "And put on your blinker."

"Dad, I got this."

I wasn't about to get involved, having earned my fair share of being called the backseat driver. This time, I kept quiet. Honestly, I wasn't sure if he actually could see behind all that hair, the same style surfers wore in the North Carolina coastal town where I grew up. They always flipped their long, sun-bleached hair to the side after riding a wave before straddling the board again. Jeremy did a similar version of the same move after he signaled and went into the left lane.

"Jesus, would you cut that hair already," I let out, even though I promised to stop bringing up Jeremy's hair in conversations.

"Honey, could you leave Jesus out of this," Greg said. If he'd been able to take his grip off the door, he would have turned around to grab my hand and give me a smile, with that look he always gave me when we both accidentally said that. I'm not sure why he cared. We weren't religious. Sure, we'd been to our share of ceremonies, but as a family we'd never gone to church.

When it came to praying, the last time was in seventh grade when I asked God for Brad Litton to notice me. My dad said I mumbled all the time, so I'm pretty sure my message got messed up because in college I wound up dating Greg Britain, whom I married right after we graduated. Besides, Brad Litton turned out to be one of those jobless surfers who aged faster than the bananas left uneaten on my counter.

Greg held on to the car door for dear life, as if he were holding onto Jeremy's hand while crossing a busy street. Jeremy was always the cautious one, the shy one, the one who never left our side. Now, instead of hiding behind my leg in an elevator, he was behind the wheel of our car, whipping his hair to the side, changing lanes on his path to freedom.

What better way to get distracted than with Jack's hysterical laughter? I leaned over to get a better look at the screen. He wore his headphones and had his nose to the screen watching funny videos. He loved them, no matter how old they were. I could tell by the mullet haircuts and oversized shoulder pads that it must have been around 1986, the same year I graduated high school.

***

I woke up to chatter then a door being slammed before realizing I'd slept the last hour of the trip. I stepped out of the back and stretched, noticing the SUV parked diagonally across two spots. College kids walked by, some smiled, others laughed at the ridiculous parking job. Greg was covered in sweat.

"That bad?" I asked.

"Only the last three hours."

"That's so not funny," Jeremy said.

Jack was still in the car with his headphones on. I knocked on the window and motioned for him to come out. We took turns pulling items out of the back, from boxes filled with snacks and bottled water to pillows, blankets, suitcases, and a desk lamp.

"Things have changed," Greg said. "We weren't allowed to have all this stuff in our room." He grabbed Jeremy's computer bag and slung it over his shoulder. "I can't even remember if I typed or handwrote my papers. Steph, do you remember?"

"Don't you mean cave etchings?"

Greg elbowed Jeremy and the two pretended to spar. Jack walked away as if he didn't know us.

"Hey you," I said. "Come back and help."

We went to the third floor and down a long hall before getting to Jeremy's room. A nightstand sat under a large window and separated two twin beds. A built-in wardrobe and two desks took up the rest of the space. His roommate hadn't arrived yet, so Jeremy chose the bed on the right and threw his clothes on it.

After lining up the snacks and bottled water, I called out, "Who's ready for lunch?" Jeremy told us to go without him, that he'd stay behind and help Ben settle in. Before leaving, I wanted to give Jeremy some last-minute advice—lock your door, hide your laptop, don't party too much, keep that zipper up, wear a condom, don't forget to change your sheets, don't get a girl pregnant, eat your fruits and vegetables. Instead, I bit my tongue and gave him a big hug, not wanting to let go. "Enjoy this time. It goes way too fast."

"Let us know if you need anything," Greg added. He looked away for a moment, his way of holding it together.

"Take care of Ginger," Jeremy said as he leaned in for an awkward hug with Jack. "She needs lots of exercise."

I turned around for one last look. The bed seemed in disarray and reminded me of how Jeremy's bed looked as Ginger jumped off when Greg would come home from work. Ginger was Jeremy's best friend, but her love remained with whoever fed her the most.

"Steph, we should go," Greg called from the hall.

"Coming."

I felt pulled. Part of me wanted to give him that last-minute advice after all, and part of me wanted to hug him again. I did neither. I took a deep breath then turned around and walked toward my two other boys who were waiting at the elevator. Greg and I glanced at each other, both with eyes like the "before" shot in an allergy commercial. As we got on the elevator, Greg glanced at Jack who was smiling.

"Why are you so happy?" Greg asked.

"I get Jeremy's room now, remember?"

***

We drove off, and Greg hit a speed bump after forgetting to slow down.

"Jesus, Jeremy," I accidentally said when my head hit the side of the door. Greg reached for my hand.

"You'll be fine," he whispered.

Those words, in that tone, were all it took. I searched the glove compartment for a tissue and snagged one that had already been used. "At least I'm not blubbering like the time we saw *Let Them Go*. Remember the ending?"

"Yeah, you were a mess," Greg said.

"Me? You bought an extra-large soda and popcorn on the way out for—what was it, four hundred bucks? Just to ease the pain," I said while checking a text message from Sveta who made sure I was holding up okay. I texted her back:

Doing fine. Jeremy's settled in. On our way to Waltersboro.

Greg and I were good at going back and forth and making fun of each other. And besides, it helped to laugh off that bittersweet moment. Jack was already far away, laughing his head off at more videos. I wanted to ask if he'd done his research to learn more about Valor of the '40s. But why spoil the moment? I tapped on his knee and asked him to share the

9

screen so that we could share a laugh. A laugh at other people's expense. Why did millions of us love that? Was it really that funny? Or was it because the people in the videos could also find the humor in themselves?

"Hey guys, look," Greg said with the excitement of an old man greeting his grandkids at the airport. "Steph, roll down your window," he added while several people in cars on the other side honked and waved.

In the right lane up ahead, a vintage car powered along. It was vintage all right, but nothing on it looked old. Polished to perfection and painted like creamy vanilla pudding, the car outshined anything on the road. The convertible top was down and tucked in the back. The walls of the tires were outdone only by chrome so bright I could have used it to put on my makeup—if I wore more.

A woman sat in the driver's seat dressed in a red blouse. She wore a matching hat and held it down with her hand. A watch with a thin black strap inched its way up her arm and, even though her other hand was on the wheel, a man dressed in a gray pinstriped suit leaned over to help steer. That hat, it seemed, was dear to her. And for some reason, I imagined her elsewhere, not in this beautiful car, but strolling down New York's Madison Avenue, stopping at every jewelry store to admire earrings and necklaces in the windows.

"Ask her if that's a '41 model," Greg demanded.

"That's embarrassing. I'm not leaning out the window like some redneck."

"Rednecks are people, too, ya know."

"Jack, where do you come up with this stuff? I asked.

"Come on, do it for me," Greg begged.

I rolled the window down all the way, and when we were next to each other, I waved. Her passenger noticed first and waved back. Then the woman looked over and smiled. Her red lips, painted in the same shade as her dress, completed the look, as if they were an elongated dot on the letter "i."

"Is that a 1941?" I yelled.

"Close. A '42," she yelled back.

"It's a beauty," Greg shouted over me.

The woman put her hand next to her ear to show that she couldn't hear. Her hat flew off suddenly, which uncovered her blonde hair done in long loose curls. Luckily, her passenger caught the hat in time. She smiled and waved goodbye as Greg let her pass. What a gorgeous woman, like one from a 1940's advertisement. I'd seen many of them when studying typography in my advertising design classes. During those semesters, I spent more time looking at the outfits than examining typefaces.

"I wish we still dressed like that," I said and glanced down at my faded cargo pants and sneakers, all a little too comfortable, a little too convenient. A woman from that era wouldn't have been caught dead in my outfit. I lowered the visor and looked at my dark circles permanently etched from too many we-need-it-yesterday deadlines at work. I smoothed down my hair and put on some lip gloss, but the circles would have to stay untouched for now.

The woman turned left at the next crossing. Greg was about to follow then stayed straight when he saw a sign for Visitor Parking. Before we got out of the car, my phone pinged with another text from Sveta:

Behave while there! Don't trade in Greg for a cute soldier… or your sneaks for combat boots ;-).

Chapter 3

We passed through the entrance and tried to keep up with our enthusiastic son. Trucks whizzed by. Small planes took off and landed on a nearby strip. Music, popular from this bygone era, blasted through loudspeakers and was occasionally interrupted by historical announcements.

Jack stopped and eagerly awaited us, pointing at a large plane up ahead. "A B-17 Flying Fortress!"

"What's a Flying Fortress?"

They shot me the side eye but kept quiet.

"So I slept through half my history classes, what's the big deal?"

As we got closer, a sign said that you could take a ride in this authentic bomber for a mere five-hundred dollars a pop.

"Can I?" Jack asked.

"For five-hundred bucks? Sure, no problem, I've got it right here," Greg joked as he pretended to check all his pockets.

With a kid in college and the owner of my advertising studio considering retirement, we'd recently talked about tightening our belts—even though I'd never spend that kind of money on a plane ride down military-memory lane.

We continued toward the Russian camp, the one Jack asked to see first, passing more soldiers, some walking slowly arm in arm with beautiful girls in dresses cinched at the waist. More red lips and hair curled and set with deep parts. Sheer stockings with black seams that went up the back of the leg. No short skirts or exposed midriffs here. Sexy had revived itself in the cleavage of an open-toe shoe.

As we approached, I heard Russian, a language I recognized because Sveta was not only my friend but a coworker. She always cursed out the account managers and their ridiculous deadlines, and she did it in Russian so they wouldn't understand.

Within the camp, Greg and Jack stopped to check out the weapons. I kept walking around since the last thing I cared about was who shot at whom and with what. A young woman dressed in a long skirt and an apron like the one worn by my childhood friend's Polish grandmother caught my eye. A flower-patterned scarf covered her black hair, which spilled out underneath and grazed her shoulders. She sat on a blanket peeling potatoes, and when done, she cut them and moved the pile into a separate pot. Next to her, a young boy dressed in an oversized uniform plucked on a small instrument that resembled a ukulele. A man stood in front of them, snapping photographs.

Earlier I'd teased about falling asleep in history class, but I knew plenty about certain aspects of the war. Pearl Harbor. The atomic bomb. And the Holocaust, from my grandfather's hasty story about being an infantryman. But there was so much I didn't know. I had no idea they allowed kids to fight. I was about to ask, but the photographer beat me to it. The young woman stopped peeling potatoes to answer.

"They weren't allowed to fight until they turned eighteen. Well, they could have lied about their age, and some did, but Yuri's only ten. He's an orphan of the division."

"What do you mean, orphan?" the photographer asked.

She continued, fully engaged in her role as a reenactor. She had a slight Russian accent, and I couldn't tell if it was put on for show or if Yuri was his real name. But nobody seemed to care. She had our full attention. "Yuri's parents were killed during the war. When the division came through, he was living in the house alone. They couldn't leave him there, so the unit unofficially adopted him. He doesn't have the love his parents would give but has food, company, and as much safety as possible."

"Does he do anything for the unit? Does he help you?" a woman asked.

"Yes, he helps me feed the soldiers, cleans up after them, and sometimes sees what lies ahead."

"Sounds dangerous," said a grandfatherly type with a white beard. By now, there was a crowd around them.

"It can be," Yuri finally piped in. "But I'm small and quick, and the Germans never see me coming."

There was laughter around the circle. I even started to laugh but caught myself. If this were real life, Yuri's situation would be tragic. Only ten years old, an orphan, not sure what the next day would hold. I reminded myself that this was an event, not the real thing, that Yuri, or whatever his name was, would go home at the end of the day, take off the uniform, and play like any other ten-year-old boy.

I felt a hand on my shoulder and jumped. Jack and Greg had caught up to me and were ready to visit the other camps.

As we turned around to leave, we overheard a heated conversation between a Russian soldier and one from another camp, a German soldier with a red swastika armband and slanted SS letters on the collar of his jacket. Standing next to them was a young boy. The boy wore a khaki shirt, dark shorts with a matching tie, and knee-high socks with lace-up boots. His shirt had several patches, one with a slanted S similar to the one on the German soldier's uniform.

"That's really disturbing," the Russian soldier said.

"It's no different than what you guys do," the German declared, pointing at the young boy on the blanket. "Or what he does. It's no different."

"Are you serious? He's dressed as a Hitler Youth."

The German soldier, who sounded American by his accent, lowered his voice and stepped closer to the Russian while we pretended not to listen. "Look, this is part of history. We can't be denied to represent it. You probably forgot it was mandatory to be in the Hitler Youth."

"Come on! You know that's not exactly true. Not until 1939 when kids had to join. You'd better get your facts straight."

"No problem, I've got plenty of facts. Don't pretend the Red Army didn't partake in their fair share of atrocities."

The Russian moved closer and stood a few inches from the German. "I think it's a good time for you to leave—before I say something I'll regret."

The German soldier and boy walked off, and as they got to the border of the Russian camp, the soldier turned around. "Don't forget, it's a free country."

"Well, don't forget," the Russian added, "you won't find any sympathy here. Like you did in France."

"*Tavarish*, calm down," another Russian called out while pouring tea from his samovar. "We will get him at the Battle of Berlin."

"And the Führer will meet his demise," the first one declared in his thick accent, with an index finger held high.

The three of us stood there, eyebrows raised, wondering what the hell happened. A Russian soldier caught our surprise and grinned. "Don't worry, comrades," he said. "There's nothing that a shot of vodka and a pickle can't fix."

"Don't mess with the Russians," Jack snickered as we walked off.

"Is it just me, or did it feel like we were extras on some Hollywood set? I almost yelled out, 'And … cut!'" Greg added.

Over the loudspeakers, they made an announcement that a reenactment between the U.S. and Japanese would begin in five minutes on the north side of the field. People rushed to get a good spot like a bunch of seniors vying for an early-bird special. Jack and Greg really wanted to see it, but I wanted to walk around and see other camps.

We decided to split up and meet in the middle by the food kiosks in an hour. I waved goodbye and stood for a moment. Not sure which way to go, I remembered the Russian and German confrontation and wondered if there was a French village here. I wasn't quite sure why I wanted to see it; I was totally on the Russian's side, agreeing with everything he said, except for the part about vodka being a cure-all.

My feet ached, and I was about to take a break when I saw French signs and makeshift houses up ahead surrounded by tanks, covered trucks, and motorcycles. To the right, a soldier walked a bicycle and a few more were cleaning and putting away their razors and combs. Another soldier, wearing a gray uniform and a hat with a skull and bones, chatted with a young woman who sat on the step of a two-story house. She bent over to fix his collar, and I noticed the same SS emblem I'd seen earlier on the German soldier in the Russian camp. When they began to giggle, it startled me and made me stop—it felt so real, as if I'd stumbled upon the enemy.

"*Guten tag*," he called out. "Please, come in. We won't bite."

The SS soldier played his part well, making me slightly uncomfortable but not uncomfortable enough to avoid asking my questions.

"This might be stupid, but why would a French woman be so friendly? Didn't you invade their country?"

"It's complicated," he said while rolling a cigarette.

16

"I'd rather cooperate and feed them," she agreed, "than be sent off to some forced labor camp."

"Well, that's partially true," he added. "After we attacked Paris in 1940, we occupied part of France, but you already know that. They helped us with certain activities."

"Like what?" I asked, wondering why someone would choose to dress like an SS when there were so many other soldiers to reenact.

"Like making parts for our trucks, like keeping the British from invading," he added matter-of-factly, as if he had practiced his answer many times before.

He handed the cigarette to the woman, and after lighting it for her, he rolled another. He continued talking with a German accent, then they giggled some more. Before turning to leave, I blurted, "Just curious. Why reenact an SS soldier?"

He took a drag from her cigarette and flicked the ashes on the dirt road. "The uniforms are cool. Besides, look around. There are all kinds of soldiers here. We're all retelling history. I chose one that had the best army and the best tanks."

If I didn't have on my sunglasses, he would have seen me roll my eyes. I'd probably never see him again but wouldn't forget his uniform, or how he rolled that second cigarette and waited to light it until he answered my questions. Just like I'd never forget the photos I found in my grandfather's nightstand. The ones that made him cry in front of me for the first time. The ones that made me, as an eighteen-year-old, wonder about humanity. "Sometimes I wake up at night," my grandfather said to me that day. "Where the images show up in my dreams to haunt me."

As I left the French village, I noticed the kiosk where we planned to meet, but still had a few minutes to spare. A flea market caught my attention across the way. Rows and rows of boots, uniforms, toy tanks, and model airplanes overflowed from tables and boxes. Belts and leather jackets hung above. I found a great aircraft poster and bought two, for Evan and Jack. Up ahead, backpacks and women's purses sat on a table. Next to them stood a big wooden bin with a sign that said "Love Letters From The War." I began searching through the piles and picked out a few.

"Hey lady," an elderly woman called out. "Careful there."

"Oh, sorry. Can I look inside the envelopes?"

"Nope, don't want you ripping them by accident, then they won't sell. They're about seventy years old, give or take."

"How'd you find these?" I moved them carefully aside, looking at the postmarks and addresses.

"Mostly estate sales. People don't keep these things anymore. Nowadays, they only care about social media."

My phone pinged with a message from Greg as I looked at an envelope postmarked with the year 1942. More letters from 1943 and a stack from '44 and '45 were underneath.

After a few more minutes, I took some from the pile, making sure they had different addresses. Some went to Washington State, some to Georgia, another to Kansas, and one to my favorite city, Boston. I slipped the posters under my arm and the letters in my bag.

"I was about to send the Russian troops out to find you," Greg said when I approached.

"I've had enough of the Russians and Germans for one day. But you're not going to believe what I found." I handed the posters to Jack and opened my bag.

"Love letters from the war," I said and fanned them out like a deck of cards.

"Yuck," Jack responded.

"They'll be great inspiration for the ancestry website I'm working on."

"Couldn't you just go online to look?" Jack asked.

"Couldn't you just go online to look at tanks?"

"Good point."

We walked out, happy to leave this pretend war behind. "I'll read the letters out loud over dinner."

"Gross," Jack said and grabbed his side, pretending he got shot.

"Fine, be that way. I'll save them for Sveta."

Chapter 4

There's something to be said about indoor camping: no frogs keeping you awake, no ticks trying to suck your blood, no unwelcomed creatures sharing your space. So when Jack wanted to camp out like the reenactors, we came up with the perfect solution. We'd bring the tent and put it up in our room at the comfortable, air-conditioned hotel. Greg and I would sleep in the bed while Jack pretended to be under the stars. The room was big enough to fit our small tent, and Jack thought it was a cool idea, which surprised me because at his age, he pretty much thought everything was gross or stupid coming from his parents.

I ran down to get the sleeping bag from the car, and while waiting for a slow elevator, the woman and young boy from the Russian camp walked through the lobby. She'd taken off her scarf and apron, and up close, she was even more beautiful. Her cheeks were flushed from the heat, her eyes as black as the liner around them. The boy, all sweaty, took off his hat and belt and handed them to her.

"Do you reenact every year?" I asked, hating that uncomfortable silence when waiting for an elevator.

"It's my third time. But I don't like sleeping in a tent, so we stay at the hotel," she said while putting the belt and hat in her bag. She still had the Russian accent I detected earlier.

I smiled and pushed the button again, knowing, of course, it wouldn't help the elevator arrive any faster. "I don't blame you. It's not my thing either."

"Is this your first time here?" she asked.

I nodded, and as the guests got off the elevator, we both went for the same button, forgetting we should have let her son push it for us. "I'm exhausted from all that walking. There's so much to see," I added.

"But you still have energy for dancing?"

"What do you mean?"

"There's a dance every year. It's the best part."

"Just for reenactors, right?"

"For anyone. It's a lot of fun. You should try to make it," she said as she walked off.

I reached for my room key and imagined how cool it would be to listen to the band, to step back in time and hear the songs my father used to play at home and when we visited my grandparents. They lived in the next town over, and we spent every Sunday with them. While my mom would have loved for me to help in the kitchen, I always escaped to the den where my grandfather kept his music.

The first time my dad caught me looking through the record collection of his youth, it became our ritual, our time together. He'd start up the player, and we'd listen to the albums. As I danced, he'd thumb through the records for gems to spin. My mom would sometimes scream from the kitchen for me to come help with dinner, but I'd pretend not to hear. The kind of selective hearing I often teased my own kids of having.

***

"Do we have to go?" Jack pleaded, asking to stay in the room by himself.

"It's part of the fun."

"There's nothing fun about dancing," he said while flipping through the channels.

"Sure there is," Greg said and attempted to do his own version of the moonwalk.

"Who knows, maybe you can get a ride in one of the vehicles," I said in my sometimes successful, change-the-subject method I'd learned the second time around with parenting.

"Can I wear what I have on?" Jack asked and rolled his eyes before reluctantly changing out of his shorts.

My blouse was at the bottom of my bag, scrunched up like a deflated football. I held the shoulders and shook them hard, as if I were trying to spread a fire. For ten minutes, we conducted a search-and-rescue mission to find my sandals. When they turned up in the tent, I wondered if our dog Ginger had somehow hitched a ride and hidden them there to chew on later.

We piled into the car and drove back across town, following the same signs as before. Greg parked along the side of the road, and we walked across the field in the direction of the music. A full orchestra took center stage, with many couples already on the dance floor. The band's leader, in his double-breasted suit and matching bow tie, conducted with one hand and slicked his hair back with the other. Musicians played their saxophones, trumpets, and trombones and stood up on cue as part of their performance. It was the summer of 2011, and the swing dance had made its way to a field on the heels of wing-tipped shoes, flirty full skirts, and strapless gowns that sparkled like a champagne toast.

I recognized many of the songs. Even though my father wasn't born until 1936, he still loved the music my grandfather played, the big-band style popular in the '40s, a groovy kind of jazz with an upbeat tempo that always made you want to get up and dance. If my dad and grandfather were alive today, they'd be the first ones to say, "That's crazy, dressing up like soldiers acting out a war." Then I'd tell them about the band, and they'd say, "Really? Tell me more."

Greg touched my elbow and moved his head in the direction of the floor.

"We haven't danced since our wedding," I said, embarrassed I'd mess up in front of all those great dancers.

"Not true." He got up and took my hand. "We danced at your office holiday party."

"That was like seven years ago. How do you remember?"

"Still feeling the hangover."

"And the cost of the babysitter," I said and walked to my favorite spot in the middle of the floor, admitting I'd need a few classes to keep up and made a mental note to put dancing on our date-night list.

"Let me lead," Greg demanded.

After a couple of warm-up songs, Greg wanted to slide me between his legs then flip me over his shoulder, but I knew he'd be too exhausted to scream *medic* for his suffering wife. While waiting for the next song, I glanced over to check on Jack. He seemed to be hanging in there, talking to other kids and playing games on my phone.

On the side stood a few SS officers with their dates. A man approached them, and after a minute, a couple of them walked off. A few stayed and stood tall. They seemed to wear their well-decorated uniforms and red swastika armbands with pride. Greg swung me around when the new song began, and I wondered why some left and some remained. Maybe they weren't welcome. Maybe the reenactor I'd overheard earlier in the day was right—that it was part of history, and they shouldn't be denied a chance to represent it. But I still had a hard time understanding who'd want to reenact an SS officer.

The band stopped playing and asked everyone to move aside. As the emcee called out veterans' names, a World War II pilot and nurse walked on stage. Cheers from the crowd surrounded us. I turned to check on Jack, but he was gone.

Even though Jack, at twelve, was no longer a little boy, I still worried whenever we were in crowds, and I couldn't see him. My heart pounded, like the time he let go of my hand at a department store, took off, and hid under a garment rack. Greg looked around, going along the rows calling out his name. As we got to the back, we saw him talking to some reenactors.

My attempt not to overreact in front of them didn't work. "There you are. I've been looking all over for you!"

"You said I could go for a ride."

"Ma'am, we'd be happy to take him around."

I elbowed Greg and whispered for him to go with them. As they drove off, Jack cracked up when the soldier blew the horn, a high-pitched sound that reminded me of the chase scenes from my favorite childhood cartoon. A minute later, they stopped and changed seats so that Jack could drive.

"Excuse me, miss."

I moved slightly, assuming I'd blocked the way.

"Miss, would you like to dance?"

A handsome soldier, with dark cropped hair and a loose-fitting olive uniform, stood with his arm held out. I started to point toward Greg then changed my mind. "Sure, why not," I said and folded my arm into his. On the way to the dance floor, we passed a few reenactors dressed in their black SS uniforms and matching caps, and I was glad my grandfather wasn't there to see them.

Chapter 5

"Honey, pass the toothpaste," I said the following Monday morning as we were getting ready for work. We loved to travel and could stay just about anywhere, but I always missed my pillow, our bed, and other comforts of home.

"Why don't you let that handsome young soldier get it for you?" Greg teased.

I laughed. "Oh, come on, what was I supposed to do? Someone had to protect me while you were off riding around acting all cool."

"I bet if he was ugly, you would have said no."

"That's not true." Grabbing the toothpaste, I added, "Okay, maybe. He did look good in his uniform."

"You know he's not a real soldier, right? He just plays one on TV—I mean on the fake battlefield."

"Actually he's the real deal." I spit and rinsed, then went to the bedroom to get dressed for work. "He's in the reserves. So I guess that means he's double-dipping."

Greg hit me on the butt with his towel. "He was dipping alright. During that Lindy Bob or whatever you guys were doing on the dance floor."

"You mean Lindy Hop." I grabbed the towel and hit him back. "Sounds like somebody's jealous," I sang before remembering it was my father's favorite dance. Greg noticed the change and pulled me close.

"What's wrong?"

"Nothing," I answered. The anniversary of my father's death was the other day and the last thing I needed was to break down right before heading to the office. Greg didn't push me to talk. He held me close and reached for the towel to get me back, making me laugh and take off to find cover in the closet where I finished getting dressed. The doorbell rang, and I ran down the hall quieting Ginger who started to bark.

"Good morning, Mrs. Britain," Olivia said politely. I'd almost forgotten she was a teenager, considering how some teenagers talked these days.

"Jack's still in bed."

"I don't blame him," she added, taking a sip from her soda.

I clasped the back of my earring. "Make him go to the pool to get some fresh air. Don't let him sit in front of the TV all day." I checked my phone for the temperature and grabbed a light sweater for the office. "Oh, there's lasagna defrosting on the counter."

"Is it vegetarian?" she asked.

"No, sorry."

"Is it at least free-roaming, organic beef?"

"It's turkey," I said while putting on my shoes and thinking, *why the hell does it matter? You're drinking soda. For breakfast.*

"Bye," I called out and dashed out the door, then remembered the letters. I ran back inside and grabbed them from my unpacked bag that would probably sit there until my next trip.

***

Like most days, Sveta beat me to the office. Born and bred in Moscow, she came to the United States years ago with her husband and son. Eight months after arriving, her husband asked for a divorce out of the blue, declaring he'd fallen in love with the owner of their apartment building. Not the type to wallow in self-pity, she said, "Sure, no problem, as long as I get full custody of Dimitry, and you find me a new landlord."

Ever since I'd known her, Sveta was a workaholic. She liked her job, and nobody waited for her at home. Dimitry was married and out of the house, so she worked day and night, if it meant a cooler website interface and a happier client. But most weekends were out of the question when she spent time with Evan and happily gave his parents a break. She loved having quality time with her grandson, and at 54, she had plenty of energy.

She was my developer, my go-to smarter-than-hell technical person on all my design projects. But a few months back, things changed for the better, and so did her hours. She met someone at the post office—of all places—where the lines were still long enough to have plenty of time to chat. She began leaving work earlier, which meant seven instead of nine. But the account managers still acted like she didn't mind pulling all-nighters, the same ones I used to pull before having kids. I told her she needed to put her foot down. Instead, she showed off her incredible work ethic by coding a little faster and making good use of Russian profanity.

"*Karova, nu pacheemu?*" she said to her computer, as if it could talk back. I knew she really meant it for one of the account managers.

"Let me guess." I paused for a second. "Goat?"

"*Nyet.*"

"Pig?"

"*Nyet.* Cow." Then she sounded out the Russian equivalent slowly—three times—as if she were my French teacher from high school.

"Another crazy deadline?" I asked, putting down my coffee.

"It's not just crazy. They didn't even check the calendar. I have PTO coming up." She put on her glasses to read the email.

"Two days to finish this piece, and we have the PatchTree Ancestry site to develop. That's a crazy deadline, too."

"Do you want me to ask for an extension?"

"No way, just a little stressed with the vacation around the corner."

"Sounds like you'll need a vacation after your vacation."

While my computer booted up, I pulled out the letters and carefully took the rubber band off the first batch after moving my coffee to the other side of my desk. All the envelopes featured script, a beautiful form that, to my recent surprise, was no longer being taught in school. I'd be the first to admit the computer made many things easier, but I sometimes longed for the lost art of letter writing. Perhaps we'd incorporate it into my designs for the PatchTree Ancestry comps, as long as the client signed off on it.

"Sveta, I know you're under the gun, but you have to see this," I said, pulling out the first letter written to a woman named Betty.

She looked over as I waved it.

"I didn't have a chance to tell you. I bought some old love letters at Valor of the '40s."

"Really? This can wait."

She got up and came into my cubicle as I started reading from the first one, dated November 23, 1944.

Dearest Betty,

I got your recent letter. Don't worry your pretty little head. Truly, I'm fine. Last night I was telling everyone about my baby, getting all sappy, and it made me miss you even more. I don't want you to worry, but it seems I may be off for a voyage soon, as long as my flying is what it should be. But I have to get my wings first.

"Ooh, a pilot," Svetlana added. "What's his name?"

I looked on the envelope and letter to make sure they matched. "Robert Blair. But he signed it as 'Bobby'. Let's grab a conference room so we can spread these out."

The first room was taken, so we went around the corner by the kitchen to grab the smaller one. Sveta brought a pen and notepad to make it look like we were working. We really were; we were brainstorming if anyone asked. I put Bobby's letter back into its envelope and took out one sent to an Evelyn Thomas from Georgia in 1944.

Dear Evelyn,
I received your letter and am glad to hear from you. Well, sugar—

"Sugar?" Svetlana said, surprised.

"You've never heard my mom say that? It's a Southern term, like honey."

"But don't you think 'honey' sounds better?"

"Not to Henry. Let's hear what he has to say. Where was I?" I added, finding my spot.

Well, sugar, we got some new girls and they cried all day long. They're already homesick. It's bonkers. Why in the world would they join up? One is a tall, round blonde and the other looks like an old battle-ax! See, you have nothing to worry about!

Sugar, I have something I have wanted to tell you for a long time, but never had the chance. I want to tell you how much I love you. I love you, Evelyn! Remember that always. These words mean an awful lot to me. I look at your picture a hundred times a day and feel safe because you're at my side every moment, day and night.

Now I'll answer your question. Yes, I very much look forward to getting married. I cannot wait to make love to you.

There was a knock on the door. Jessica, one of our project managers, walked into the room. We changed the subject and started talking business, how we wanted the functionality of the ancestry website to work, and how we might incorporate some of the letters into the design.

"Hey, ladies, do you think you'll be long? I booked the room for a meeting and need to set up in about ten minutes," she said, holding her agenda book.

"Five minutes, tops," I said and, after she left, picked the letter back up and began where I'd left off.

Yes, I very much look forward to getting married. I cannot wait to make love to you. Remember the time your mom went to the store? I can still picture our kisses on the sofa. Never mind all this talk, or else you-know-who might stand up at attention!

I'd better close for now. Up early in the morning for another long day. A thousand kisses your way. Please take care of yourself and write me real soon.

"Awww," we both said in unison as I folded the letter.

"That's hilarious. 'You-know-who might stand up at attention,'" Sveta said. "I can't believe he wrote that. Naughty boy."

We discussed the PatchTree project for a moment, and she agreed it would be great to incorporate the letter idea into some of the designs. We'd meet again in a couple days to discuss the details.

"Let's look at one more," Svetlana added. "Not sure if we can top the other one, though. That was so romantic, and a little raunchy. My kind of guy."

I looked through the piles and chose the letter that was by itself, not attached with others by a rubber band. It was the one I'd picked from Boston.

"This one's interesting," I said, looking at the envelope, turning it front to back. "Sent to Boston much earlier, in 1941, to an Arnold."

The writing on the envelope looked different, in script, but fancier with the number seven crossed in the middle, the way Europeans wrote. It looked like the person who wrote it had only one piece of paper, cramming every possible word on the front and back.

"Hmm," I said. "This one's in a different language. Can't tell which one."

"Let me see," Svetlana said. She looked at it closely. "I need my glasses." We walked back to our cubicles.

"Interesting. Very interesting."

"What?" I said impatiently.

"It's written in German. From a Camp Gurs. If you give me a little time, I can translate it for you," Svetlana said.

"Seriously? That makes four languages. What can't you do?"

"That's easy. I can't relax. Been trying to figure that out for years." She looked at the letter again. "The words are really small, lots jammed on the page. But it shouldn't take too long. I'll do it when I'm on vacation."

My mind started to wander as I tried to put those two together: a love letter written in German and a Camp Gurs. The camps, at least the ones in Europe during that time, had nothing to do with love or leisure. While waiting for Sveta to translate the letter, I had to find out more.

Chapter 6

Stinky, sweaty, and loud. That's how I always described Jack's taekwondo class. Set in the lower level of a fitness center, Western Warriors helped kids who had a hard time focusing—a last-ditch effort, with many parents joking that the studio was to distracted kids what milk was to chocolate-chip cookies. They belonged together. They helped make everything seem better, even for the moment.

In our case, it was different. We stumbled upon the studio when Jack got invited to a party there three years ago. He loved jumping, board breaking, and screaming, all the things a mom prone to frequent headaches cherished. But Western Warriors' name was misleading. They didn't quite make warriors out of our kids, considering the way some earned their black belts— faster than the shutter action of my best camera.

But all that changed when Master Reynolds, a thirty-something with a fifth-degree black belt, took over. He was especially tough on them and made it harder and the process longer to move up through the belt levels. On occasion, he let the younger kids get away with being silly right before class. But not the older boys like Jack. I wasn't bothered by the tough love and extra time for him to become a black belt, although my bank account sometimes disagreed.

"No, Brian, like this," Master Reynolds bellowed and replayed the move, kicking his leg above his head and holding it there while all the moms watched.

"Taylor, work on your flexibility. That will help your kicks," he said while slowly dropping to the floor. "You're not warming up enough. You need to spend time doing that before you get here," Master Reynolds demanded before working his way into a complete split. "Class, the more flexible you are, the fewer injuries you'll have."

By this time, the one and only dad lifted his head, joining the rest of the moms who no longer had an interest in their phones or magazines. But even with his good looks and amazing flexibility, Master Reynolds couldn't keep my attention for long. I always used Jack's class as a way to catch up on my to-do list, like I used kids' movies to catch up on my sleep.

This Thursday's class was no different. Every few minutes, I'd look up to see Jack's forms in between checking email and ordering my weekly groceries. I added strawberries to my online cart when I got a text from my mom who recently traded in her flip phone for a halfway-smart one.

Can you talk?

That was Mom's way of saying, "Can you spare a few minutes?" when texting wouldn't cut it.

Before leaving the room, I passed by stinky shoes, duffle bags filled with sparring equipment, and Master Reynolds' elasticized torso. The hallway would be my makeshift phone booth, so the grunts, heavy breathing, and *hiyahs* wouldn't compete with our conversation.

"Mom, is everything okay?" I asked.

There was a pause, and I knew she was upset and didn't want me to hear her voice crack. She always paused to try to hold it back.

"Mom, what happened?"

"It's stupid."

"Tell me."

"I got in an argument with a lady over a parking space."

"That's so out of character. You're like a saint behind the wheel."

She sighed. "I got upset for no good reason. It didn't help that I was already a little down because of your dad."

The anniversary of his death was hitting my mom hard. She still relived his passing, thinking she could have done something more to help. It had been two years since his death, and though she was trying to look and stay busy, she was still hurting. Some people put a time limit on grieving, like a college exam you didn't quite finish or an expired coupon you never got to use. I didn't want to be that kind of person, the kind who told you that time was up, to go back to being happy, even if you had to fake it. But I also didn't want to pretend I didn't notice the toll it took.

"Mom, don't be upset that I bring this up, but maybe you should talk to someone?"

"A shrink? What could they possibly say? That I'm being too hard on myself because he died right in front of me? I know I feel guilty for no reason. I know there was nothing I could have done. Some days, it's just hard."

"I know. I worry about you."

"It's not that I'm totally against therapy. I'd rather try staying busy."

"Like the time you started posting funny dance videos?"

We laughed, but I could feel her pain and tried to change the subject when she mentioned how together I was. For a moment, I wanted to pretend to be the one who had it all together. But I was also hurting from the loss of my dad, the man I loved dearly, whose voice I still heard when he told a joke—whether it was funny or not—and his contagious laughter that would spread to everyone around him. I held back the tears, and before going into the studio, I looked up at the light in the hallway to intimidate them, to make them go back to their hiding place.

Tucking away the bittersweet memory of my dad, I watched Jack while walking back to my seat. The extra work seemed to pay off with Master Reynolds who announced Jack would test for his black belt soon. I sat down and, instead of finishing my online shopping, started on the next item on my list—researching Camp Gurs.

In a long list of search results, the second entry caught my eye. The website described Gurs as one of the first and largest concentration camps established in prewar France, about fifty miles from the Spanish border near the foothills of the Pyrenees Mountains. If it hadn't been listed on a history website, Gurs and its location could have sounded nice, like somewhere you'd take the family for vacation. But why would someone write a letter in German from Gurs in southern France?

As I read further, it started to make sense. In October 1940, German authorities deported thousands of Jews from southwest Germany across the border. Officials of the Vichy regime interned most of them in Gurs. The site said that of the 7,500 Jews, about 1,700 were eventually released, 750 or so escaped, around 1,900 were able to emigrate, and 2,800 men were enlisted into French labor battalions.

If it were a German Jew writing a letter, how would he or she get the correspondence out? Besides, I didn't even know Jews were allowed to write letters in concentration camps. I pulled up the calculator and noticed there were about 300 not accounted for. Maybe the person who wrote the letter was one of them, the unaccounted for that somehow didn't make the list.

But there was more. Between August 6, 1942, and March 3, 1943, Vichy officials turned over about 4,000 Jewish prisoners to the Germans who sent many to Drancy, located in a suburb of Paris. It went from bad to worse. From Drancy, they were deported to extermination camps like Auschwitz. All in all, about 22,000 prisoners passed through Gurs. It made me anxious knowing the letter was written in 1941 and, from the looks of it, before the German Jews were sent to Drancy.

But I had to stay positive. For all I knew, it was a person from France who spoke German and had German relatives in Boston. I had to stay positive, even for a complete stranger who caught my eye with beautiful handwriting and number sevens crossed with lines in the middle. On the other hand, how could I be so naïve? I thought I knew about the Holocaust from school and my grandfather, but never realized they had concentration camps in France. Had I slept during that lesson? Or did my high school history teacher Mr. Greene skip that important part?

"Turn around and face your families," Master Reynolds yelled. Jack bowed out, had a quick joke with a few friends, and grabbed his shoes and sparring bag.

"So what do you think of Master Reynolds?" I asked on the way home after turning down the music.

"I like him, but he's pretty strict."

"That's tough love. It's a good thing."

I drove down our street and thought more about the letter. "Jack, when do you study World War II in school?"

"This year, I think."

"I wonder why they wait that long."

"I guess to teach everything in order? Hey, can I stay up later tonight?" he asked, changing the subject, avoiding the slight chance we'd talk about his grades.

"Okay, but just a half hour."

We pulled in the driveway, and as Jack ran in the house, I called Jeremy. He didn't answer, but a minute later, he texted saying he was out with friends and would call me in the morning. I smiled, mostly because I knew he wouldn't call. But it didn't matter. His text was enough to ease my mind and not worry, letting it wander and wonder again about the letter from Gurs.

Chapter 7

Sveta was gorgeous, but with her deep tan, she came back from her vacation even more stunning. In a sense, it was my first day back too, since Jack's summer break had officially ended. Jack survived his first year of middle school and transitioned fine to seventh grade, although I was the one who needed a little help.

"So, how was it?" I asked while putting my bag in the drawer.

"Unbelievable. The beaches were great, and they have this Old San Juan area with amazing restaurants."

"Sounds like heaven. Now back to the routine, huh?"

She nodded. "I went through two hundred emails, and I have another hundred. Oh, before I forget," she added and got up from her desk to hand me a piece of paper. She stopped and held the paper behind her back. "On second thought, I'm not sure if it's the right time."

"Oh shit," I whispered. "Please don't tell me you're giving notice."

"Are you kidding? You and me, we're like this," she said while crossing her fingers. "It's the letter. I'll email it to you, but thought you'd want to read it printed out first."

As I was about to start, there was an announcement that Sam wanted a quick meeting in the large conference room. He did that every now and again when he got back from an important meeting. The letter would have to wait.

"*Boje moi*," Sveta said under her breath. I'd heard this phrase many times and no longer needed a translation.

"Oh my God" said it perfectly. Often when Sam called meetings, he'd ramble on, turning a ten-minute gathering into an hour.

Our office consisted of eighteen full-time employees, and when we needed extra help, we'd call in designers, writers, and programmers. The freelancers always joined us in these meetings because, as Sam put it, they were part of the team. But Sam's assistant told them to sit this one out, which made the full-timers nervous.

"First things first. Stephanie, how are the PatchTree comps coming along?" Sam asked as he plopped into his chair. It caught me off guard, but I was ready with a response.

"It's going great. We're about ready to present."

"Great. With those few tweaks from the internal review, the client will love either one. And the email campaign for the university?"

Jessica, our account manager, perked up. "I just checked the results on open rates and click-throughs, and the second round of emails are about to launch."

"Okay, let me see the results before you show the client. I want to be prepared to ask for more business. So..." Sam rubbed his hands together and looked down at his notepad. "I wanted to share a couple things. The week before Labor Day, I had a great meeting with the marketing director from Casa Koolers. They're moving ahead on their sparkling juice line, so it looks like we've got more work."

The room erupted in cheers, hoots, and claps. Everyone seemed relieved that new business was coming our way.

"Second thing. Whenever rumors go around, people think I don't hear about them. But, I do. I know there's been a rumor about me retiring. I wanted to let you know that, yes, I've been thinking about it. I've had this firm for thirteen years after putting in twenty-five at other companies, during which I survived a nasty divorce and the Internet bubble bursting. Not sure which was worse, but that's beside the point. So here's the deal. Two companies approached me, but I turned both offers down. And the reason I wanted to tell you is—you have nothing to worry about either way. If I decide not to sell, we're doing fine—we're getting new business and all looks good. And if I decide to sell, all of you will be fine. But, again, as of right now, there is no offer on the table." He paused and looked around. "I really mean it when I say you have nothing to worry about." He paused once again then asked, "Any questions?"

There was silence. Nobody wanted to bring up what was really on their minds. I knew they were concerned. I'd heard coworkers whispering in the hallways on more than one occasion.

"No questions? Okay, as trite as it sounds, my door is always open. Let's get some work done and lunch is on me. Pizza in the conference room at noon."

We walked back to our cubes, and Sveta took her sun-kissed legs and spun them around in her chair to continue the daunting, after-vacation task of plowing through her inbox.

I read Sam's detailed email about Casa Koolers and learned about my first deliverable: to develop a creative strategy for the team. But before starting, I had to finish preparing for Thursday's PatchTree comp review. Normally we'd show comps on the computer, but the client wanted them mounted on boards like it was still 1998. While waiting for the designs to print out, I read the letter.

27 January 1941

My Dear Arnold!

My last letter must have reached you. I hope you are all healthy. Yesterday I received your package and you cannot imagine our joy. Since October 1940, we have been away from our home. Every day we have to worry. For the first time, from the Swiss help organization, we got a cup of milk, a piece of cake and jam. There are thousands of people here. But I worry about Isadore; he is very pale. I am also very worried about our sponsorship. Nobody helps us. Arnold, did you offer a sponsorship? Please, if you haven't already, I ask that you sponsor us. If you can, you could also send us another food package? That would help us reduce our unhappiness. Please also write to Gertrude and ask for us. We cannot write to everyone. Leo is in the men's barracks, separate from me and Isadore. It is worthless to write about anything else. We sit here left to our grim fate with misery all around us.

I stopped right before getting to the end. A couple weeks ago I told myself to stay positive about the letter, that maybe a relative was communicating about life in France. How naïve could I have been? Before continuing, I looked up at Sveta.

"I know. I've read it a hundred times."

"It's horrible," I said. "Part of me doesn't want to know what happened."

"Let's talk about it later," Sveta added before attacking her emails. "It deserves a stiff drink."

Maybe they were some of the lucky ones who escaped, as the website described. Could they have finally made it to Boston? This plea for sponsorship made me worry because not everyone could emigrate, or had enough time to coordinate it.

I continued to read the rest of the letter. In every curve of the writing, fear and desperation soberly united with hope. But toward the middle, desperation outweighed everything else. Even if the person had survived, she would most likely be gone by now. But I still wondered about their fate—especially the fate of Isadore, who I assumed was their son.

At the bottom, still hoping for sponsorship, she had put their birthdates. At the time, Isadore was just five years old. Too young to take care of himself. Too young to escape on his own. Too young to worry, which was, in a way, fortunate.

"Sveta," I said while holding the letter, "this Isadore she talks about…"

"It's heartbreaking, more like heart-crushing."

"You'll think I'm crazy, but I need to find out if he's still alive."

"*Daragaya*, why would you want to torture yourself, digging up the past of the Holocaust? It's so sad."

I paused and looked up at the light, hoping again to push back the tears. "Do you believe in fate?"

"Of course, I do."

"Then you'll understand why." I walked over to her cube, laid the letter on her desk, and pointed to the last paragraph.

> *In case you can get us sponsorships, here are*
> *our birthdates:*
> *Leo: September 3, 1901. Hanna: October 27,*
> *1905. Isadore: July 12, 1936.*
> *We will wait and see what happens. I send you*
> *our sincere regards.*
> *Hanna*

"Because that boy shares the same birthday as my father, down to the year they were born. July 12, 1936. I have to find out what happened."

"Wow," Sveta said. "Let's look him up." She pulled up a web browser and typed Isadore. "What's his last name?"

"I need to check the envelope. Did you bring it?"

"You only gave me the letter."

"Are you sure?"

"Absolutely. I insisted you make me a copy, remember?"

"I can hardly remember what I had for breakfast."

"Me too." Sveta turned around and paused before adding, "This kid and your dad. What if they're the same person?"

"You know how crazy that sounds, right?"

I leaned on her cubicle wall. No way it could have been my dad. He had a thick southern accent. And his family had been in North Carolina since the early 1900s. Intriguing, yes. Likely? Not a chance.

But it wasn't just chance this letter found its way to me. It couldn't have been. Before picking up the comps from the printer, I put a reminder in my phone to find the envelope to start my search for Isadore.

Chapter 8

I used to love cussing. But after having kids, I passed on my swear-like-a-sailor title to my friends and coworkers. Occasionally, I'd still let out a few in front of the kids. Jeremy usually ignored it. Jack, on the other hand, always came running to help because a stubbed toe, massive paper cut, or a computer crash often accompanied my salty language. This time, I spewed profanities at an envelope.

I sat on the living room floor with the letters in piles, trying my best not to mess up their order. I'd found the envelope from Gurs, but the top was ripped and part of the last name was missing.

"What's wrong?" Jack asked.

"Look." I handed him the letter. "This is so disappointing. I wanted to find out the last name of the person who wrote it."

"That's easy. Do you have the original letter?"

I nodded, and after he explained what he wanted to try, Jack sat down with me on the floor. He took the envelope, put a piece of paper behind the back, and rubbed a pencil over it, then took a blank paper and rubbed a pencil on that really dark. Part of the name started to show. It took some patience, but Jack didn't give up. He kept at it until we could see the full name—Hanna Fischer—written in block rather than the beautiful script found on the letter.

I got up and hugged Jack. "You're a genius."

While many of us couldn't imagine life before marriage or kids, I couldn't imagine life before the Internet. We used it for practically everything in our house except searching medical conditions because reading worst-case scenarios about something as benign as a bug bite made me cringe. Nothing brought it home quite like online images, which made me once think I was about to die from a mosquito bite I got on a camping trip. But the search engine was an antidote for everything else.

I used it to find recipes to make quick meals, learn more about competitors during pitches, and discover the Camp Gurs I'd recently known nothing about. That's where I decided to start, by entering Isadore's name and adding Camp Gurs behind it. Nothing came up. Next, Isadore Fischer in France. Nothing. On a long shot, I tried Germany. Again nothing. Finally, Isadore Fischer - Boston. A few matches came up, one from a Winchester University in Virginia. I clicked on the link and went to the university's website. Isadore Fischer, adjunct professor in the Foreign Languages Department, bachelor's and master's from South End College of Massachusetts. *Good for him—seventy-five and still working.* That is, if I'd found the right person.

The website listed his email address, but he'd probably trash my message right away—if he opened it. Who wouldn't ignore a complete stranger asking about a decades-old letter and a possible connection to the woman who wrote it? It would take me days to come up with a subject line that didn't scream *stalker.* Calling him seemed like a better idea, and within seconds, directory assistance helped me locate an Isadore Fischer in Stevensonville, Virginia. I wrote down the number, as the doorbell rang.

"Wine, anyone?" Sveta asked and headed through the hall toward the kitchen.

She put the bottle on the counter and grabbed two glasses from the cabinet. Once a month on Fridays, Sveta came over for our version of Happy Hour. We'd start with wine, nibble on some snacks, then go back for more wine. By the time Greg got home from the gym, we'd be halfway through the bottle. Often he'd hide in the family room while we continued with girl talk and watched videos.

"So what's your favorite concert of all time?" Sveta asked and poured wine into both glasses.

"Don't make me choose! It's like asking someone's favorite movie. But the craziest? When the band only wore beanies."

"Wait. What do you mean they only wore beanies?"

"You'll get a hoot out of it," I said, doing a search and clicking on the first video that came up. Completely naked except for knit caps and high-tops, the bass player and lead guitarist ran around the stage and jumped from the drummer's platform numerous times. Sveta got a kick out of it and said it was more like "decent exposure" since they were all in great shape.

We pulled up more videos, and I gave her a quick lesson on music from my youth. Guitar solos and teased hair. Off-the-shoulder sweatshirts and shoulder shimmies. And a bunch of new wave songs my college roommate played nonstop. Total '80s and total amusement, especially as a chaser to the wine we were consuming.

"Now it's my turn," Sveta said and took control of the mouse.

She closed out the browser accidentally and the university's website popped up. She stared at the screen for a few seconds before realizing what she saw.

"*Maladetz*, you found Isadore?" Sveta asked with excitement. "That was fast! Thank you, Internet gods. I guess my crazy idea about it being your dad was a tad far-fetched."

"Agreed. Although I haven't tried contacting him yet."

"I can do it, I'm the biggest nosybody out there."

"Busybody," I corrected.

"Nosybody. Busybody. Who cares?"

Talking about Isadore made me think about my mom. Maybe I was being too overprotective, but I didn't want her to get more upset about Dad's passing. Hearing about the shared birthdates would be another reminder he was gone. So for the time being, I decided not to tell her the news.

***

After Sveta left, I stared at Isadore's number. Maybe emailing would be better than calling after all—or not even contacting him. Like Sveta said, why dig up such a sad past? Most likely, it wouldn't be the same Isadore. What would be the chance he'd end up in Virginia? Then again, what if it were him, and he never knew about the letter Hanna wrote? Would he want to know, or would he want to forget about his past like so many people?

The letter could sit on a shelf, along with Isadore's number, collecting dust, becoming less meaningful to me as the months and years went by. It could sit there, out of reach, a place I'd hardly look. But my belief in fate was strong, one that I couldn't shrug off with apprehension. While Greg and Jack played their video game, I went to the kitchen and dialed the number. A man answered right away.

"Hello, Mr. Fischer?"

"Who's asking?" His voice was scratchy, like my dad's when he'd laugh at our dog Bugle who often chased his tail. A Boston accent affected Isadore's voice without the slightest hint of a French or German one.

I got nervous and blurted out, "My name is Stephanie Britain calling from Maryland. I'm looking for an Isadore Fischer. Are you—"

"Can you please take me off your list?" he asked, interrupting me. "I'm not interested in buying anything. Goodbye." Then he hung up.

That went well. Do I sound that much like a telemarketer? Something struck me when he said the word "off." It didn't quite sound like a Boston accent; there was something different about it, like how Sam's father, who was from Belgium, sounded on every tenth word or so. I had to call back.

"Mr. Fischer, please let me finish."

"Only if you're not selling something. I don't need any life insurance."

"I'm not selling anything."

"Good, glad to hear."

"I'm calling because ... well ... let me first say this may sound strange and out of the blue. But by chance are you Isadore Fischer who was born on July 12, 1936?"

"That depends. Are you planning to empty out my bank account after this call?"

"No, but my mom might," I said, and he laughed.

"What's your name again?"

"Stephanie Britain."

"Miss Britain, why do you want to know?"

"Because I found a letter you're mentioned in that has your name and full birthday. It might have been written by your mother when she lived in France in 1941. At a Camp Gurs."

There was a pause, this time much longer. I knew I shouldn't have said lived. It was more like deprived, separated, detained, devastated.

"Mr. Fischer? Are you still there?"

"My mother wasn't from France," he said. "Miss, I have to go."

"Please, don't hang up. Hanna Fischer, was that your mother's name?"

"I said I have to go."

"Okay, sorry I bothered you. Have a nice evening."

We hung up, and I began cleaning up the dishes. In the morning, I'd continue my search for the right Isadore. But the way he paused, the way he changed his mood, the way he abruptly asked to get off the phone. Was it because he was surprised about the letter? Was there a chance he survived, but his parents didn't?

Greg came to the kitchen and grabbed a glass from the cupboard. He put his arms around my waist and kissed the back of my neck.

"Let me guess. You came to help me clean up," I teased.

"Can it wait? I'm in the middle of killing aliens."

"But you're in the kitchen. Where are they now?"

"They've retreated."

"Did you ask them for a five-minute break?"

"Something like that."

The phone rang and, since my hands were wet, Greg answered and chatted with my mom before handing the phone over.

"Hey, you doing okay?" I asked, referring to our last chat about Dad.

"Doing more than okay. I have my moments, but today's a good day."

Greg ran out of the kitchen when Jack called for him, realizing his five-minute reprieve was over. Ginger came in with her nose to the ground searching for crumbs. She stopped in front of me and leaned her head against my leg demanding a neck rub.

My mom told me all about her upcoming trips the following month, all planned during the holidays, which meant she wouldn't make it for Thanksgiving again. She hadn't been since my father passed, with a noticeable emptiness at the table these past two years without them. We said good-bye and as Ginger eyed her treats on the counter, the phone rang. I quickly answered, thinking it was my mom.

"Did you change your mind about Thanksgiving?"

It wasn't my mom, though. It was a man's voice. "Miss Britain?"

"Mr. Fischer?"

"Call me Izzy."

"Sorry, I thought it was my mom."

"I guess I shouldn't have swallowed all that helium," he said and when I laughed hard, Ginger jumped in place and startled me.

"Sorry for my rudeness earlier. After you called, I did a search on you."

"You did? Find anything good?"

"If I'm right, you work in Stantin, a town about 30 minutes from DC. You're a senior art director at a branding and design firm. You have a husband, two kids, and a dog. At least that's what the Internet told me."

"The Internet's been good to both of us. That's how I found out you live in Virginia and teach at Winchester University."

"Well, it looks like we're even. Except I lied to you about my mother. Please tell me about the letter you found."

Chapter 9

Set within Virginia's foothills and literally split in half by I-66, Stevensonville lies two hours southwest from our home in Maryland and is considered a bedroom community by many who commute from there to DC. The Saturday we traveled to meet Izzy, the idyllic countryside shared space with RVs and eighteen-wheelers, while cows grazed near the highway and clouds rubbed shoulders with mountains. On the way, we passed signs for Luray Caverns, a place I'd always wanted to visit.

"Why couldn't you mail him the letter?" Jack asked as we sat on a bench inside Krista's Pantry, a small restaurant near the highway.

"Watch the attitude. This is important to your mom," Greg said as I walked toward the showcases filled with assorted pastries and pies. They beckoned a closer look to narrow down my choice for dessert.

"You should try one of each," a man said behind me.

"Hey, Izzy, I guess you missed us," the cashier said while ringing up a customer. Before turning around, I checked out his topsiders, the kind made popular in the coastal town I used to call home and where my mom still lived.

Even with two-inch heels that pushed me to five ten, Izzy was still about an inch taller. As he took off his baseball cap, a full head of silver hair fell about and several sunspots made an appearance when he lifted his hand to flatten a few strands. He wore a windbreaker that I imagined covered his gut many men over fifty—or even forty—get. But, he proved me wrong when he unzipped and uncovered his slender build.

"Doesn't look like you eat too many of those," I said.

"I eat the sugar-free version. Doctor's orders."

"That's no fun."

"Tell me about it. But for special occasions, I'll order one—or three." He continued, "You must be Miss Britain."

"That's me," I said as we shook hands.

"I pictured you shorter with blonde hair."

"Got the red hair from my Irish grandmother."

"Or the milkman," he said and we both laughed.

"Oh—before I forget." I pulled out the envelope.

"Later. We have plenty of time for that. Suzy, it's two today," Izzy called out while holding up two fingers in the shape of a peace sign.

"Actually, four," I corrected.

Greg and Jack walked over. Izzy smiled and gently tapped Jack's head. If I'd done that, he would have rolled his eyes. Instead, Jack grinned.

"Let's feed this kid. How old are you? Fourteen?"

"Twelve."

"Good lord, they need to stop watering you," Izzy guffawed at his own joke, and with his contagious roar we laughed along. What was there not to like about a seventy-five-year-old man with a sense of humor?

We followed the hostess to our table, and along the way several patrons greeted Izzy by name. I knew it. Izzy was a regular. I always loved them when working at Gemma's in high school. Regulars were always the best tippers. Depending on the day, they'd come in for an early breakfast and sit for hours reading their newspapers. The longer they sat, the more they'd tip. We never pushed them to give up their tables, and when one of the regulars, Mr. Thomas died, we mourned like he was part of our family.

The hostess gave us all a menu except Izzy, and when the waitress took our order, she asked if he wanted his usual.

"I feel a little weird knowing about you from the letter. It's like I invaded your privacy," I said while putting the napkin on my lap.

"It's no big deal, how else would you have found me?"

"How did you end up in Virginia?" I asked.

"My wife. She vacationed here as a kid and wanted to come back. She was tired of the rat race."

"And you?" Greg asked. "Which do you prefer?"

"Can you guess by this view?"

"I don't blame you," Greg said as he looked out the window.

"I was talking about the hostess." He waved at a woman with long dark curls. "I'm half-joking," he added.

When I asked Izzy about being an adjunct lecturer, he said it was the perfect part-time job, giving him the luxury of working twenty hours a week with big breaks in the winter and summer, an ideal situation, as he put it, for someone who should have retired years ago but wasn't quite ready.

He told us a perfect day included teaching two French classes, driving to Krista's for lunch, then another hour-long tutoring session with a student who needed extra help, at the campus or his house. He enjoyed the fifteen-minute commute, hitting only a few traffic lights along the way, and if there were more than two cars waiting at a red light, it was considered a traffic jam.

After we finished our meal, I handed him the letter.

"If you're not in a hurry, why don't we get some dessert and have coffee at my house?" He leaned in to whisper, "The coffee here won't win any awards, but the pies are amazing."

"I don't know," Greg said. "We've got a long drive ahead of us."

Izzy wiped his lips then put the napkin on his plate. "That's okay. They only allow people from Maryland to stay two hours, tops."

"Seriously?" Jack asked.

Izzy pounded on the table in a classic drumroll. "Just kidding. Did I get you on that one?"

"A little," Jack confessed.

The waitress cleared our plates and asked if we wanted dessert. I looked at Greg then Jack. "Which pie is the best?"

"Lemon merengue," Izzy and our waitress said in unison.

"Okay, one of those to go, please," I requested.

Izzy drove up to our car in his silver SUV and rolled down the window. "Just follow me. And stay close. There's a lot of twists and turns."

"Looks like Izzy and my mom went to the same driving school," I said a few minutes into following him. "What's he doing? About seventy?" I asked, adding, "I bet there's a lot of roadkill around here."

"Yeah, like the one I just hit."

"Dad!"

"I'm kidding. It was a bump."

Jack sat up and looked out the back to make sure. The drive to Izzy's house took us around several curvy roads, like he said, past huge farmhouses, red barns, and more cows and horses grazing by the road. Along the way, Izzy waved at cars that passed, and we did the same to keep company.

Several minutes later, he slowed down and stopped by a row of mailboxes. Izzy pulled the mail out of the last box and turned onto a gravel road that had a privacy sign at the edge. After a slight bend, the river cradled the left side, with a few men in fishing boats and a few more kayaking. Steep driveways sat on the right and houses perched on hills. We passed a dead-end sign and turned up the last driveway. It was a steep hill that wound around to the left. In front of us stood a sizeable cottage made out of stone with floor-to-ceiling windows. All you needed was a little snow and a family dressed in parkas, and you'd have the best advertisement for a ski lodge.

Izzy pulled into the garage, and we parked by the front door then got out to take another look. It was already fall, and the leaves had changed to the color of ripe peaches. It seemed like Izzy or the previous owner had chopped down a few trees on the left because you could see across the river to the houses on the opposite side.

"Come on in," Izzy said when he opened the front door.

"This is amazing," Greg said.

"Now you know why I don't miss the big city."

We entered a small foyer, and to the left was a large living room with a kitchen in the back. A teenager with long hair sat on the sofa playing a video game. He moved his head to the left to get the hair out of his face, reminding me of Jeremy.

"We've got company," Izzy sang. "Dylan, this is Stephanie, Greg, and Jack Britain."

"Hey, nice meeting ya," he said without taking his eyes off the screen.

"Is that *Undone*?" Jack asked.

"Yeah."

"Which release?"

"Third."

"What's your kill-death ratio?"

Dylan shrugged. Jack walked closer and stood to the side of the sofa, adding, "My kill-death ratio is probably way better than yours."

"Then pick up a controller."

Jack looked at Izzy. "Can I?"

"If it's okay with your parents. That stuff can be addictive. I set the timer for thirty minutes."

"You play?"

"Sometimes," he admitted.

"See, I told you," Greg said, as if he was trying to get buy-in from me when he got glued to it at home.

Jack plopped on the sofa, and we went to the kitchen. Izzy made coffee and pulled out plates for the pie.

"Is Dylan your grandson?"

Izzy shook his head. "He's a college student. I rent one of my bedrooms during the academic year."

"Your wife doesn't mind, I guess," Greg added.

"Diane passed away a few years ago. We never had kids, so it was her idea to start renting out to students. Are you ready for the world's best lemon merengue?"

As he poured coffee, I told him about the reenactment, conveniently leaving out the part about how he shared the same birthday as my father. I wasn't sure what his reaction would be; maybe he'd think it was an odd reason to contact him.

"You know, I was really young before the war, but I remember so much, especially about my mother. She was very loving and a wonderful cook. She made the best chicken dumplings."

"What happened to her?"

Izzy paused. "Should I top off your coffee?"

I wasn't sure if he was being hospitable, or if he was trying to change the subject.

"No thanks," I answered and got up to look at several photos on the side table.

Izzy slipped away for a minute and came back with photo albums, one from their engagement party with pictures of the two of them, their family and friends, newspaper postings mentioning their upcoming wedding, and a dried corsage. Izzy was skinny in his twenties and had dark brown, wavy hair with short sideburns. The other albums showed their travels throughout Asia, South America, and Canada. I noticed there weren't any photos of Germany and didn't dare ask if he'd been back. The doorbell rang, and Izzy dried his hands before looking at his watch.

"Oh shit, it's three already?" Izzy walked to the front door. A student came in with her backpack. She pulled out her notes and textbook and set them on the desk by the window.

"Olivia, give me a few minutes." Izzy turned back to us. "You're more than welcome to stay. I'll be done in an hour."

"We should be going. Jack, time's up." He didn't respond. "Jack," Greg said louder.

He put the controller down and stretched.

"I hope you'll come back again," Izzy said while walking us out to the car. "Do you want Dylan to show you to the highway?"

"It's okay. We'll find our way, thanks." Greg extended his hand and shook Izzy's.

"Stephanie, thank you for the letter. It means a lot."

"I wish I could do more."

We got in the car, and Izzy leaned on the passenger door. "There's nothing else. Besides, I'm seventy-five. I've got other things to do than live in the past."

"Like playing *Undone*," Jack said.

Izzy leaned in more and looked at him. "Smart kid you got there."

We said goodbye, and as Greg started down the driveway, I rolled down the window, turned toward Izzy, and yelled, "If you don't have plans for Thanksgiving, why don't you join us?"

"I'm a busy guy. Let me check with my two personal assistants," he yelled back and waved as we drove off.

"That was kind of spontaneous, asking him to Thanksgiving," Greg said.

"I felt bad with his wife not being around anymore. Don't worry. He probably won't show up."

"He's totally gonna show," Jack said as we continued down Izzy's driveway and onto the two-lane road.

Chapter 10

Jeremy pulled away from our hug within seconds, but I wouldn't let go that easily. After all, it had been three months since I'd last seen him. His hair was still a little too long, his skinny jeans a little too low. The dark circles etched like steady waves showed that late-night studying got the best of him. Most likely they'd be gone with a few nights' rest since neither kid had inherited the ones that found their home on me in fifth grade and stayed once I turned forty.

"Mom," Jeremy called from the hallway after I'd gone to the kitchen. "What happened to my room?"

"Honey, you're in Jack's old room now," I answered after checking the turkey and closing the oven door. "Jack," I yelled. "Come down and help Dad set the table."

Every year, I was in charge of the turkey, stuffing, and gravy. Sveta would bring the sides and alcohol. When my parents came for Thanksgiving, they'd bring dessert. For the past two years, though, Mom was off traveling, a hobby she took up after Dad died. Seemed she'd rather eat gelato in Florence or stroll the cobblestone streets of Montreal than spend time with her grandkids. Maybe she was running away or making up for lost time. This year, Izzy would join us and bring Krista's famous pies with him.

I heard a commotion in our driveway, and Ginger started barking. Greg looked out the peep hole then opened the door.

Instead of Izzy, my mother walked in and plopped down her luggage.

"Ciao, darlin'," my mother, Katherine, said in her southern drawl as she reached out to kiss both cheeks.

"Mom, I thought you were in Greece?"

"The weather was awful. By the way, nice to see you, too," she snickered. "It was so hot and humid, my clothes hung on me like shrink wrap. But don't worry. I'm leaving tonight for Charleston."

She walked to the living room after handing me her coat. At sixty-five, Mom still looked great thanks to her daily regimen of vitamins, smoothies, and exercise.

"Where are the boys? Jack? Jeremy? I've got presents," she sang out as though they were still toddlers. Jack came sliding on his socks across our hardwood floor.

"Give Grandma some sugar," she said and planted several kisses. "Look at you. What have you been eating?" She stood next to Jack and measured him. "Already up to my forehead, my goodness. Where's that brother of yours?"

Jack shrugged and called out for Jeremy who came down the hall slowly, his head buried in his phone, texting away. He looked up and smiled when he saw my mom.

She put her hands on her hips. "Well, look at you. You're a sight for sore eyes. Must have to tear the girls off. Are you enjoying school?"

"Yeah," he said and returned to his texting.

"Yes, ma'am," Katherine corrected. "Steph, you've had them out of the South so long they've lost their manners."

"They were never in the South. I left after high school, remember?" I turned around and pretended to fix the tablecloth, giving me a chance to roll my eyes.

"Exactly my point. You can't forget where you come from."

I escaped to the kitchen to check on the turkey. The doorbell rang, and before I could set down the oven mitt, Sveta dashed in and plunked several bags down on the counter. "Just met Izzy in the driveway. He's kind of cute."

"Nice, Sveta, nice."

By the time I got to the foyer, Mom had already struck up a conversation. Izzy had traded in his alma mater's baseball cap for a gray wool derby and his windbreaker for a burgundy cardigan. He followed me to the kitchen and placed the pies on the table.

"They were out of lemon merengue, so I brought pecan and apple. They're also to die for."

"Yeah, I'll probably die from stuffing my face with them. Greg, honey," I called out. "The turkey's ready."

Greg came to the kitchen, shook hands with Izzy, and poured Svetlana and my mom a glass of wine. There were seven of us—eight including Ginger, who waited patiently a few feet away in case we accidentally dropped food on the floor. We never let her get too close, but the kids always tried to give her a treat when I turned my back. Jeremy and Jack were already at the table listening to my mom's stories about the cliff-side town of Santorini as Greg filled plates with turkey, stuffing, green beans, and carrots. Izzy passed on the carrots when Greg got to his plate.

"I don't like them either," Jack said.

"They're good for you. I'd eat them, but I'm allergic."

"I should use that excuse." Jack moved his carrots around and cut them in small pieces to make it looked like he ate a few. I was on to it but didn't want to call him out, not in front of everyone.

"So, Izzy," my mom said. "What do you do?"

"I'm a French professor."

"Ooh-la-la," she said.

Izzy smiled. "Everyone says that."

She continued. "How do you know Stephanie?"

My mom was a twenty-questions kind of person, always good at making small talk.

"She found a letter written by my mother from a concentration camp."

"Can you believe it was mixed in with a bunch of love letters from the war? At least that's what the sign said."

"What sign?" my mom asked.

"From the flea market at Valor of the '40s. Remember?" I said, even though I knew I hadn't told her yet.

"No, first time hearing it. I'm the one who's supposed to have senior moments, not you."

"Reminds me of a joke about senior moments. Wait. What were we talking about?"

"Good one, Svetlana," Izzy said before adding mashed potatoes and gravy to his plate.

When my mom asked more about Valor of the '40s, Greg sprinkled in stories about the tanks and reenactors. I told her about the flea market, dance, and vintage dresses.

"Can't believe I'm saying this, but it actually sounds like fun, especially the dance," Izzy said.

My mom finished off her wine and lifted her glass toward Greg. "Izzy, what happened to your parents?"

"Mom," I whispered.

"No, it's okay. Honestly, I really don't know exactly what happened—except that a woman who helped hide children during the war got me out of the camp, then I lived with a Christian woman for a couple years who pretended to be a relative. After the war, I moved to Boston."

"But if you don't know what happened, how do you know your parents didn't survive?" Jack asked.

"Because they tried reuniting families after the war. I guess they couldn't find my parents, so my uncle from Boston adopted me. That's the story, and I'm sticking to it."

Jack added, "I'd want to find out what happened. What if your parents were stressed out from the war and had amnesia?"

"You've been watching too many movies," Jeremy said.

"It does sound a little far-fetched, but let's go with it for a moment. Even if they survived, they wouldn't be alive now, so what's the point? I'm thankful to the American Army who liberated us, and my uncle who raised me."

"Here, here," my mom said and lifted her glass. "Y'all, we have to drink to Izzy. And the people who helped save him."

After the toast, I started clearing the table. My mom followed me to the kitchen and moved some of the leftovers into containers. She opened the fridge to make room on the top shelf.

"I'd really like to read his mom's letter."

I put the dishes in the sink and turned around. "Not sure if that's a good idea. I don't want you to get upset."

"Now why would I get upset?"

"Izzy's mom put their birthdates in the letter in case they could get sponsorship."

"Okay, and?"

"Izzy and Dad share the same birthday."

"We do? You didn't tell me that!" Izzy said, carrying dishes to the sink. "Must also be handsome, like me," he teased.

"Was," I answered and started crying.

"Oh shit, what have I done?" Izzy said in a soft voice.

"It's not your fault," my mom added. "Steph's father died a couple of years ago."

"Look at me, all weepy about my dad. You lost yours when you were so young."

"It doesn't matter when or how you lose a parent. It always hurts." Izzy paused. "But guess what? That's why we have pies from Krista's. It's a cure-all."

"What's going on in there?" Greg called from the dining room.

"We're deciding on dessert," Izzy winked.

"Only a small piece for me," my mom said. "Or I'll have to find the nearest water aerobics."

"Water aerobics?" Jeremy called out.

My mom poked her head out of the kitchen. "Are you making fun of your grandma? You should try it instead of having your nose in that phone all day."

***

Later in the evening when my mom left, it reminded me of the time my parents once waved goodbye from a cab on their way to the airport. How I missed seeing my parents as a couple. How I missed my dad and the unconditional love he always gave. Watching her leave left an emptiness, an emptiness that made me seek comfort in photos that adorned our hallway.

Photos of my parents filled both walls, some when they were young and recently married. I stopped to take a long look then wiped the dust off the frame before going to the family room. Jeremy sat on the floor and, as usual, texted away. Jack and Izzy took over the couch. Izzy wasn't joking when he said he'd team up with Jack the next time they got together. They were killing aliens, and Greg was on the sidelines rooting them on, like a soccer dad hoping to crush the other team in overtime.

"He's hiding behind the wall! See him?" Greg screamed.

"Oh crap, he got me. I'm gonna respawn," Jack added.

"I didn't see him either. Even with these four eyes," Izzy said and looked my way for a second before returning to the screen. "Stephanie, one last kill," he continued.

"Play all you want," I said.

"You never say that to me!" Jack exclaimed.

"That's because Izzy never has homework."

"That's a fail," Jeremy laughed and looked over at Jack. "Dude, how many times have you died already?"

Izzy put the controller on the table, got up, and stretched.

"That's enough for me. Tomorrow's Friday, and my heavy metal band gets together in the morning to jam."

"Really?" Jeremy asked.

"Nah, but sometimes I let Dylan and his friends play at the house. That's when I run around looking for my earplugs," he admitted.

Izzy said goodbye to the boys, and the two of us went to the foyer. Izzy grabbed his keys and put on his hat. I slipped into my flip-flops, and we walked to the driveway with Ginger by our side. Izzy took out a small box from the back and handed it to me before closing the door.

"You're the only one who's really shown interest in what happened. To be fair, I don't really talk about it, so not that many people know."

"Maybe it would help to talk?"

He paused before opening the driver's side door. "I really don't want to live in the past so that's why I'd rather give you this. Diane encouraged me to write, but I didn't get very far. Who knows. Before I die, I might become rich and famous, and you can sell my journal to the highest bidder."

We said goodnight and Izzy backed out of the driveway. He honked and waved as he took the turn off the cul-de-sac. I called for Ginger, who was sniffing by one of our bushes, then locked up and went to my bedroom to take out the journal.

Chapter 11

The box was small but had enough room to hold a leather-bound journal and a few photos. Dust covered the top, proving it had been a while since Izzy looked inside. The photos, all in black-and-white with fancy white edges around them, reminded me of the ones I used in the ancestry comps, the ones that meant nothing to me, the ones with faces of strangers.

The photos in Izzy's box had brief descriptions on the back. There was a photo of a very young Izzy with his parents and another with a girl who looked about ten. The words "Isadore and Rebekkah, 1939" were written on the back. Could Rebekkah be Izzy's sister? He never mentioned having a sibling, and Hanna hadn't written about her in the letter. Could something have happened to her, and that's why she wasn't brought up? I put the photos back in the box, picked up the journal, and turned to the first page.

Long ago, whenever I told people about my childhood, they often asked, how can you remember so many details that happened when you were so young? I always answered that question the same way—I remember everything, well, almost everything. I remember our apartment in Staufen, the way my mother made chicken dumplings and my favorite toast with butter and jam, my grandmother who sang German lullabies, and Rebekkah who played hopscotch with me on the sidewalk. I remember it all—the good and the bad. I recall things that happened to me when I was three. Some say it's a good trait, to remember moments from such an early age. Looking back, I've often thought not remembering might have been better.

The Gestapo came to our apartment when I was four years old. I believe my parents tried to leave Germany, but couldn't get out. On that day the German police came, we were taken by train to a camp in southern France. It was a long ride, hot and cramped. When we arrived, they took my father and put him in separate barracks where they kept the men and teenage boys. I stayed with my mom, and whenever there was a chance, I'd sneak between the barracks to send messages back and forth between them. I was just four years old, and I was their go-between, mostly to tell each other that everything was okay.

Earlier I said I remembered everything. But I don't remember the reason my mom told us we had to leave our home. Maybe she didn't tell me. Maybe she didn't have time.

I didn't know the exact location of the camp. My mother received a few boxes filled with goodies. It came in handy because what they fed us was a broth we'd call dishwater soup. Sometimes, when we were lucky, there'd be a single carrot floating in it. On the days my mother had a carrot in hers, she'd fish it out and give it to me. When she sang me "Happy Birthday", we pretended one of the carrots was a candle. I pretended to blow it out then ate the soggy vegetable.

After a while, we escaped, not sure how, but out we went during the night. We lived on a farm and used haystacks as beds, similar to the way we slept in the camp. We were all together for a short time, a short happy time, until we were discovered and sent to another camp in France. And that was the last time I saw my parents.

The journal entry ended abruptly. I had so many questions and couldn't wait to call Izzy. Greg came into the room and picked up a few photos from the box. I handed him the journal, and he sat down next to me.

"Can you believe I served carrots? What the hell is wrong with me?"

He came closer, put his arm around me. "You invited him to Thanksgiving. After meeting him once."

"I thought you were okay with it? I did kind of blurt it out without asking you first."

"Babe, you're missing the point. The carrots didn't stand a chance against your hospitality."

"Maybe I should call him, let him know that I read his journal."

"Wait a few days, let it sink in."

***

On Monday, after making sure Jack got on the bus, I called Izzy on the way to work.

"Hey Izzy."

"I'm not Izzy. I'm his twin brother Fizzy, named after all the seltzer they gave me as a kid."

"Ha ha, very funny," I said and turned out of our neighborhood and onto the main boulevard that led to my office. "I read your journal."

"Already?"

"Now I know the real reason you don't eat carrots."

"Darn, you figured me out."

"You should've told me. I wouldn't have served them."

"Don't be silly. I just didn't want people to feel sorry for me. I don't want anyone feeling sorry for me. Even though it started out lousy, I've had a blessed life."

"For what it's worth, I loved your journal—*loved* isn't the right word, but you know what I mean. It makes me want to know more. But I want to respect your privacy."

"I know I said that I didn't want to live in the past. But on the way home, I thought about what Jack said."

"About what?"

"About finding out what happened. I tossed and turned all night and decided, 'Why the hell not?'"

"Really? So you've changed your mind about your parents?"

"Not about my parents. About the woman who saved me. I want to find out if she's still alive. And pay my respects. She'd be in her mid-eighties now so it's a long shot."

Izzy started to fill in some of the holes, or at least as much as he could, considering he was only six years old when he last saw his parents. One day, his mother pulled him aside and told him to behave himself. That was all he remembered from their conversation, and it was the last time he saw her.

Hearing Izzy's story, I couldn't help but think of Jack, who was a few years older than Izzy at the time. Could I have done something as courageous as Hanna? Could I have given up Jack like that, in hopes that he'd have a chance to survive? Hope seemed so distant. Survival, so impossible. If I'd never found my grandfather's photos as a teenager, I would have never seen the many who, as his unit discovered, were left lifeless. Railroad cars near the entrance filled with dead bodies, some clothed, some naked, all emaciated. "The stench of death" he and his army buddies called it. A scene so horrific it made grown men cry.

Izzy continued, "Many orphans about my age were with older girls, maybe about fourteen or fifteen. They took care of us, taught us how to make a bed, helped us cut up cardboard boxes for picture frames. I didn't have any photos, so I helped other kids place theirs in makeshift frames."

"Sounds like they tried to create a so-called normal life while war waged around you."

"They did, but we were always on our toes. I didn't know what to call them at the time, but partisans warned us as Germans got close, and we had to move quickly for somewhere else to stay. When this happened, we broke up in smaller groups, and that's when I went to live with a woman named Madame Simone who pretended to be a relative. She risked her life to save mine."

Izzy paused and cleared his throat. I wanted to chime in, maybe change the subject in case he started to feel uncomfortable, but he continued.

"On the way to her house, I had to learn a new name and story and repeat it over and over again so I wouldn't forget it. They even prepared false papers for me. My name was Henri and I came to stay with Madame Simone because it was dangerous where we lived."

"I can't believe you remember all that. You were so young and brave."

"I'm not the brave one. The woman who got me out of the camp and set everything in motion, that's who's brave. Maybe you can help me find out what happened to her? The problem is," he continued, "I don't have any information, not even her name."

"I'd be happy to help," I said, continuing my drive on a dreary day.

Set on automatic, my wipers slowed to a crawl as the rain turned to a drizzle then stopped. The sun tried to make its way through as I turned down the street and into our building's garage. Having a short commute kept me sane and sometimes allowed me to run home at lunch to let Ginger out when our neighbor couldn't make it.

The parking attendant greeted me and as I walked to the elevator, I knew I couldn't rely on the Internet for my search, like I'd used it to find Izzy. We had to start somewhere. But how would we find someone without a name?

Chapter 12

Sam stood in the conference room awaiting the presentation for PatchTree Ancestry. I set up my laptop and pulled down the screen after placing the creative boards around the room. Normally, we projected the comps on the wall, but the client liked to take something tangible back to show at the office.

The redesign for their website had gone well so they threw us some more business—this time, to build a mobile app. We'd planned to show the comps and go over naming ideas. Katie, our copywriter, walked into the room with Svetlana, as I pulled up the presentation on my computer. Sam left to meet the client in the lobby and came back to the room with Susan, their marketing director, and Allan, the technical lead who'd partner with Sveta to develop the app.

"Hi, everyone," Susan said. "Whatcha got for us?"

"So, I hope you like what we've done. We have three ideas to show you," I said as everyone took a seat.

We kept in mind the direction from the website and also the users' goals: They want to find out about their family and past generations, but they also want to connect with relatives who are still around. Katie came up with some great name ideas for the app. I clicked to the next page to show the choices.

"Oh, those are good," Susan said. "They all have a nice ring, but I'd like to choose something warm and fuzzy."

I clicked to the next page. "You can always use your company name for brand recognition and one of these names underneath to market the app." I got up and turned the board around. "Here's the first idea. This is what the main screen will look like, with three buckets of information. We kept the same color scheme as your website."

"We'll need to develop a few different versions for compatibility across platforms," Sveta said.

"She never leaves the office," Sam chimed in, attempting to make a joke.

I could tell Sveta wasn't amused, but she smiled instead, adding. "That's right. They're planning to install a shower just for me."

I presented the next design choice, and our account manager answered questions about the timeline. Susan liked two of the three comps and said she would get back to us with a decision by the end of the week. She had a good eye for design and expected a lot, partly from her experience, partly because it was a fairly new company. Like any business, they had to prove themselves and choose the right branding and positioning.

After Sam left the conference room, we chatted a few minutes about the name and taglines, then I walked the client to the lobby. We waited for the elevator and when Susan mentioned how much she liked the use of the old photos, I told her about Izzy and how he asked for my help.

"I'd love to be able to say, 'Use our site to find the info you need.' But right now we only have records on ancestry in the United States. We're planning to do more, but England and Ireland are the only others in the works. If I were you, I'd start with the Holocaust Museum. They have a great resource center there."

"And they're practically in our backyard. I mean, how great is that?" Allan added.

"You're right. Not sure why I didn't think of that," I said. "Do you think they'd help me, even if I'm not a relative?"

"Of course, the resource center is open to the public. And if they don't have what you need, I'm sure they'll lead you in the right direction."

As she pushed the button to the lobby, Susan added, "Have you thought of contacting someone in France? Maybe someone there knows what happened to the woman? That might be an option if you can't find anything. But if I were you, I'd start with the museum. They might have everything you need."

***

It had been many years since I'd been to the Holocaust Museum—eighteen to be exact—when my grandfather was invited to the opening ceremony in 1993. He asked me to come along and pointed out his army division's flag, one of the many that formed the backdrop that day, one of the many divisions that helped liberate concentration camps.

When I discovered the photos in his nightstand, my grandfather reluctantly told me how his division came across Dachau and what remained there. I couldn't understand what he'd gone through, the pain and disbelief to come across a camp that, just days before his division's discovery, had been guarded by Germans who left behind these tattered souls, some dead and damaged, some barely breathing.

That day at the museum, in 1993, we held hands, his holding mine so tightly that it made me turn to look at him, to check on him. He looked back, with his blue eyes red and swollen. *My grandfather was forever scarred.* What could it have been like to discover something so tragic as the remnants of a concentration camp? Do you tell yourself, *Thank God, I was able to save them?* Or, do you think, *Why didn't we come sooner?* How can a person recover from the acts of people, from the acts of war?

We never made it into the building that day. It was too much for my grandfather to handle, so we left right after the opening ceremony. This second visit, on the same day Susan recommended their resource center, would be my first one inside. I left the office early, drove into the city, and snagged a parking space two blocks away by sheer luck.

After walking through a long line at security, I entered a red brick atrium that reminded me of a train station's depot. I saw kids as young as seven and wondered if they'd truly understand what they were about to see. The attendant in a burgundy coat pointed toward the resource center housed on the second floor, but first I wanted to see the Permanent Exhibit.

I rode the elevator up to the fourth floor where the first part of the exhibit began. A "Search for Refuge" poster caught my eye. By 1940 viable escape routes were closed, and in October 1941 it was officially forbidden. The photo showed Viennese Jews in 1938 waiting in line at the police station to obtain emigration visas.

Around the bend, snapshots of captives in their vertical-striped uniforms covered a wall. I stopped and searched for Hanna's face. Would she look the same as she did in the photo with Izzy and his father? Or would she look emaciated? Tired? Scared? Worried? Alone? Even if her picture hung there, would I recognize it as her?

I continued along the hall and came to a display of hundreds—maybe even thousands—of shoes stripped from people from concentration camps. One of their last belongings, a testament to the lost souls of the Holocaust.

After watching films about liberation, I entered a hall called "Children" where we learned that one million children died during the Holocaust. There wasn't much about hidden children, but there was a photo and caption about a Swiss organization saving Jewish children from deportation to Auschwitz. I made a mental note to tell Izzy.

After visiting the exhibit, I went to the resource center on the second floor. A man behind the desk was talking to a woman, and as I waited, I sat down at one of the computers that lined the side of the room. I typed Izzy's name in the registry and an entry came up. A page popped up with his full name and Germany as his birthplace. For the heck of it, I searched for his parents and nothing came up.

"Ma'am, may I help you?" the attendant asked.

"I was looking up a friend and don't see that much information. I don't see his parents either."

"Why don't you come up to the counter. Let's see what we can find out. Name, please."

"Stephanie Britain."

He typed it in. "Hmm, I don't see anything for a Stephanie Britain."

"Oh sorry, that's me. I thought you wanted my name." He looked up above his bifocals and scratched his head. "No, I need the name of the person you're researching."

"Yes, of course. Izzy, I mean Isadore Fischer. And his parents, Hanna and Leo."

"Here, let's see. I found Isadore but didn't find Hanna and Leo. Did you find Hanna and Leo in the registry on the other computer?"

"No, only Isadore."

"Did they survive? Because that register is only for survivors of the Holocaust."

"How would you get his information?"

"Most likely he attended an event or some sort of survivors' reunion. But let me check something else." He pulled up a new page and in the search bar typed in Izzy's name. A page that looked like a scanned document showed up. He moved his screen toward me, and I leaned over the counter. "Okay, here we go. See that date on the back? Looks like that's when he might have requested U.S. citizenship."

"Let's look at the front again," he added and pointed to the text as he read through it. "Born in Staufen, taken to Gurs, then to Rivesaltes."

"Sounds right and matches what he told me. He said he was saved by a woman who helped him escape from the camp."

"That makes sense. There were many who worked underground to help save children during the war."

"Is there a way to find out what happened to his parents or get information on the woman who saved him from the camp? He wants to pay his respects, if she's still alive."

He moved his glasses to the top of his head. "There was a child welfare organization during the war that helped save thousands of children. That's a good place to start." He paused again and asked, "Do you want me to still look up his parents? What were their names again?"

"Leo and Hanna."

I watched as he typed in the same search box at the top right. But the results came up empty. He pulled up a separate page and put their names in a form on a different memorial site.

"Here we go."

I leaned in even closer. It was another scanned document, a page with a long list of names on it, their birthdates, and a convoy number at the top with a date.

He got up and went to a file cabinet. He pulled out a book and held it up with two hands.

"Has Isadore seen this?" he asked. "It lists all the Jews who were deported from France during this time, including Jews from other European countries who were brought to France. That's a page from this book."

Returning to the computer, he said, "Convoy 19. August 14, 1942." He pointed to their names and continued. "Unfortunately, the timing was especially bad for them. Very few survived from this convoy. The ones who did were mostly men kept for labor. Izzy is very lucky to be alive. If I were him, I'd also want to pay my respects. There were a lot of very courageous people who risked their own lives to save the lives of others. If he does find her and thanks her, it's very honorable. A lot of people talk about it but never go through with it."

We chatted some more about the museum, how long he'd volunteered there, and his stamp-collection hobby that took up his spare time. Our conversation turned to Izzy, and why he didn't want to live in the past or talk much about his childhood. The volunteer told me about other survivors and the stories they'd shared with him at the museum over the years.

"Look," he added. "it's none of my business, and I can only imagine how hard it is to talk about it, but we have very few survivors left. We need to hear their stories. Young people need to hear their stories. And those stories need to include what happened to those who didn't make it. We have to remember not just the survivors, but the ones who were murdered."

"He always says, 'What good would it do?'"

"Tell him he should do it for his parents."

I thanked the attendant and started to leave. As I watched him walk over to help some teenagers at the computer, my phone pinged with a text message. It was from Jack.

Where r u?! Have to be at TKD soon.

I ran down the stairs and out the door to my car. *Shit.* Master Reynolds will put me in a headlock for sure, if we're late.

Chapter 13

We walked into Western Warriors, and I could tell by Master Reynolds' expression we were in trouble. I lowered my head and walked to my usual seat until he called us into his office. It might have been easier if he just stood us in the corner. He reprimanded me for being late and reminded us how seriously he takes his class. I looked straight at him and could feel Jack steaming next to me.

"Master Reynolds, I'm very sorry. I was stuck in traffic."

He picked up his pen and began tapping it on the desk. After placing it back down, he informed us that Jack was supposed to test for his next belt level fifteen minutes prior to our arrival, and for him to get to first degree, which could be this summer if he worked hard, he needed to perform in front of five judges who would score his forms, techniques, and kicks.

Master Reynolds looked at his watch then got up from his chair and walked out of the office to talk to the other instructors. He came back, pulled on the bottom of his uniform, and snapped his belt. As he sat down, he told us that he'd make an exception, this time, since Jack had never been late before. We walked out of his office and took a seat. Jack rolled his eyes.

"I know, right," I said, sounding like a disagreeable teenager. "Traffic? Stuck in traffic?"

"Well, I couldn't say I totally spaced out. He would've chopped my head off."

"You should've taken me with you. It's our next unit anyways," Jack said.

"In your history class?"

"Yeah, I mentioned I know a Holocaust survivor."

"And?"

"My teacher wants Izzy to come talk. Do you think he'd do it?"

"Sweetie, I don't know." I remembered the man at the Holocaust Museum telling me how young people needed to hear the stories, the stories about the survivors and their loved ones who weren't so lucky.

"Can you ask him for me?"

"You should ask. He's already bonded with you over video games anyways."

"Please?"

"Do you want him to come, or is it because the teacher asked?"

He looked down and fixed his belt. "I want him to come. But, I don't wanna push him."

"How about this: We'll call him when we get home, and we'll ask once. We won't push."

***

Later that night, it didn't take long for Jack to set up video chatting with Izzy. Jack was a little shy, but he needed to ask him face to face and the best way was between him and his computer. Izzy grinned with excitement as he shared his plan to use video chatting for French lessons when students couldn't make it in person, then he teased how he'd never have to leave the house again with this great technology. Izzy propped his laptop on the kitchen counter, and we could see Dylan walk by in the background.

"Dylan, come say hi to the Britains."

Dylan leaned in and waved, and when he did, his hair fell in front of his face. He moved his hair to the side, hitting Izzy's forehead in the process.

"Oh man, you okay?" Dylan asked.

"Don't worry, that's my bad eye anyways," Izzy joked.

Dylan disappeared from the screen after another wave, and I knew it was subtle cue for me to do the same. If I stayed, Jack would rely on me too much. I went into the next room and sat by the dining room table. Before they started, Izzy asked some questions about upgrading his computer, maybe to make Jack feel more comfortable.

"So, your mom tells me you're doing well in school."

"Sort of. I guess."

"What's that mean? Are you flunking out?"

"No."

"Anybody picking on you?"

"Nah."

"Then you're doing well in my book, kiddo."

After some more back and forth, Jack finally got up the courage to ask Izzy about coming to school to speak.

"Will it be kids or a bunch of boring adults?"

"Just kids. And my teacher."

"Do you know when?"

"I think February?"

"You know what?" Izzy added. "I'll do it. Gives me plenty of time to prep and fly my wardrobe stylist in from Paris. Now, my biggest question is," Izzy continued, "how do I set up this video chatting thingamabob with my students? And how the hell do I turn it off? Or do we sit here and stare at each other all night?"

Chapter 14

Getting into Jack's middle school was almost as tough as a middle-ager getting backstage for a close encounter with her favorite rock star. We passed through two checkpoints and provided photo identification, parent verification, and a criminal background check through their computer. I was about ready to give my blood type when my visitor pass printed out. Izzy went next, and it took a little longer since the secretary had to call up to Ms. Beauregard's room to make sure he was expected.

I looked around, tapping my fingers on the desk. "I go through this every time. You'd think it would be easier by now."

"I should have brought Krista's pies—they would've put them into a sugar-induced coma and we could've snuck our way in," Izzy whispered while putting his driver's license back into his wallet.

The secretary hung up the phone. "Okay, Mrs. Britain and Mr. Fischer, you're all set. Do you know your way?"

"We'll find it, thanks."

"Room C107, down the long hall, turn right, then another right. Are you sure? Carlos can show you. Right, Carlos?" she said and turned to a student sitting with his head on the table.

Izzy removed his hat and pointed to his forehead. "No need. I have a permanent GPS implanted in my brain. You said C107, correct?"

The secretary smiled then turned to another student who walked in. "You got it." She stood up and put her hand on her hip. "Nathaniel, why aren't you in fourth period?"

"Mom's picking me up early," he said and handed her a note.

We could still hear Mrs. Pine chatting it up with students as we took off down the long corridor. Rows and rows of beat-up lockers and bulletin boards framed both sides. Artwork and student-council results took up space on the walls. We turned right and eased our way into the math hall, which made me cringe remembering the high school and college courses I barely passed. We turned left near room C105 and knew we were getting close when we saw world maps and pictures of George Washington and Abraham Lincoln on the wall.

The door to Mrs. Beauregard's room stood ajar. Jack sat by the window looking out as a PE class ran through drills. Not such a great spot to sit when you're trying to learn all about history. I knocked gently on the door. Mrs. Beauregard turned to us and smiled.

"Please, come in. Class, Mr. Fischer's here," she said and pushed a button on a remote that lifted the projector screen. The white board behind her held photos of Izzy and maps of France and Germany. The class closed their books, and several students said, "Hello, Mrs. Britain" in unison.

Mrs. Beauregard put her index finger to her lips as the room turned quiet. "Class, as you already know, Mr. Fischer is here to talk about his experience during World War II when he was a child. We'll save all our questions until after he speaks, okay?"

She stepped to the side and sat down by her desk. "Mr. Fischer, whenever you're ready."

Izzy took off his hat and coat then sat in a chair in front of the room. He ran his hands through his hair and pulled a piece of paper from his chest pocket. He opened it up, took a quick look then looked up at the class after clearing his throat.

"Hello, class."

"Hello, Mr. Fischer," they responded.

"Call me Izzy. This is algebra class, right?"

They broke out in laughter, and a girl with blonde hair and a squeaky voice called out, "No, Izzy. It's world history."

"I know, I know, just kidding. Thank goodness it's not algebra. I'm trying to keep you kids awake, not bore you to tears."

After a minute making a few jokes in light of a very serious topic, Izzy turned the subject to the heart of the story, asking how many students had heard of the Holocaust before this year. Three kids raised their hands; one was Jack. Izzy glanced around the room and began counting, as if he were a teacher making sure all kids were accounted for on a field trip.

"Three out of thirty, not so bad. Well, I don't blame you because who really wants to hear about war and destruction? But I'm living proof that miracles do happen, so without further ado, let me tell you a little more about my life in Germany and France during World War II," Izzy said then started reading from his notes. "But before I tell you about my experience, I have a confession." He paused and looked at me. "This is my first time talking about it, so you'll have to be patient. I'm a bit shy, even at my old age."

Izzy looked back down at his sheet of paper and began.

"My name, as you know, is Izzy. My full name is Isadore Fischer. I was born in 1936 in Staufen, Germany. In December 1940, the German police arrested my parents and me in our apartment. I was four years old. We were taken to a central location where we waited at a railroad station with several hundred other Jewish families. When the guards were ready, they shoved us into a train and took us on a long journey to southern France, and detained us at a place called Camp Gurs.

"At Gurs, they separated men from women, but because I was young, I stayed with my mother. The living arrangements were very, very bad. It rained a lot, and there was so much mud that some people lost their shoes in it. Many people wouldn't be able to get their shoes out, so they had to go barefoot. Can you imagine not having an extra pair of shoes? We were also hungry all the time. They fed us a broth that, once in a while, had a carrot slice floating in it. My mom always fished hers out and gave it to me. Because of this, to this day, I still can't eat cooked carrots. Once in a while, we would get milk and a piece of bread. And we had to sleep on the floor on top of haystacks. To say the least, it was very uncomfortable."

At this point, Izzy shared parts of his childhood that would have been in his journal if he had continued writing. He told the class that his family managed pretty well for a while before the French police found them hiding and took them to Camp Rivesaltes. By then, two years had passed since they'd been taken from their home in Staufen. After that, his parents and thousands of other Jews were rounded up and sent by train to Auschwitz.

He paused for a moment before telling the kids how lucky he was that he didn't get on that train and about the courageous woman who risked her life to save his. When Izzy began speaking about his mother, a few girls in the class got teary-eyed.

"Before my mother was sent on that train," he continued, "the young woman who saved me approached her and said something like, 'Where you're going is very dangerous. Give me your child so I might try and save him.' At least that's what I'd been told. I was really too young to remember exactly what happened. It was, as you can imagine, a very difficult choice for my mother—to keep me with her or allow this woman, who was a complete stranger, to take me. So, in a desperate act, my mother—who was very brave—turned me over to this woman.

I believe, very deep in my heart, that my mother had only one choice. To give me up.

"By that time, I was six years old. We had to move around a lot, especially when we were warned that the Germans were coming. I was hidden in a small French town and lived with a Christian woman. I had to take on a new name and pretend to be somebody else. I had to do that so nobody would find out I was Jewish and turn me in to the authorities. This brave woman took me in at the risk of her own life because it was very dangerous to hide Jews."

Izzy paused and his voice trembled. "I will never forget her as long as I live."

"Mr. Fischer, would you like to take a short break?" Ms. Beauregard asked.

He turned to her and said that he was okay while wiping a tear from the corner of his eye. I looked at the students and could see several girls doing the same. Izzy put the tissue back in his pocket and continued. "With this new identity I was able to go to school for the very first time. I learned how to read French, how to write, and I learned French history. When not in school, I would help in the garden. I lived this life for almost two years. In 1945 when I was nine, I saw my first American soldier when they came to liberate us. I will be eternally grateful. Everyone was shouting as the army rolled by. The organization that helped save me assembled all the hidden children and brought us to orphanages. Then they began to try and find survivors to put families back together. My uncle was already living in America. He found out I was alive and brought me here.

"When I came to America, I was ten years old. I spoke only French and had to learn English fast. I was just a couple of years younger than you. Although I was safe and had plenty of food, it was very hard to cope because I didn't know exactly what happened to my parents. I longed to see them and often cried myself to sleep. I tell you this because it's important to understand that it's okay for boys to cry and show their emotions. Often, even now, I try to act tough, but sometimes you have to let it out.

"I went on to finish high school, then college, and became a professor at a university. I still work part-time and live in a small town in Virginia. I am very grateful to all the people who helped save me. I will never, ever forget them. Well, that's my story. Thank you for listening."

Ms. Beauregard came to the front and shook his hand. She started to applaud, and the kids joined in. They continued to applaud, and Ms. Beauregard went around the room with a box of tissues. A few girls grabbed some and wiped their tears. "Okay, any questions for Mr. Fischer?" she asked.

Several raised their hands at once. "Brittany."

"Did you ever see your parents again?" she asked and half the hands dropped.

"No, I didn't. This woman who approached my mom was right. It wasn't going to end well."

"Maybe they survived?" another student asked.

"Yeah, maybe they jumped off the train and took on new identities."

"Brian, show some respect. This isn't a Hollywood movie."

"It's okay," Izzy said. "I mean, look at me. If I wasn't here to tell you from my own experience, it would be hard to believe all the things that happened."

"Natalie, what stood out in Mr. Fischer's story?" Ms. Beauregard asked.

Natalie wiped a tear. "Not having his mother. And the mud. Getting stuck in the mud."

"That was something else," Izzy said with a smile. "We had only one pair of shoes, so you could imagine how some felt if they couldn't get it out of the mud."

"Makes you wonder if you really need those expensive sneakers," the teacher said, and Jack looked over at me because he often wanted the expensive ones, and I wouldn't dare spend more than fifty bucks on a pair of shoes, for any of us.

As more questions—some silly, some more considerate—went around the class, I thought of the book I'd received that the museum volunteer showed me. It was in my trunk, waiting for the right moment to give to Izzy. I'd memorized the page number where his parents' names were mentioned: page 470, out of 760, in type so small you'd need a magnifying glass to read it well. With hundreds of names on each page, a book so large and heavy it took two hands to carry. There'd never be a good time to give Izzy the book, but it also wasn't right for me to hold on to it. I assumed he'd be upset, that he'd react a certain way when finding his parents' names. But how would I know for sure? Maybe it would be a way for him to find closure.

The bell rang, and the kids gathered their books. They thanked Izzy, by first name, and stumbled out of the room. It was the last period of the day, so we followed Jack down the long, crowded hall to his locker where he picked up his jacket and backpack.

On the way home, they talked about the new video games being released, something I hadn't heard since their last match a couple of months ago at Thanksgiving. It saddened me that Izzy had no kids, no grandkids with whom he could share his stories, skip down memory lane, or leave a legacy.

I wondered why he and his wife never had children, but it wasn't my place to ask. Then I remembered my dad and how he didn't have the chance to finish out his role as grandfather. Jack was ten when my dad died, and I'd be lying if I said I wasn't a bit resentful that he was taken away, just like that. I'd be lying if I said I wasn't upset that my mom had taken up traveling the world instead of sticking around to spend more time with her grandkids.

Construction took us on a detour to Jenifer Avenue, a few blocks away from the building where I got my first job after college. It was back in the day, before computers, where we'd lay out ads on boards using our blades and pencil-drawn illustrations—and heard lots of yelling and profanity. We were yelled at about deadlines, about doing work that wasn't epic or award-winning material. We were yelled at, period. But I still loved the business and couldn't imagine doing anything else.

Now, working for Sam Lewis, whom I met along the way and who hired me away from his competitor, some things had changed. Computer graphics had taken over illustrations and deadlines were even crazier. Over the years, coworkers would come and go, so I got used to constant change. But Sam's possible retirement meant someone I'd respected and known for more than a decade could be replaced by someone with a different personality and work style, or someone who might bring in their own senior-level creative staff. The advertising business had always been a revolving door, one that I'd revolved around throughout my twenties. But I wasn't twenty anymore. Or even in my thirties. You could say I was in my mortgage- and college-paying years.

We pulled in the driveway, and I popped the trunk before turning off the ignition. Reaching in, I grabbed my computer bag as my purse fell off my shoulder and into the trunk.

"Well hello, sweetheart. Come give Grandma some sugar."

Wearing one of my warm and bulky sweaters, my mom stood on the front porch next to Greg who smiled then shrugged.

"Mom, I thought you were in Miami until April?"

She kissed Jack and put her arms around him. "Darlin', it's a long story."

Chapter 15

Still glowing from the Florida sun, Mom stood in the kitchen taking sips of ginger ale in between bites of her turkey sandwich. She took a few more sips then put the can back in the fridge. It would last a week, and even if the fizz wore off, she'd still drink from it before opening a new can. Often, when he was around, my dad would finish the rest so that she could start a fresh one.

She sat down at the table and crossed her legs, revealing numerous sunspots that, in her case, marked a good life spent on the North Carolina coast.

"So what happened in Miami? Something with George?" I asked.

"Turns out he wasn't actually visiting family when he went to Vegas. He was going to the casinos."

"So?"

"He lost a lot of money."

"How much?"

"Doesn't matter. What matters is that he lied to me, and I'm done."

"So, you're walking away? Without giving him a second chance? It could've been worse," I said as I put dirty plates in the dishwasher.

"I'm too old to deal with that. Lie to me once, and that's it."

"So, now what? You're going to leave, off again, time after time—stopping here along the way? Seems like you're always on the go now. Since—"

"Since what? Since your father died? You're too young to understand that life is too fleeting."

"Mom, come back."

"Let me talk to her," Izzy said as he walked out of the kitchen to follow her.

The two of them spent the next hour on the screened porch. Izzy came in a couple times to fetch her a jacket and some snacks. He made Mom smile and laugh, adding the kind of glow to his face that seventy-year-old men get with a little attention. Our screened porch was similar to Izzy's in Stevensonville. His had a much better view, though, as it reached out to visually touch the water. I imagined him and his wife sitting on that porch, like birds on a branch, talking, laughing, maybe even crying. Was it there, where they talked about their childhoods? Was it there, where they shared Krista's pies and marveled over the river and mountain views? Was it there, where they spent her last days?

I still didn't want to give Izzy the book, realizing quickly there would be no good time. Life was too short, as I'd already known without my mother pointing it out. I took the keys, went to the car, and lifted the book out with both hands, using my hip to steady it while I closed the trunk.

"Working over the weekend again?" Izzy closed the door to the porch behind him.

"Not exactly," I said as my keys slid off the top of the book and onto the side table. "This is for you. I've had it for a couple of weeks."

"Oh, a present. I like presents," he said as he put down a can of ginger ale.

"I wish it were. Remember how you asked me to find out what happened to the woman who saved you?"

Izzy nodded.

"Someone recommended that I visit the resource center at the Holocaust Museum. The guy gave me some printouts showing where you were last documented, and he told me about this book." I handed it to Izzy.

He put it on his lap and looked at the cover. He lifted off the sticky note, where I'd written "76,000 names, page 470 for Izzy."

"Once, eons ago, I went to an event for hidden children from the war. I never attended another. Too damn depressing."

"Makes sense. The guy mentioned that maybe you attended a reunion and that's why you were in their system."

He half-smiled and looked up at me. "He called it a reunion? That's funny."

The volunteer gave me a lot of information that day, some of which I hadn't remembered. But I remembered "reunion," thinking it sounded weird to call it that. Izzy turned to page 470, ran his finger across the names, and stopped about halfway down.

"Leo Fischer and Hanna Fischer." He turned to the previous page and read the introduction about this particular convoy, an introduction I'd read numerous times. More than a thousand were in this convoy, including one hundred children under the age of sixteen. It had made a stop at Drancy before going to Auschwitz, its final destination. From the looks of it, there was only one survivor from this train, a train Izzy would have been on if it hadn't been for the woman who helped him escape. The survivor wasn't one of Izzy's parents.

"Good Lord, what happened? Why the long faces?" my mom asked as she came into the living room.

Izzy turned to her. "Katherine, everything's okay, just filling in some of the pieces from my childhood." He continued looking through the book.

"I'm sorry, Izzy. First your mom's letter, now the book. I should've kept it to myself."

"Don't say that. I've been the one avoiding it all these years, never wanting to talk about it."

"Well," my mom said. "it's not a walk in the park. It's hard to talk about."

"So many survivors say that we should never forget." Izzy put down the book and reached in his pocket for a handkerchief. He'd used it often to blow his nose after a sneezing fit. This time he wiped a tear away, like when he spoke in Jack's class. "After reading this, more than ever I want to find the woman who saved me."

"I know." I said and looked over at twelve-year-old Jack who joined us. When Izzy was twelve, he was adapting to his new life without his parents.

"I'm on it," I added. "I've already contacted one of the organizations, waiting to hear back."

"Good. Now enough of this sad stuff. How about a game of *Undone*?"

"Multiplayer?" Jack asked.

"Sure, but don't act like Dylan. He's always yelling 'hacker' and using profanity that would make a ship full of sailors blush."

***

By the time he and Jack finished their missions—killing aliens and respawning, as they called it, to kill more—it was almost eleven. I'd seen Izzy drive before, and although there wasn't anything wrong with it, if you were a professional racecar driver, I was afraid he'd go around one of the turns too quickly near his house.

We offered for him to stay the night, and he agreed after a little convincing. Greg gave him a T-shirt and some pajama pants and showed Izzy to the guest bedroom for the night. My mom stayed in Jack's room, and we put Jack on the sofa.

In the morning, like every morning, I reached for my phone to check the weather and emails. On the top was one from an unfamiliar name.

Dear Ms. Britain:

Mr. Laine forwarded your email in regards to Isadore Fischer and his desire to pay gratitude to the woman who saved him. It's wonderful to hear that Isadore is well. There is a woman who went into the camps who currently lives in Italy. But she is not the only woman who saved children during the war, as you probably know. I will need more information, any information he has, specifically the dates he was detained at the camp, and where he was taken after that, if he can remember. The more I know, the better I can help. I look forward to hearing from him. If he'd rather have you communicate with me, that's fine, I'll just need him to let me know.

Regards,

Jennifer Ginsman

I threw on my robe and went to the kitchen. Greg was at the stove covered in flour, and Izzy, who wore one of my floral aprons, tried to keep the mess at a distance.

"You look cute," I said.

"Not too girlie?" he asked, pointing the spatula to the floral print.

"What's that grin for?" Greg asked.

"Oh, nothing much. Just got an email from the children's welfare organization."

"Already? And?" Izzy replied.

"Let's sit down. I'll read it."

"Come on, you always want me to sit down. I can't stop now. I'm on a roll."

Izzy peeled up the side of the crepe with the spatula to check it then put the pan in his hand, and made a quick move with his wrist to flip the crepe over in the air.

"Nice," Greg said.

"See, can't stop me now."

Greg added a crepe to the pile, and when it started to lean, Izzy pressed the spatula to the side, holding the crepes up while he grabbed another plate to split the pile in two. I poured a cup of coffee and read the email out loud. Wearing a sweat suit and sneakers, my mother walked in when I was halfway through.

"Ooh, Italy. If you go, I insist on coming along."

"You've been, what, about five times?" Greg asked.

"It's my favorite place in the world."

"Mom, you say that about almost every place."

She laughed then took a sip of coffee. "Darlin', you're right. I do."

Jack stumbled in, rubbing his eyes before fishing out the cereal from the pantry.

"I'm hungry."

"Of course you are. You're twelve," my mom said. "By the way, mister," she added, "where are your manners? What happened to 'good morning'?"

"Good morning."

My mom got up and gave him a big kiss. "That's better, sweetheart. Now, all you young'uns, I'm off to an aerobics class."

As soon as she turned away, Jack wiped the wet spot she left on his cheek, as he'd done for the past couple of years with me. He was ten when he started backing away, the same age that Izzy, who'd been orphaned for already four years, boarded a ship on its way to the United States. There were so many questions I still wanted to ask Izzy but hadn't. When did he realize his parents weren't coming back? What does he remember about being liberated? Or about disembarking the ship and stepping on new soil? Instead, I put the focus on my new projects at work and staying in touch with Ms. Ginsman to find the woman who saved him.

Chapter 16

After seeing Jack off at the bus stop on Monday, I warmed up my coffee for the drive to work. It was the end of February, and spring was around the corner teasing me. Time passed so quickly and in a few months, Jeremy would be back home for the summer. I often became nostalgic, wanting at times to push the pause button and replay all my first moments. My first kiss. Watching the kids take their first steps. The first day we brought Ginger home. Seeing my dad's face when he first held Jeremy.

I wanted to relive some of those. And I wanted my dad back. People told me time heals when you lose a loved one. I wasn't sure if I believed that, and often thought those who said it had never lost a loved one. But meeting Izzy helped me realize how lucky we were to have my dad for all those years. Anytime I felt sorry for myself, for not having him around, I thought of Izzy and what he went through with his parents.

When I got to the office, there was a flurry of activity. Young, budding account executives and project managers scurried around. Jason, Sam's assistant, checked cubes, carrying a garbage bag in one hand and used coffee cups in the other. Everyone else checked their walls for inappropriate photos and pulled them down while shoving paper into piles on desks. This could mean only one thing—a client visit. I walked to my cube and eyed the mess and stacked-up coffee cups in the corner. Sveta's desk never needed a cleanup. She was the queen of neat.

"Did I miss the email? Is a client coming?"

"Sam has a meeting this afternoon," Sveta said. "Not sure who's coming, but you know Sam—makes us drop everything."

"I didn't see a meeting on the calendar."

"He could be bluffing to get us to clean up."

"Stephanie, I need you," Sam called out from his office.

I whispered, "You watch. He wants me to find some ad we did ten years ago to show to a potential client. I'll spend hours searching instead of meeting actual deadlines."

"Of paying clients," Sveta added.

"Exactly," I said and walked toward Sam's office. I knocked before entering.

"Hey you, good morning." Sam moved his coat from the chair and hung it on the hook behind the door. He sat back down and dunked a biscotti into his tea to soften it up. "I got an email from a guy named Mitch Sefferd this morning. He's starting his own chocolate company."

"That's cool. What's it called?"

"AshLynne Chocolate."

Sam still hadn't told me why Mitch reached out, but I'd already repeated the company name in my head twice, imagining how it would look on the packaging. AshLynne Chocolate. Each word was on the long side but it wasn't too bad. Long company names, especially ones with four or five words, always challenged me to work a little harder so the design wouldn't be compromised.

"Mitch has a lot of experience," Sam continued. "He's been with several food manufacturers and knows a lot about running the business. They're almost ready to go to market and need help with branding, logo development, the works. Could be huge."

"Why us? Why not one of the big guys?"

"He likes our work. Plus, there's a connection. My stepson Owen went to college with him."

"That always helps."

"Yep, but we still need to win them over. That's where you'll do your magic, as usual. We need some ideas for a meeting next week with their marketing guy. If he likes it, then we'll meet with Mitch."

"No pressure, right?" I said knowing I'd be working all weekend, along with the entire creative team. It was a chance to bring additional food-and-beverage clients into the mix. We had Casa Koolers, and if we won, it meant we could compete with the big shots already in that market. My brain switched quickly from business to creative as teal and orange came to mind as background colors. But I'd need to find out more about the company, the reason behind the name, and the target and market we'd go after.

Sam smiled, dipped his biscotti again, and began reading his email. I got up to leave.

"Steph. If it works out and we get the account, there'll be a nice bonus for you."

It wouldn't have been the first time Sam waved a bonus as an incentive, and he always kept his word if we won. But winning was the key word. He told me, as he'd done many times in the past that, if all went well, we'd be looking at a big-dollar account. The truth was, though, we'd bust our asses to create comps and get the business only about half of the time. Still, it was the best way to get clients, show our creative ideas, and compete against other agencies and design studios.

I asked him to keep me posted and when I got back to my desk, the phone rang. It was Mom, saying she was headed to Miami. Turned out George couldn't live that long without another trip to Vegas, so she wanted to pack up the few items she'd left behind without him being there. And as a surprise to me, she decided to go back to North Carolina to give living on her own a try once again. Greg and even Izzy asked me not to be so hard on her for wanting to live her vagabond lifestyle. It wasn't her fault that Dad died, Greg said—in a much more diplomatic way. And it wasn't her fault that I was the one who left North Carolina and moved away from small-town living.

It was in that small town where I learned how to ride a surfboard and swear like the guys. Where I spent my summers deciding which surfer to kiss under the pier waiting out a storm. But boredom settled in. After high school, I traded in the small town for the city. My parents weren't too keen on the idea of out-of-state tuition and begged me to go in state, so I wouldn't have student loans. But my heart was set on Baltimore, so they slowly warmed up to the idea that their eighteen-year-old daughter would be leaving for the big city.

I wished my mom a safe trip back to Miami and finished the creative brief for AshLynne Chocolate. I set up brainstorming sessions with the team, where we'd throw out ideas, passing on some, finally giving the go-ahead on three that we'd present the following week. The twenty-somethings didn't mind working on weekends, as long as they were done in time to make it to the clubs. I gave final direction on one of the ideas and, after they left, called to check on Izzy. His phone rang and an unfamiliar voice picked up.

"Sorry, I think I have the wrong number. I was trying to reach Izzy Fischer."

"Yeah, this is Izzy's cell."

"Oh, who's this?"

"Dylan."

"Oh hey Dylan, it's Stephanie." I sat down and held on to the side of the chair. "Is everything okay?" My heart pounded. "Did something happen?"

"Izzy was in a car accident. But, he's okay…"

"Jesus. How bad is it?"

"He'll be fine. Just some bruises, that's all." I could hear a lot of background noise, people talking. "Izzy said not to worry. He's fine. They're going to release him tomorrow."

"He's in the hospital? Tell him I'm on my way."

Chapter 17

Traffic was at a standstill going west at any time on Fridays. People loved getting a head start on the weekends down I-66. They, along with the eighteen-wheelers, hogged the road and got in my way. To help pass the time, Sveta arranged a conference call with the team, and we finalized plans for the AshLynne pitch.

The hospital stood by the interstate with the parking lot close to empty making me believe—whether real or not—that it was a slow day. I flew down the hallway and heard laughter coming from one of the rooms.

"Ouch, don't make me laugh. It hurts," Izzy said. Several college students sat around his bed and on the two chairs. They turned around as I entered the room.

"Stephanie, you didn't have to come."

"Nice seeing you too, Izzy," I joked and walked closer. He wore a bandage on his left hand, and his arm was bruised.

"How are you?"

"Could be worse."

"So what happened?"

He wouldn't answer me, even after asking twice.

"He was texting," Dylan said.

"Are you crazy? What was so important?"

"I wasn't exactly texting." He put his arms on the side of the bed and lifted himself up. "I was going down the driveway and heard that ping your phone makes when you get a text. I went to grab the phone and looked away for a second and ran into the tree in front of my house."

"Jesus, Izzy." I put my bag down and sat on the bed next to Dylan. Even in the hospital, you had a gorgeous view in central Virginia. If I were on my death bed, this would be the view I'd want to be my last. Dylan stood up, and the rest of the teenagers filed out.

"Izzy, you need anything?" Dylan asked after grabbing his jacket.

"Nope. Oh wait—yes, stop by Gerry's and ask him to come get rid of the tree."

"That tree didn't stand a chance," Dylan added.

"Ouch, stop making me laugh. Tell him I'll pay him tomorrow."

"Cool. Call me if you want me to pick you up."

"See ya, Izzy," a couple of students called out before leaving.

Izzy looked at me with his bloodshot eyes before turning his head to gaze out the window. His worried expression hit me. Maybe he was scared about what happened but didn't want to say so. Lying in his hospital robe, he looked all of his seventy-six years. He didn't have his baseball cap or brown leather jacket to fall back on to help fade his age. Life crept up on him, as it had on everyone.

"Where does it hurt?" I asked.

"I'm fine."

"Izzy, you can tell me."

He turned to face me again. "Mostly my hands and my right leg. I guess I tried hard to stop."

"It's okay. Happens to the best of us."

"At least I wasn't sexting. Wouldn't want to make anyone jealous of my physique."

After a few jokes, our talk turned serious. He called the accident his wake-up call, not the kind you have when you're young and you have to change your life around. Or, in middle age, when you realize you've haven't done much with your life. It was the kind you get when you're older and realize you have nothing in order. He confessed that he hadn't updated his will since his wife died a few years ago. He'd planned on doing it, but time flew by and life took over.

"I'm calling my lawyer first thing in the morning."

"Do we really need to talk about this now?"

"It's as good a time as any. I'd like to make you executor, if that's okay."

I took a deep breath. I knew from several friends how much work it involved.

Izzy read my mind. "I know it's a big responsibility—but I'm going to make it easy. I don't have any living relatives. I had a childhood friend, Rebekkah, but she passed away several years ago. She has two daughters, one in upstate New York and one in Chicago." He paused to fix his hospital bracelet. "We don't really stay in touch. They have their own lives."

Rebekkah. That was the name of the girl in the photo with Izzy, the photo I found in the box he gave me months ago. All this time, I'd wanted to ask about her but was afraid to bring up too much from the past. Greg always said to take it easy on him with the questions. Turned out Rebekkah lived in the same town in Germany and was also a hidden child during the war. They found each other many years later when they both attended a mutual friend's wedding. Rebekkah passed away a few years back, and Janet, one of her daughters, called him on occasion.

"Why not ask Janet?"

"We're not close. Stephanie, you're family to me."

I had to chase the tears back to their hiding place before I could answer, "That's sweet." It sounded pathetic, what I said, as if someone's giving you a compliment and you don't know what to say.

"Well it's true. I've had a good life. It started out crappy, but turned out great. I met the love of my life and had many great years with Diane. I've had an amazing career. I love this small town and all the college students who keep me young. But meeting you—you're like the daughter I never had."

"Okay, now the flood gates are opening."

"Look, I have to get things in order because what if I hit another tree or drop dead after getting run over by a two-headed buffalo."

"A two-headed buffalo?"

He smiled, and it made me smile back. That afternoon he shared more stories about Diane—where they met, the day they got married, and how they fought over the foster dogs and cats she'd bring home, some that pissed all over the house. She'd always win the fight, by saying how Izzy was an orphan and how could he, in his right mind, turn away these precious animals. They negotiated, and as long as she could housebreak them, they could stay. Each time, within a week, Diane would train them and take the dogs to nursing homes to spend time with the inmates, as Izzy called them.

He shared stories of his college housemates and how at first he wasn't used to seeing them in their T-shirts and boxer shorts, drinking orange juice and milk out of cartons. It reminded me of Jeremy and the many times I yelled at him to put something on and grab a glass like a human being.

"So you'll let Dylan pick you up tomorrow, right?" I looked at my watch. "Promise?"

"Promise," he said. "Now go home. You have a long drive."

I picked up my bag and called Sveta to let her know I'd be in on Saturday to work on the AshLynne Chocolate pitch, along with the rest of the team.

"Stay out of trouble." I leaned down and gave him a soft hug, paying attention to his injuries. On my way out, I thought about my dad. He never had a chance to make it to the hospital that day. No chance for a second chance. Many say it was a blessing the way he died, that he didn't have to suffer. Some people who tell me that have never lost a parent.

"Meribel!" Izzy called out, startling me.

"You scared the crap out of me. Who's Meribel?"

"Not who, what. I remembered after all these years. It's Meribel. The street I lived on with Madame Simone in France."

"The woman who took you in?"

"I can't believe I remembered. I should be in a car accident more often."

Chapter 18

Two weeks after visiting Izzy in the hospital, I got a letter in the mail from a lawyer. In a short paragraph, he wrote that Izzy had appointed me executor to his estate. Being an executor was all new to me, and I had to learn more and get prepared.

"What's that, a love letter?" Greg teased as he came into the kitchen.

"Yeah, from a lawyer."

"Steph, you don't have to say yes." he said after reading it.

"He doesn't have anyone else."

"I know you really like Izzy. And I really like Izzy. I'm just concerned."

He picked up a furniture catalog from the coffee table and started skimming through the pages.

"Concerned about what?"

He put the catalog down. "Steph, you can't replace your dad. He's gone."

I wanted to look up at the light, my cure-all for tears, the way I'd always get them back to their hiding place. But looking up meant looking at Greg, and that meant I'd cry even more. His big brown eyes had a way of getting to me.

"I'm not replacing my dad, that's ridiculous."

"It came out the wrong way." Greg sat down next to me and pushed a piece of hair behind my ear. "I don't want you to get hurt."

I knew what he was trying to say, in a nice way. Izzy might die, and Greg would have to pick up the pieces. But we couldn't go around not having people in our lives because we were afraid we'd lose them one day. We couldn't go around pretending we didn't care and that we didn't need anyone to care about us.

"He's nothing like my dad. No one could replace him. But don't you think it's fate that I found that letter, and they share the same birthday? Maybe it's a sign that I was supposed to find him?"

I could tell by Greg's silence that he didn't want to hurt my feelings. Once before, he said it was just a coincidence, that millions of people shared the same birthday. But I'd always believed in fate. Maybe I shouldn't have this time. Maybe meeting Izzy was a coincidence, a chance, even luck. And that was okay with me. Some things weren't meant to be, but some were. This attitude kept my life sane, especially in my career, having to spend hours on pitches, winning some and losing others.

"So are you ready to kick some ass on the chocolate pitch?" Greg asked, changing the subject and knowing I'd made up my mind about Izzy's request.

"Hell yeah, kicking ass and taking names." I laughed remembering how Sveta got hooked on the caramel and sea-salt truffles the potential client had sent, popping one after another like popcorn at a matinee.

Greg raised his eyebrows and whispered, "Want to practice on me? I'll pretend I'm the client. You could wear one of your silk blouses and sexy librarian glasses."

"I was thinking more like wool socks and granny panties."

Greg smiled and led me to the bedroom, convinced he could help me relax for the pitch, as he'd done a few times before.

Chapter 19

The next morning the boards were set up, the research was done, and headlines, taglines, and copy were written and on target. We were ready to go up against the other firms when Kevin, the marketing director for AshLynne Chocolate, came down from Pennsylvania to narrow it down. As usual, Sam wanted me to take the lead presenting the creative. He was there to schmooze and back me up.

New business pitches were a little nerve-wracking at the beginning, but not anymore. I'd done dozens throughout my career, and I was more than prepared for AshLynne Chocolate. I knew why they considered their chocolates different and more flavorful. I knew why they chose the name, which was a special tribute to the owner's wife named Lynne and his daughter Ashley. And I knew which market they needed to go after from the research our account manager had provided.

While preparing at my desk, I kept looking down at index cards. They became a staple a few years back when I noticed they helped Jack when doing presentations in school. We put a few talking points on each card to help us get unstuck and keep going. It worked like a charm, although it didn't always help us win the business. There were so many factors involved. Price and budget were just two of many. Sometimes all it took was a cute girl to win the client over. In our office, Jessica could fit the bill, but we never used that trick. We wanted to win on our merits, experience, and creativity.

"AshLynne is here," Sam's assistant, Jason, whispered as he approached my cube. Sveta and our copywriter Rachel walked ahead of me. When we got to the conference room, Jason introduced us to Kevin, the marketing director, who looked no older than twenty-five. *They're getting younger every day*, I thought as I extended my hand to greet them.

"So, we're really excited to see what you've done," Kevin said as he took a seat.

"I believe we're waiting for Sam, our fearless leader. Can we get you some tea or coffee?" I asked as I poured a cup of water and left it by my notes.

"No, I'm good," Kevin added, "Actually, Sam said to start without him."

"Okay, great." I turned the board around and pulled down the screen for the presentation. The first idea showed a mom looking out the window waving to her kids playing in the backyard.

"We discovered from our research that there's a sweet spot. No pun intended, really. That sweet spot is somewhere between single people in their twenties who binge-eat it, and older folks in their sixties and seventies who love chocolate but eat it in small amounts or the sugar-free versions. This other market—families with young kids and teenagers—isn't being tapped."

I flipped to the next screen showing logo designs, a home page of a website, and ideas for social-media platforms. We wanted to integrate everything, not only for branding purposes, but to make sure we got more than one project.

"Price-wise, AshLynne isn't in the same category as candy bars you'd find by the register at a convenience store. And it isn't priced like the more expensive ones, which are heavily marketed to business purchases or special occasions. This is AshLynne Chocolate. The everyday sweetness in life."

As I flipped to the next screen, the door opened, and Sam walked in with a man who looked familiar. They sat at the side of the conference table, and I continued with the presentation, showing the boards and additional slides for email campaigns, if the time came for a larger advertising budget.

"Nice work, Stephanie," Kevin said.

The gentleman sitting next to Sam got up to glance at the screen. He still looked very familiar, and I tried to place him.

"Great job with the research, and I love the creative approach and what you've built around the brand. My wife, Lynne, would love it, too." He turned to shake my hand. "We haven't met. I'm Mitch."

He stared for a moment. "You look very familiar. Have we met?" he asked.

I didn't expect to meet the owner during the first presentation. He looked mid-thirties and taller and more slender than I imagined, with sandy blonde hair and green eyes. His rectangular-shaped glasses, similar to the ones Greg used to wear until he got contacts, worked well with his angular features and wide forehead. "I was thinking the same thing. Maybe at one of Sam's parties?"

"Sam, you've had parties and haven't invited me?" he joked. "I'm sure we'll figure it out," he added. "Either that, or you have a twin roaming the streets."

"Not that I know of, but I should ask my mom." I shook his hand once more before he and Sam left the room. Kevin had a few questions about the campaign, but I couldn't concentrate. I never forget a face, and it was driving me crazy.

I gathered the equipment and took it back to my cubicle.

"*Daragaya*, why are you staring into space?" Sveta asked.

"Nothing, trying to place Mitch. He looks so familiar."

"He's pretty cute."

"You think everyone's cute."

"Maybe he looks like one of your ex-boyfriends?"

"Nah, not my type. It's driving me crazy, but I'll figure it out."

I went back to work, still trying to place Mitch, and found an email from Jennifer Ginsman. The good news—the woman from Italy was still alive. The not-so-good news—it wasn't the woman who saved Izzy. She helped save several Jewish children, but from a different part of France. Her email turned more promising at the bottom. With the information Izzy provided, she had found Izzy's savior. Berneen Powers was still alive and living with her daughter in Charleston, South Carolina, and would be thrilled to meet with him.

Charleston, of all cities. I'd been many times while growing up in North Carolina. Izzy would finally have a chance to meet the woman who risked her life to save him and who knew how many other children. What were the chances she'd still be alive and able to remember the details from so long ago? After grabbing my bag and asking Sveta if she wanted some coffee, I walked to the nearby café and reached for my phone, excited to tell Izzy the news so he could plan a trip to meet Berneen—if he hadn't changed his mind.

Chapter 20

Izzy sat on the sofa while I ran around making sure everything was packed. I made a stop in Jack's bedroom. Ginger sat by Jack's feet while he did his homework. It was the morning before school, but he'd forgotten about an assignment and scrambled to finish up. Jack typed away, with his headphones on, playing music you could hear several feet away. I didn't want to startle him, so I went around to the side until he noticed. He paused the music and lowered the headphones around his neck.

"It's too loud."

"Mom, it's fine."

"Are you going to give me a hug before I leave?"

He smiled when Ginger came up and rubbed against my leg. "Wow, she understood you."

"Not Ginger, silly, you. So, still no hug? When are you going to grow out of that?"

He shrugged and looked back to his computer. He'd grown up so fast, faster than Jeremy who was out on his own tackling freshman classes and probably chasing girls. The house had become quiet since Jeremy left. No more disputes or jealousy two brothers sometimes created. I wasn't sure if Jack missed Jeremy or was happy to be the only kid in the house. I bent down to give him a kiss, and he tried to move out of the way.

"Take care of Dad while I'm away."

"It's only a few days, right?"

"Yep, so have some boys' fun. Do things I normally hate."

"Like video games?"

"Yep, get it out of your system because when I get back, it's back to the thirty-minute limit. And make sure you do your homework while I'm gone."

Greg came up behind me and put his arms around my waist. "I'll miss you. But it's exciting for Izzy."

I nodded. "Can't wait for him to meet her. I'm dying to know how she saved him."

"With her ninja-like skills," Jack said before putting his headphones back on and drowning us out with his music.

***

Charleston wasn't anything like I remembered as a teenager. In high school, my friends and I drove there for some surfers we'd met the weekend before. We packed into Carla's beat-up station wagon for the five-hour trip and told our parents we were staying at her aunt's house, which was partially true. When we realized her aunt lived an hour from Charleston in a sleepy town named Ladson, we changed our plans and got a hotel room closer to the beach.

We'd spend the day at the beach, then go back with the surfers later at their beach house. Naturally, one of them knew how to play guitar—a few chords that charmed Carla into giving up a lot more than the rest of us. Since my dad was a great guitar player, it took more than three major chords to impress me.

This time, instead of staying near the beach as I did in my youth, we chose a hotel off of Meeting Street, since Berneen lived with her daughter in the historic area.

We turned on King Street, the main road that runs through downtown, and stopped at a red light. College students with tans and tank tops passed on their bikes. Tourists strolled by carrying their boutique bags and ice cream cones. Young locals sat weaving flowers out of cornstalks, hoping to make a few bucks. We continued on King Street then turned and pulled into the hotel's driveway.

"Darlin'," my mom called as we pulled our suitcases out of the trunk.

She was also sun-kissed, like the college students. Except on her, it left many sunspots, and, if you sat with her long enough, you'd hear a few good stories about her life on the coast. Dressed in a pink and orange floral top, white pedal pushers, and pink ballet flats, Mom fit right in with the Charlestonian ladies. She'd gone even blonder than before, which made her tan look even deeper.

"I'm already checked in. Been hitting the stores." She got closer and put her hand out. A new topaz ring adorned her finger. A matching necklace completed the set. "Izzy, I've got to take you to one of my favorite restaurants. I hope you like seafood."

"Sure, who doesn't?" he said.

My mom pointed at me.

"I know, can you believe it?" I said. "Grew up on the coast, and I won't touch the stuff."

"Well, more for us," Izzy said as we walked through the lobby to check in. It was bustling with tourists, some carrying even more shopping bags than the ones we saw on King Street. Filled with light, the atrium warmed up the lobby so much I had to take off my jacket and stop to fan myself.

"Darlin', you're too young for menopause."

"It's not menopause," I whispered, and a lady smiled and nodded as if she related.

"Sweetheart, you don't have to be ashamed. The hot flashes will pass."

I sighed and turned away. It was not worth the argument. Obviously, my mother knew more about my body than I did and had become a medical expert on the subject.

"So what's the plan? Shopping then dinner?"

"Mom, maybe Izzy wants to rest a little."

"After sleeping half the way down? I feel great and would love dinner, but my treat."

"You will do no such thing. Charleston is practically my second home. You're my guest," she said.

"Okay, then I'll treat for breakfast."

My mom smiled, her mischievous smile that made me scared to ask for more details. "Another time? I'm meeting an old neighbor who moved to Charleston a few years ago. Steph, you remember Walter Edsyl?"

"Mr. Edsyl? My high school English teacher?"

"Steph, we're just friends."

Izzy touched my arm and grabbed my attention. He looked at me and lowered his brow to show a distaste for my questioning. Maybe the look was his way of saying, "Take this time with your mom and enjoy it. Tomorrow she might be gone like your dad." I backed off when we got to the elevator, not wanting to take away from the reason we were in Charleston—to meet Berneen.

The elevator door opened, and we piled out. Izzy decided to join my mom for some shopping, and I plopped down on the bed. My phone vibrated and awakened me later with a text from Sam.

> *We made the cut for the AshLynne biz.*
> *It's down to us and one other agency.*
> *I'll want them chomping on something else*
> *before they make a decision.*
> *We'll talk first thing Monday.*

Chapter 21

The next morning, Izzy sipped his coffee and nibbled on a muffin without a word. We were on our way to meet Berneen, and I was sure he had a lot on his mind. Had he prepared any questions or did he have only one: How did you save me?

After breakfast, we walked the few blocks to her daughter's house, crossing over King Street and passing the College of Charleston before turning down Coming Street. We passed beautiful two- and three-story Charlestonian houses painted like pistachio and lemon sorbet. I imagined families sitting on their piazzas drinking sweet tea while fanning themselves in the summer heat. Several of the large homes had been divided into apartments and rented out to students who turned the beautiful porches into storage for their bikes, skateboards, and empty soda cans.

We turned down Montagu Street and walked past a few houses before stopping. A wrought-iron fence surrounded a beauty bathed in vanilla stucco sitting high and framed by palm trees on both sides. Karen's house, the most modest on the block, reminded me of houses near my college in Baltimore.

"You're quiet," I said as we walked up the sidewalk to her house.

"I've got the jitters," Izzy said and put out his hand.

"We don't have to do this if it's too hard. You're shaking." I took his hand in mine.

"Must be the vodka I drank right before breakfast."

I fixed his jacket lapel. "I can explain that you're not feeling well, and I can get the answer for you."

"I'm fine, really. Let's do this."

We walked up the stairs and rang the bell. A woman, who looked to be in her fifties with a dark blonde bob that fell to her chin, answered the door. She smiled and put her hand on her chest.

"Izzy, Stephanie! Please come in. I'm Karen, Berneen's daughter. So nice to meet y'all."

"You have a beautiful house," I said, looking around the hall and toward the living room.

"Well thank you. Please, have a seat in the living room while I get my mom."

Many photos lined their foyer. Most were family portraits in black and white and it reminded me of the remembrance hallway in the Holocaust Museum with photos of a family from Eastern Europe. Later in the museum, we learned they all perished during the war. That could have been Izzy. It might have been Berneen. But they were both here to remember the ones who weren't so lucky. I walked over to Izzy, who was looking closely at a photo of a young girl with her parents.

"Maybe that's Berneen?"

He nodded, and, after we glanced at a few more, we walked to the living room, which was filled with wall-to-wall windows. You could see a small garden in the back. A swing sat under a weeping willow tree with a red wagon parked next to it on the brick patio. Either Karen had kept the wagon from when her children were young, or maybe she already had grandchildren. Either way, I imagined weekends filled with happy, laughing kids running and playing tag in the backyard while Karen and Berneen watched.

"Mom, this is Izzy." We turned around to face Berneen. She stood, with one arm holding on to Karen and her other hand on top of a chair. She walked a few steps toward Izzy and

116

got teary-eyed. She pressed a tissue against her lips. Her nose turned red as she tried to hold back the tears.

"It's so wonderful to meet you." Berneen held out her hand, and they stood there looking at each other, holding on to each other's hand.

"My, you've grown," she said then chuckled nervously.

"Yes indeed. And, thanks to you, I've been able to lead a fantastic life."

Berneen looked at him for a moment longer then sat down. She was eighty-six and still beautiful. Her hair, now white, was parted in the middle and pulled back in a bun. As with women from her generation, she was dressed beautifully and completed the look with rouge and red lipstick. She even had on navy patent leather pumps that matched her green and blue plaid skirt.

"Izzy, tell me about yourself. What did you become?"

Izzy spoke about growing up in Boston, meeting Diane, becoming a professor, and his life in Virginia. While Izzy continued about the letter and how we met, Karen brought us some cookies and iced tea, sweetened perfectly like my mom's.

Izzy took a few sips and set it back down on the table. "Enough about me. You've had the most amazing life, I'm sure."

She smiled and asked him to speak up a bit before she answered. "My life has been adventurous. Somewhat too adventurous at times."

"Like the time she jumped out of an airplane on her sixty-fifth birthday," Karen said as she passed around a few cookies.

Berneen giggled. "Once was enough."

We laughed and talked about some of life's most daring moments. Izzy still looked nervous, so I continued. "What you did for Izzy was the most daring of all, beyond brave."

"I did what was asked of me. What Izzy's mom and hundreds of other mothers did, now that was brave. I remember I was seventeen, working at the camp as a nurse. They started getting people ready to board trains. We had to act fast, so I started approaching mothers as they were leaving."

"What did you say to them? To my mom?"

"I knew you would ask that, and I wish I could remember the exact words. I remember telling them that they were going to be taken somewhere that wouldn't be safe. I felt so bad having to be blunt, but I had to act fast, and they had to make a heart-wrenching decision so quickly. Could you imagine? Having to make that choice? And trusting a complete stranger with your child, not knowing what would happen?"

Berneen turned away and toward the French doors that led to the backyard. Izzy, who always had a way with words, struggled. His eyes welled up, and Karen passed him a box of tissues. He took one, wiped his eyes, and blew his nose.

Berneen looked backed at Izzy. "I told myself I'd keep it together, be strong when I met you. But you're the first hidden child I've seen since the end of the war. For many, many years I couldn't sleep. I kept picturing these mothers and what they must have gone through as they left the station on those trains. I wouldn't have been able to survive the journey with such a horrible pit in my stomach, the worry of not knowing what would happen to my child. Forget about me—they could take me, do whatever they wanted—but how could they do this to children?"

Berneen's lip began to quiver. She sighed heavily and began to weep. Izzy leaned forward and took her hand. They both hugged and cried together.

"I'm sorry," she let out.

"I'm more grateful than I can ever say, for what you did for me."

Berneen looked up and stared ahead, as if she were thinking. "There was one mother that I had to ask more than once, then finally, I grabbed her daughter. We were fairly certain she wouldn't survive if she stayed. That tore me in half to have to do that. I can still see the mother's face."

Karen came from behind and rubbed Berneen's shoulder.

"I'm so sorry you had to go through all that," I said. "I can't imagine how hard it must have been, and now you have to relive all those details."

She wiped her eyes again. "It's okay. Izzy, you wanted to know, how did this crazy lady get the kids out?"

"I wouldn't say crazy. Fierce is more like it."

"Fierce. I like that." She continued, "I wish I could tell you exactly how I got you out. But it depended on the situation. Sometimes we hid the children under our capes, and sometimes we took them out at night and hid them on a wagon. We told them to be quiet and behave, but I never mentioned their parents. I wouldn't give them false hope."

"That's the bravest thing I've ever heard. Do you know how many children you saved this way?" I asked.

"Oh, I don't know. One would have been enough. Even if I just saved Izzy, it would have been worth it."

"Izzy, are you okay?" I asked.

He nodded. I could tell this was taking a toll on him.

"Izzy," Karen asked. "Were your parents taken to Auschwitz?"

He nodded again.

"That's what I thought," Karen added. "I'm very sorry for your loss. On one hand, it was the worst part of my mother's life. On the other, I'm so glad she was able to help."

"What about your family, Berneen? What happened to them?" Izzy asked.

"My family is here. Did you see the pictures of my grand-kids on the credenza?" She pointed toward the table by her side. She may have been trying to distract us. Maybe she didn't want to talk about what happened to her family during the war, or how she ended up here in Charleston. Maybe she was like

Izzy in so many ways and didn't want to talk much about it. But then she shared more of her story.

"Right after we were liberated, I met a handsome soldier, and he swept me off my feet. He was from Charleston, and after he retired from the army in 1965, we moved back here to raise our four kids."

"You had your hands full," I said.

"Yes indeed. Nine grandchildren. Karen is the only one who still lives in Charleston. The rest have flown the coop."

"They all do that," Izzy added.

Berneen spoke more about her family and especially grandkids. She called it her bragging rights.

"Would it be okay if I took a few photos of you with Izzy?" I asked after she finished her stories.

"Of course, that would be wonderful. And get my good side, which quite frankly, is any side," she said, giggling.

"Same here," Izzy said. "I especially look good in my bell bottoms and platform shoes, which I forgot to bring along. You know, senior moments."

I fished out my camera and made sure it was set on automatic. "You guys are too funny."

Berneen took a sip of her tea and set it back down. "You need a sense of humor when you've gone through a life like Izzy's. Makes everything better when you laugh. Right, Izzy?"

"Laughter is the only medicine," he said as he helped Berneen out of the chair and walked her over to the window.

"Let's take the photos in the backyard. It's such a beautiful day," she added.

We walked outside, and the two of them sat in a large lounge chair on the brick patio. I made sure to get the red wagon and swing set in some of the photos.

"Mom, it wouldn't hurt to smile," Karen pleaded.

"I'm going for my sexy look," Berneen said before laughing, which made Izzy laugh, which made the best photo of all.

Chapter 22

The ride home with Izzy was quiet. Berneen said she was adventurous and a risk taker, but at the same time she didn't see herself as a hero. Did being a risk taker really have anything to do with saving lives? If it did, she wasn't just saying this. She lived it. Before we arrived in Charleston, Izzy told me he just wanted to find out how she saved him and to pay his respects. Other people hid him, fed him, protected him, cared for him. But Berneen set it all in motion.

What made people do the right thing? Choose not to turn a blind eye? Risk their lives to save others at any cost? What made them different from the rest, the ones who didn't take that chance. Fearlessness? Bravery? Empathy? And was the reason different for everyone? Doing the right thing to help a neighbor, a friend, or even a stranger. But doing the right thing could have jeopardized their own lives and the lives of their families. Some were caught and faced horrible consequences. Others were lucky, like the children Berneen saved.

After Izzy headed to Stevensonville, I came back to an empty house and found a note left by the boys that said, "Gone to a movie. Be back soon." I took a quick shower and read an email from Sam, with more details about AshLynne. Luckily, we weren't required to do another round of presentations. They'd decide between two design firms based on the presentations already done. Sam said we'd know by midweek.

Whether we'd win or not, I could relax for the rest of the weekend.

I took the memory card out of my camera and placed it in my laptop to see the photos we took in Charleston. A folder popped up, and before clicking on the recent ones, I came across a folder from Valor of the '40s, the reenactment from last summer. It dawned on me that I never went through the photos. Between Jeremy going off to college, meeting Izzy, my crazy work deadlines, and making sure Jack stayed on top of his homework, it had slipped my mind. I opened up the first one of Jack and Greg standing next to the Flying Fortress. *Wow, Jack had grown a lot since last summer,* I realized before clicking through more pictures. The Russian woman and young boy sitting on the blanket peeling potatoes. A few shots of women dolled up in their fishnets and red lipstick. American soldiers leaning against their vehicles.

Ginger looked up at me, begging for her Sunday walk. I reached over to pet her then got up and peeked outside. The month of May had brought warmer weather, the perfect time to spend with my furry companion while the boys were still at the movie.

"Let's go for a walk," I said without turning around. Ginger knew these words well and knew what to do. She hopped up and came toward me, burrowing her head against my leg, with her tail wagging.

We took our usual path, stopped to look at some house renovations, and walked uphill to the playground where all the kids came running to pet her. We were quite popular with all the kids. Ginger loved the attention, and when they left to continue their sliding and swinging, she jumped in place as if she were stomping her feet to get attention.

We bought our house when Jeremy was two. It had been years since I'd taken the boys to this playground, but now it was Ginger's turn. Every year, there were new faces, younger parents, and trendy strollers.

I took a photo of Ginger and sent it to Jeremy. Texting was our favorite way to communicate. He was a responsible texter, meaning he'd always text back. After a minute, my phone pinged.

Aww. I miss her.

I texted: *And your mom?*

Which one? He texted back with a smiley face.

Having boys, one thing was for certain: They communicated with very few words. They'd never go on and on about their friends, their feelings, or who upset them on any particular day. Jeremy's texts assured me, comforted me, let me know he was okay. If a one-word text was all there would be, I'd take it any day. Jack turned out the same way, unless I asked him about one of his video games. Then, he could talk for hours.

When we got home, Ginger plopped down next to me as I continued looking through the photos. Ginger started to snore, and I smiled, thinking back to when she'd spend time with Jeremy and they'd take naps together. How I missed that. How I missed Jeremy and my family of four and even though we often were in separate rooms, I knew we were all happily coexisting.

I scrolled back to find the photo of Jeremy in his dorm room before clicking back to the reenactment. More young women freeze-framed in their fishnets and red lips. Men in uniforms smoking cigarettes on the bumper of their vehicles. Russian soldiers eating bread and sausage.

Then I got to the photo of the French camp, and the one I'd taken of the German soldier and French woman sitting on the makeshift stoop talking to each other. Until now, I'd forgotten all about that SS officer. Even though the event was make-believe, how could someone want to dress up like that? He'd mentioned the cool uniforms. But, how could it be the

123

only reason? To reenact a Nazi because the uniforms were cool? To choose to portray someone in history who was responsible for such tragic consequences. It didn't make sense to me. Then again, war in general didn't make sense to me either.

Something in the photo caught my eye. The French girl's shoes were very worn, and her stockings were torn. Was she trying to depict how it looked during the war or were the dirt-covered shoes from the day's dusty events? As I clicked to the next picture, the one where they turned to face the camera, something else caught my eye and those earlier feelings of familiarity were confirmed. The SS officer who encouraged me to come into their camp, the one who seemed to enjoy his role and who spoke with a German accent so freely was Mitch Sefferd, the owner of AshLynne Chocolate.

Chapter 23

Monday mornings were always grueling, and Greg's snoring and Ginger's panting woke me up several times during the night. By the time I got to the office, I needed a second cup of coffee. My daily routine of booting up the computer and checking emails came before making my rounds. Many from the creative department, especially the younger ones, crawled in about ten. They never minded staying late, but cringed if there were early morning meetings. Svetlana sat at her desk, programming away, cussing at her computer when it was acting up.

Sam's weekly recap about client development mentioned we were still waiting to hear back from AshLynne Chocolate. I deleted the email and remembered the reenactment. It really wasn't a big deal, or any different from an actor portraying a Nazi in a film. It was a role, an act. But every time I pictured him in that uniform—rolling the cigarettes, sharing his make-believe beliefs about the German army—the memory of my grandfather liberating one of the worst camps in Europe, and Berneen's somber expression when she talked about taking the children away from their mothers, filled me with sadness.

If we didn't win the AshLynne account, we'd be fine. Casa Koolers loved our work and promised to throw us new projects. But even so, it wasn't the nature of the business to sit and be content. You never knew when a client would cut their budgets, no matter how much they loved you and your work.

Even a happy client would leave if their sales dropped for any reason, even if it had nothing to do with the marketing and advertising. That was the nature of the beast, the nature of the career I chose.

As I hung up my sweater, Sveta spun around in her chair. "Darling, how was your trip to Charleston?"

She lifted her arm and wiggled her fingers, then put her hand out. She was sporting a new ring and bracelet. "I took a road trip, too. To the jewelry store. Rob bought them for me for my birthday."

"I thought you guys broke up."

"We did." She smiled. "Then we made up. It was fun making up."

"You mean making out."

"That too. Actually that was more fun."

"What was fun?" Sam asked as he came up the aisle.

Sam listened to the story about how Sveta couldn't decide what to choose and how Rob practically fell asleep in the chair as she tried on different rings. Sam was easily distracted and most likely would have been diagnosed with ADD as a child if they monitored kids back then. His mind was fleeting. He looked around, asking questions about different topics.

"Well, good for you, Svetlana," he said, and as soon as he started asking questions related to work, the few girls who'd come to take a look at the ring retreated to their cubicles.

"Stephanie, I need you for a minute," he added. I knew he hadn't come over to hear the news about Sveta.

"Close the door," Sam said before plopping into his chair after we walked over to his office. He spun around to look through his email and check his phone for messages.

"I got a call from Susan this morning."

"Is everything okay?" If Sam was calling me into his office and closing the door, I knew I had to prepare myself for something big, most likely the worst.

"They're pulling their projects."

"What? I thought they were happy with their ancestry app."

"They are. But they're a start-up. They've run out of funds and need to slow down on some projects until they get more. There's not much I can do about it."

"So, what does that mean?"

"You know what it means."

He was right. I knew what it meant. It meant I'd have to let someone go. Sam hated conflict and giving bad news. He could never let anyone go personally, so I had to do the dirty work.

He looked up at me as he took a sip of his tea. "You decide. Definitely one of the freelance designers, and maybe one of the copywriters."

"But we only have two writers. Whoever stays will be overwhelmed."

"I can't afford both."

"I have an idea." He stared at me, hoping I'd come up with something fabulous, but really, it was a stalling technique. "Let's wait a little, maybe two or three weeks before we make a decision. If nothing pans out by then with more work or new business, I'll take care of it."

Sam tapped on the desk and looked at the calendar on his laptop.

"Okay. Two weeks. But do it on a Friday, without notice, and give the copywriter a sixty-day severance. It's tough out there."

As I left, a few colleagues were huddled outside his office. It was the usual few who always stood waiting, pretending to talk shop. I smiled, not wanting to show any worry. We were a small company, and it felt like an extended family, even when it came to the freelancers. I was halfway down the hall when Sam called out, "Stephanie!" *Shit. Now what? Did we lose more work?*

"This is friggin' amazing."

"What's amazing?" I asked when I stuck my head in his office.

"I just got two emails. One from Casa Koolers. Listen to this: 'Sam, we love what you guys did for the website launch and social-media campaign. Numbers are looking great. We're ready for a car banner design and a new email campaign to drive even more traffic to the site. Do you have the bandwidth?' He's asking if we have the bandwidth? Hell yeah, we have the bandwidth."

"So glad we don't have to let anyone go," I whispered.

"Actually, we might need extra help. The second one's from Mitch. He wants to hire us as the agency of record for AshLynne Chocolate. Looks like we'll be busy."

Chapter 24

I always looked forward to holidays, especially after Jeremy left for college. They were often the best times for the four of us to be together, when all of us were more or less free of work, school assignments, and other parts of our lives taking over.

It was Memorial Day weekend, and we'd planned a cook-out and invited Izzy and Sveta. Jeremy slept in after being out late visiting his high school buddies. When he was home, Ginger would trade in Jack's bed for Jeremy's. Ginger missed him, and it didn't hurt that he spoiled her with long afternoon walks. Sometimes I'd join them, and even though we didn't talk much, being together reminded me of years ago when I pushed Jeremy in the stroller. We didn't have Ginger then, but our brown Lab, Bailey, couldn't get enough of our walks. She'd wag her tail every time we brought the stroller out. She knew it was time to go.

She stayed by our side, never pulling us. She gave us a sense of security through the neighborhood but mostly provided us and the other kids great company at the playground. Bailey even helped potty train Jeremy by leading him to the bathroom and staying there while he sat on the toilet. She was a remarkable companion.

When I was pregnant with Jack, we got a new neighbor who had a cute little Maltese. Bailey fell in love with her. Over the years, I'd forgotten the dog's name. It was as if the horrible incident erased my memory of it. One day, Bailey heard the

Maltese bark and ran to the front door. She wagged her tail and looked back at me. Bailey wanted out. I always made her wait for the leash, but this time—who knew, maybe it was the pregnancy—I didn't follow my usual routine. I tried to blame it on something other than my stupidity. That day, I opened the door, and Bailey ran out with a mad dash across the street to say hello to the Maltese. By the time I grabbed the leash that hung steps away on the closet door, I heard the brakes screech. I didn't want to look. I was too scared to look.

Jeremy was six years old, and that dog was his everything. He was too old to lie to, too young to completely understand. But I had to tell him. I still remembered the look on his face, how his upper lip first trembled then hid under the bottom one, how his tears flowed, how he hid his face in the pillow and curled up after throwing the blanket over his head. He let me console him but didn't hug me back.

I'd soon have my hands full with a new baby, but we couldn't live without a companion. I also knew it would be too much for Jeremy to handle, so that's when we surprised him with a new puppy. We spent the day deciding on a name, settling on Ginger after she jumped in Jeremy's lap when he said it the first time. Ginger was twelve now, and though she had slowed down quite a bit, she still loved our walks.

"You used to love going down that slide," I said to Jeremy as we passed the playground. "You were always negotiating to stay longer."

I looked over at him, remembering those times and our beloved Bailey. She was long gone and so were the days that Jeremy would stand next to me and put his hand out to see how much he'd grown over the summer. In about eighth grade, he passed my height and now was several inches taller than me.

"Remember Bailey?" he asked after looking at the playground and back at Ginger.

"Of course, she was an awesome dog."

"I still remember what happened."

"What do you mean?" I didn't tell him that I'd just been thinking about her.

"When Bailey got hit. Did she suffer?" he asked.

"I was a coward. I couldn't do it."

"Couldn't do what?"

"Go get her. I had the neighbor pick her up and wrap her in a blanket." I paused for a second to compose myself. "She was gone by then." I paused again then asked, "How do you remember everything? You were so young."

"She was my best friend. Until Ginger." He reached down to pet her as we stopped at the corner. "Mom, it wasn't your fault. She ran out so fast."

"It was, not sure what happened to me."

As we walked up our street, he added, "At least her last thought was Cookie."

"You even remember her name," I said as we watched the kids run down the block.

"She loved that dog way too much. Nothing stops love. You should know that."

It was amazing how much insight a nineteen-year-old could have. He was right. Nothing stopped love. And nothing stopped the memories—good or bad—even when you're six years old.

***

"Wait until you see the color turn on the burger before flipping them. That's the trick," Sveta said to Greg by the grill.

"And don't flatten them out. All the juices will escape, and they'll be all dry and tasteless," she added.

Greg, who donned an apron with an image of Michelangelo's David in boxer shorts, held up the spatula and smiled at both of them. He was biting his tongue, most likely wanting to say there were too many cooks in the kitchen, or in this case the backyard, but he did the right thing by staying quiet. You'd never win a battle against the ladies, especially a feisty Russian one.

Izzy picked up on it and walked to the cooler. "I think our chef needs a cold beer." He took off the cap and handed Greg the bottle. "Nice apron. I used to have a body like David's."

"Really?" Svetlana said curiously.

"Yep, my six pack was completely made out of marble." As usual, Izzy laughed at all his jokes. But this time, we beat him to it and laughed first.

Evan ran up to Sveta and threw himself in her arms. "*Baba*, I'm hungry."

"Soon, *Vanetchka*. Uncle Greg has to cook the burgers, and once they're done, we'll eat, okay?"

Jeremy crept up behind Evan, scrunched down, and got on all fours. Evan was too busy hugging Sveta to hear him coming. "I'm hungry too!" Jeremy exclaimed, and he started tickling Evan, who let out a guffaw so loud that it woke Ginger up from her nap. She barked and slowly trotted over with her tail wagging. Evan grabbed on to Ginger and tried to get on top to ride her. Even in her older age, she didn't mind because she withstood it all those years with our two boys. She was used to having a little boy try to ride her like a horse.

I opened the sliding door and went to the kitchen to put the salads into bowls. I grabbed the ketchup, mustard, and pickles from the fridge and set them on the counter.

"Can I help?" Izzy asked and put his beer on the table.

"No, I'm good. Actually, if you could grab those two bowls over there, I'll dump the salads into them."

"Potato salad has feelings too, you know."

"I don't get it," I said.

"You said you'll dump them. That's not so nice, being dumped."

"Sorry, I have a thing for coleslaw this week."

"Okay, but break the news lightly."

I smiled and turned to him. "Have you spoken to Berneen since our trip?"

"We spoke yesterday. She's doing great."

I put the paper plates and utensils in a bag to carry out to the backyard. "Can I ask your advice about something?"

"Sure, shoot." He sat down at the kitchen table, grabbing a few potato chips.

"We bid on this new business at work and we won. It's a large account, a chocolate company, could be thousands of dollars in billings."

"Do you need an old guy for your ad? You can pay me in chocolate."

"I'll let you know. Remember the reenactment in the summer where I found the letters? I didn't tell you everything."

I grabbed a few chips and told him all about that day—the different camps, the evening dance, and my short, but memorable encounter with the German soldiers, one in particular who happened to be our client.

Izzy chimed in. "I don't get it. You don't have to be his best buddy or care what his hobbies are. You just have to market his chocolates. Anyways, it's not like he's a real SS guy."

I picked up another handful of potato chips before hesitantly adding. "I'm surprised you don't think it's a big deal."

"Because it's pretend. They reenact wars so people don't forget what happened. It's history. At least they're acting it out so people who don't know much about it can learn something. Kind of like watching a movie. Have you thought of it that way?"

"That's what Greg said."

"How could you see it any differently?"

"But what if he's really an anti-Semite?"

Izzy wiped his hands with a napkin. "I learned long ago not to live by 'what ifs'. Besides, there are plenty of anti-

Semites out there we don't know about, and I doubt they're wearing SS uniforms. We're not going to change how people feel and what they believe in."

The screen door opened, and Jeremy was busting Jack's chops for something. They were always pretty competitive, and even though Jeremy hadn't been home for long, they were already at it, getting testy over something. It could have been the smallest thing like who's going to take out the trash. This time with them getting older, it almost sounded as if a dad and his son were bickering. Jeremy's voice had changed years ago, becoming deeper. Often, I'd get Greg and Jeremy mixed up if they were in different rooms unless Jeremy added "Mom" to the front of his sentence. Jack's voice hadn't changed yet, but it was getting scratchy. It wouldn't be long before his voice would start to confuse me as well.

"Mom, the burgers are ready. What are you doing?"

"We're coming. Grab some of the salads."

Izzy got up and took a few more chips. "These are addictive."

"I know, that's why I don't usually keep them in the house."

Jack grabbed a handful on his way out. "Mom, live a little. They're just potato chips."

"Stephanie," Izzy said after Jack left, "I'm sure there's nothing to worry about."

He picked up his beer and stuffed the bag of chips under his arm. "I'll tell you what. You helped me find Berneen. Let's see what we can dig up on this client of yours. And, if there's nothing, you'll forget about it, deal?"

"Deal."

"Good, because a lot of guys are into reenacting. It's a hobby."

I'm sure Izzy was right. Mitch was keeping history alive, choosing to show a contemptible side of the war. But curiosity got the best of me, and I wanted to see what we could find out.

Chapter 25

Now with his freshman year complete, Jeremy was home for the summer. He'd have a chance to sleep in for a few days before working at the grocery store to save money for his sophomore year. Jack, still in school and being tortured by standardized tests for the rest of the week, begged to stay home and also sleep in. We negotiated—he'd sleep an extra half hour, and I'd drive him to school. Considering the car was where we did most of our talking these days, I didn't mind.

He scarfed down a peanut butter and jelly sandwich, drank a glass of milk, and ran to the front door to put on his socks and shoes. Once in the car, Jack threw his backpack on the floor and put on his seatbelt.

"Can we take the long way?"

"Why?"

"So I don't have to sit in the gym waiting for the bell. It sucks."

"Honey, the year is almost done."

"Why does Jeremy get so many breaks? Can I skip high school and go straight to college?"

"I don't think you're ready for that."

"So I'm not smart enough?"

"That's not it. It has nothing to do with smarts and studying."

"I know—you think I'll drink all the time and fail my classes."

"That's not it, it's just a little too much fun in college."

"What do you mean?" He paused. "Oh, I get it. Never mind."

I stopped at the light and turned to him, trying to get more details. "What do you think I meant?"

He didn't answer and bent down to fish out his phone and headphones from his backpack. Obviously our conversation was over. I could resuscitate it if we changed the subject to video games, but instead I took a few sips of my much-needed coffee and waited for the light to turn green.

"I keep getting emails about Valor of the '40s. Should I unsubscribe?"

"Up to you. Anything interesting?"

He shrugged. "I usually delete them."

"Well, then how do you know?"

"I should unsubscribe. There's probably a link on the bottom, right?"

"Yeah, in small print only teenagers can read."

"It's just news stuff. Says the reenactment is moving to June with more airplanes and vets telling their stories. Do you want to go?"

"Been there, done that, ya know?"

"It'd be cool to see more planes. Maybe Izzy wants to go? He could hear the vets tell their stories."

"He did say it sounded like fun. Let me think about it."

Taking the long way, I pulled up at the back of the school and waited for several buses to zoom by to the front. "Now go learn something. You only have one week left."

"One week too many." He pushed his hair out of his face and picked up his backpack. Soon his hair would be as long as Jeremy's, and we'd have to cut it, if he'd let me.

My phone beeped with a text. It was from Sveta.
Where are you? Sam's been by twice, needs to talk.

I looked at my watch. It was close to nine. After I parked, I grabbed my bag and headed across the lot to the front door. We shared a building with an architectural firm, an insurance company, and a bank on the lower level. Usually the parking lot was packed, but with summer approaching many people had already started their vacations. The bank manager waved to me as she unlocked the front door.

I texted Sveta back.

> *Relax, I'll be there before u down two shots of vodka.*
> *Walking to the elevator.*

"I already drank those shots, so you didn't beat me," Sveta said when I reached my cubicle.

"I can tell by your red nose."

She smiled and grabbed a tissue from the holder. "I wish. Allergies."

Two folders sat next to my keyboard. I opened the blue one, the one that held two cards for June birthdays, and wrote a short message on both before signing my name.

"Any idea what Sam wants?"

Sveta shrugged. "Didn't say. Must be important, considering he walked over twice."

I put the cards back in the folder and walked to Sam's office. "Shit, don't they realize you're going to burn your friggin' tongue off," he exclaimed, trying to take a sip from his coffee.

"That's why they put the warning on the side." I pulled the chair out and sat down.

Sam had a huge office with windows covering the entire wall. There wasn't much of a view, but the amount of natural light made up for it. Industry awards lined his credenza, and photos of his kids sat on the side table with books he most likely never read.

"If I waited for it to cool down, it would be afternoon tea time. I think my tongue is scarred for life."

I smiled.

"You probably wouldn't mind that, me not being able to talk for a while," Sam said and got up to close the door.

He was in his mid-sixties, and his regular exercise and five-cups-a-day coffee habit helped him stay slim. Most days he wore gray straight-legged slacks with crisp button-downs in pastel colors many men avoided. He always tucked his shirts in and made sure they were ironed perfectly. "You never know when a client might show up on our doorstep, so you have to look put together," he'd always say. Today, though, he wore jeans, an eggplant-colored sweater, and driving loafers. On those rare days when he wore jeans, he usually planned to leave the office early.

He picked up his cup, took off the top, and blew on it before taking a sip. "You've been with me a long time, what has it been?"

"Eleven years."

"Longer than anyone. You know, I respect you so much and your incredible talent."

Uh-oh, what's coming next?

"Have you ever thought about buying the business?"

"That came out of nowhere," I said, startled at first. "I've never really considered it. But I definitely don't want the added stress of owning a business. Why are you asking?"

"I received another offer. And this one looks tempting. But I wanted to ask you first if you were interested."

"No, no worries on my end. Definitely not interested. So what's different with this one?"

While taking a sip, Sam used his other hand to show the money gesture, rubbing his thumb and index finger together. I'd been through this before with Sam. For all other offers, and there had been about five, he grabbed me from my cube, closed the door to his office, and shared the news. It seemed like I was the only one he confided in, maybe since I'd been with him so long. This time, he shared more details.

"It's an all-cash offer. I won't have to worry about losing it in the market."

All cash. Not bad for thirteen years in a business of winning and losing accounts over and over again. Rinse and repeat. Rinse and repeat. Revolving clients, revolving freelancers. Not bad for someone who was willing to take more risks than the rest of us.

"So, you're taking it?"

"Think so. This might be it—you know, get out while the going's good? When I can still enjoy my retirement and while people still remember me as a nice and great-looking guy."

"And modest, too," I teased.

Sam laughed. And when Sam laughed, he laughed hard. He never held back. He didn't care if people turned around and gave him a look, that same look you get from people when you're talking too loud on your cell phone.

I looked out the window. It was a beautiful, sunny day. Sam's office took in the light, and dust settled on the furniture. I got up and ran my finger across the desk and wiped the dust on the upholstered chair. An architectural magazine with a green cottage nestled atop a cliff graced the cover and sat on the table next to the window. I picked up the magazine and skimmed through it.

"What's on your mind?"

"Nothing," I said while flipping the pages.

"You always go for the magazines when you're deep in thought. What's going on?"

"Wondering what it will be like without you here," I said, worried about a new boss and what that would mean.

"I know you're tired of me telling you about the offers and them not working out. Do you want to know the real reason why I never take them?"

I shrugged.

"I always tell them I wouldn't even consider unless they gave you a percentage of billings. You've been with me practically since the get-go."

"That's so generous, and thoughtful, thank you." I hesitated, leaning on the side table. "Do you think I'd be able to help choose which clients to bring in?"

"Why's that important? Billings are always good, right? Unless they're treating us like crap, but we've worked with assholes before and lived through it. Remember that guy from … shit, what was the name of that company? The guy who yelled all the time and never wore deodorant, smelled like a fourteen-year-old kid after PE class?"

"How soon we forget our shitty clients," I said.

"Yeah, as soon as we cash their checks," he added.

I put the magazine down and opened the door to leave.

"Oh, we need to present to AshLynne in three weeks. They want to see the first part of the campaign, so let's get started on that. Kick-off meeting this afternoon, okay?"

I left the door open and walked back to my cube thinking about the offers Sam declined. Why did he feel the need to tell me the reason? Did he really want me to buy the business? For me, buying Sam's studio wasn't an option or even a desire.

"So, what did he want?" Sveta asked quietly when I got back to my cube.

I was about to fill her in when I got a text from Izzy.

Found something interesting.
Don't worry. I'm not driving and texting.
I'll show it to you when we see each other next.

Even though Izzy was being a bit cryptic, there was only one thing he could have found. Something on Mitch.

Chapter 26

School was officially out for summer, and we were on our way to Valor of the '40s. Izzy joined us and was one of the reasons we decided to come back for a second time. He wanted to see how it was portrayed, go to the dance, and maybe rummage through a barrel of letters to see what he could find.

Jeremy was at the wheel, and even though he didn't make me as nervous as he did this time last year, he still changed lanes too often for my taste. He'd cut his hair a few days before our trip and no longer needed to whip it out of his eyes. A cropped cut that actually looked great on his heart-shaped face had replaced his surfer look.

Izzy started singing some of his favorite tunes, while the rest of us were a road-trip's version of party poopers.

"You guys are no fun," Izzy called out after asking us to join in.

"Okay, okay, I didn't want to outshine you," Greg said and sang along.

"Dad, you're going to make all the dogs yelp."

I elbowed Jack and mouthed for him to stop. Greg didn't have the greatest voice—the dogs would literally cry—but it reminded me of our family trips from years ago when the boys were younger, and we'd sing and play silly car games.

Both kids had changed so much within the past year. Jeremy started to phase out of his teenage stage, and Jack, approaching my height, had long hair like Jeremy's in high school. Master Reynolds didn't approve of the hair, but there was no talking Jack out of it. He had his mind made up, and at least it saved us money on haircuts.

I turned to Greg and smiled. He reached for my hand, moving it up and down, trying to encourage me to sing along. If it were the four of us, I might have considered having my lousy voice on display, but now we had Izzy along for the ride, which was a good thing, since it kept the farting at bay from my household full of boys.

After another hour, we pulled into the hotel parking lot, got out, and stretched before grabbing the luggage. It was a gorgeous day, and the weather called for mid-seventies, an improvement from last August's event, which at ninety degrees made guys in their uniforms joke about sweating bullets. I hadn't seen any reenactors at the hotel but hoped to run into the young woman from the Russian camp. I wondered if she'd bring the boy along and how much he'd grown.

This time, at Greg's request, I packed a nice '40s dress and shoes so I could fit right in for the evening dance. We loved dancing before we had kids, and that night at last year's dance was a step back in time.

As we got out of the car, we heard honking from the street in front of the hotel. It was a familiar honk, one I heard driving to the event last year. Three vintage cars, one in vanilla like before, one baby blue, and the other in black, passed by. The tops were down, and ladies in the passenger seats wore colorful scarves around their hair to keep it in place. A scarf flew off, and the driver slammed on his brakes and pulled off to the side. We watched as the woman got out and ran in her high heels to pick it up from the parking lot.

Izzy stopped and turned. "I don't remember girls looking like that during the war. I'm a sucker for a girl in fishnets."

"What are fishnets?" Jack asked. "I take it back, don't want to know."

"When I was your age, I was already chasing girls. That's why I'm so skinny. I kept chasing and chasing but never caught them."

"It's a good way to stay in shape," Greg added.

"Can we change the subject?" Jack said, walking ahead of us to the lobby.

"Sure," Izzy said. "Tell me about the tanks we'll see."

Jack slowed down and waited for Izzy to catch up. "The Russians and the Americans are the coolest. And wait till you see the planes."

Before going to our floor, Izzy asked me to stop by his room. I told the boys to go ahead. Once we were inside, Izzy opened his duffle bag and handed me a thin folder.

"On a scale of one to ten, how bad is it?" I asked, assuming it was all about Mitch.

"I don't know, about a nine?"

He pulled out a shirt and a pair of pants from his bag and put them in the drawer. "I was going to say about a fifteen. But, it was a long time ago."

"I should have kept it to myself," he added as I walked toward the door to leave.

"Why?" I asked.

"Because I don't want you confronting him."

Chapter 27

Jeremy sat texting away by the window, and Jack was on one of the beds watching TV. I plopped down next to Greg with the folder Izzy gave me. It had one of those circular ties on it that seemed to take forever to unravel. Inside were several documents and photocopies of a few articles.

As we skimmed through them, Mitch's name was sprinkled throughout and on the byline of articles from 1995. Several headlines caught my attention. "The Race Game" and "It's All About the Power," both written by him, both about the power Jews have in the country. There were a few news articles at the bottom of the pile. "College Student Denies Personal Property Damage." "Sophomore Allegedly Threatens Bodily Harm to Members of Jewish Fraternity." Under those, an arrest report with a mug shot of him, from 1994, completed the contents. From the looks of it, Mitch had been arrested, but the case was dropped.

"I didn't expect this," Greg whispered.

Within these few pages, I had my answer, even if it was almost twenty years ago. Even if he was only a college student at the time. It was clear to me that Mitch wasn't a guy who reenacted an SS officer just for history's sake or because he liked the uniforms.

"You think Sam knows?"

"Not sure. But not sure it would make a difference, considering he told me billings are billings, as long as we get paid."

"Yeah, but this is different, right?"

"I hope so, and I'm trying not to lose my you-know-what over it. My grandfather would turn in his grave if he knew about this."

"What about turning in his grave?" Jack asked.

"Hey, those are cool graphics. What's the show?"

"Dad, stop changing the subject."

"Me? Changing the subject? What are you talking about?"

Greg jumped over to the other bed, landing on his knees, and sat next to Jack. They watched TV for a few minutes as I changed into more comfortable shoes and put the folder in my bag. We locked up and headed down to the lobby to meet Izzy.

We piled into the car and drove over to Valor of the '40s. When we got to the entrance, Izzy insisted on paying our fee. He called it his contribution for gas since we wouldn't let him pay along the way. I couldn't remember the last time anyone gave me money for gas, and it was cute when he offered.

"There go the Americans," Izzy said as a few passed by in their vehicle as we walked along the dirt path. "I remember them coming down our street in France. I'll never forget that day as long as I live."

"It's kind of like time stood still," Greg said.

"I think it's great that they're educating the public." Izzy grabbed Jack's arm. "Plus, your mom found the letter, and now I get to bug you." Jack smiled and surprisingly didn't pull away like he would have from my hugs.

We continued down the field and watched the soldiers stop a short distance ahead. They all got out, and two leaned against it while the others sat on the bumper. One of the soldiers took a drag from a cigarette and passed the pack to his buddy who chose a cigar instead. It reminded me of my grandfather who used to hang cigars from his mouth and, in between telling stories, would spit out the soggy end.

We had to move out of the way several times as more trucks made their way down the dirt road. Izzy smiled as he caught a glimpse of two girls ahead in A-line dresses, cinched waists, and short gloves barely covering their wrists.

Izzy tapped Jack's arm and pointed. "There up ahead, see the girls? Those are fishnets."

"They look weird, like they forgot some fabric."

"That's the point," Greg added.

"Guys, leave him alone. Can't you tell he doesn't like girls?"

"Shut up, dumbass," Jack said to Jeremy.

"So, guys, which camp first?" I asked, choosing distraction instead of getting on Jack's case for bad language.

"Russian," both Jack and Greg said in unison.

"*Da*. The Russkies," Izzy added.

"I bet they have some cool rifles."

"Jeremy, I didn't know you were into guns?"

"Mom, chill. I'm not into guns."

"I am chill. I asked a simple question."

Greg stopped and turned around. "Don't get all attitude-y with your mom."

Jeremy rolled his eyes. "You both need to chill. Geez."

"I want to see the rifles too," Izzy added.

"Yeah?" Jeremy caught up and walked with him.

Izzy turned around to Greg and me, shrugged, and mouthed "not really." He was trying to squash some family drama that was about to begin with a teenager and his parents who obviously didn't understand him.

Up ahead, the Russian flag decorated with a hammer and sickle waved as the wind tore through it. As we got closer to their camp, Russian music blared.

The soldiers, young and old, stood talking to visitors. Their uniforms, already wrinkled and grubby from wear, would have been a drill sergeant's excuse to whip them into shape. But this was World War II, and who had the time to make it all perfect? They were probably lucky to be alive—even as a historical make-believe.

The young woman with raven hair from last year sat on a blanket. I was happy to see her and remembered how we spoke briefly by the elevator. This time around, she was with a young soldier. They chatted, he smiled, she twirled a piece of hair that fell out of her scarf. It was obvious they were flirting, and what better time than when you may not live another day? I looked around for the young boy who sat next to her last year but didn't see him. Chances were, I wouldn't have recognized him anyway, considering the way kids grew at that age.

All of a sudden, the soldier on the blanket jumped up after hearing a command in Russian. He grabbed his rifle and ran to join a formation. The commander stood in front of the line speaking Russian, and his unit stood upright like a dominos set. One false move and they'd all tumble down. Upon orders, the soldiers moved their weapons from one shoulder to the other then relaxed their stance. There was one woman in their ranks. When called on, she walked forward. The commander shook her hand, and the two exchanged words. After she saluted, she rejoined the formation and stood at ease with the rest as the commander turned toward the crowd.

"Today, we honor Lieutenant Mirchenko who volunteered to join the Red Army when Germany invaded the Soviet Union. Skilled as a sharpshooter, she became one of the best women snipers, ever. Mirchenko is being honored for her service and for killing not only eighty-seven German soldiers, but also nine enemy snipers. She is a true hero, and Comrade Stalin is very proud of her allegiance to the Mother Land," the commander triumphantly shouted in English as his thick Russian accent crept through.

We continued to watch as the Russian soldiers marched off. Some people started clapping for their performance. The commander smiled and, while trilling his Rs, barked out, "Comrades, we need some good, strong partisans to fight for our cause, to fight the filthy Nazi regime. Who's ready to fight for Mother Russia?"

We glanced at each other, but nobody moved forward. He took his hat off and wiped sweat from his forehead. He continued in his thick Russian accent. "You Americans. So comfortable at home. Where were you in 1941 when we needed you?" He immediately broke a smile. "I'm kidding. Don't look so scared. Come, it's time for a shot of vodka. Or two."

"Crazy Russian," Greg said under his breath.

"But they outsmarted the Germans. Speaking of Germans, where are they?" Izzy asked.

"What about the American ones, or Japanese?" Jeremy asked.

"I'll go with the boys, and we'll meet up in a bit," Greg said before walking off with Jeremy and Jack.

"Izzy, you're a bona fide detective, that mug shot of Mitch is a classic," I said.

"Whatever you decide, you're not going to change his beliefs."

"It doesn't mean I have to work with him."

"It's a tricky situation. Don't you think it's really up to the owner of your firm, whether *he* decides to work with him?"

Izzy had a point. It was up to Sam, and with Sam, it was all about the money and the bottom line. But, what if he did wind up selling? Would my new boss be willing to give up a lucrative account? And would I have the guts to bring it up?

"So, are you ready?" Izzy asked.

I nodded, and we walked out of the camp, leaving the boys behind.

Chapter 28

Throughout the field, we passed a few American camps, a Japanese one getting ready to reenact a conflict, and the flea market where I found Hanna's letter the year before. Around the bend, an elderly woman, with silver hair that matched the tips of her scarf, sat behind a table. Spectators were gathered around, listening to her stories and looking through photo albums. Each page of the album had a handwritten header that read "Dachau April 1945."

"I worked for a doctor's office before joining the Army Nurses Corp," she said. "I saw a lot of action when we got to Europe. Helping the injured troops and then taking care of survivors at Dachau." The woman continued her story, sometimes fragmented, as if she wanted to leave out details, as if she didn't want to remember parts of her story. "Oh, I don't know," she answered when a local reporter asked for more details. "There were many still alive. And a lot of them had typhus. We had to help them and get them out of the camp."

The photos were different from the few my grandfather took, the ones of the deceased. The nurse had photos mostly of survivors, who were so emaciated their eyes bulged and their faces sunk to the depths of sorrow. I put my hand on Izzy's arm as we continued to listen. We looked at each other, and he moved his head to the side as if motioning for us to leave.

"I'm sorry, we should have kept walking." I was about to tell him about the photos I'd seen in my youth, to share how my grandfather was one of the liberators.

Izzy grabbed my arm and stopped. "I hear French music. Let's listen and see where it's coming from."

"I can't hear a thing," I said.

"Shhh, I'm trying to listen."

"Okay," I whispered as Izzy looked in the distance.

He pointed to the right. "It's coming from over there."

Izzy pulled a handkerchief out of his pocket and wiped his brow. For being in his mid-seventies, Izzy was in great shape, slim and fit. His habit of walking three miles a day came in handy for these kinds of weekends. As we got closer, I pulled my sunglasses out of the bag and put them on, even though it was overcast. My need for huge sunglasses could only be understood by a celebrity's desire to go unnoticed. Izzy wanted to see my client. But I didn't.

Up ahead and like last year, houses were lined up in an imaginary French village. In between, a post with signs showed French city names and the kilometer distance to them. Women sat on porch steps, and Nazis leaned against rails. Some soldiers rested near motorcycles and rolled cigarettes. Others sat playing a round of checkers.

As we walked closer, they looked up but didn't stop their activities. They continued to chat with the girls, smoke their cigarettes, and try to beat their opponents in checkers. Izzy looked around and I followed him. Suddenly, the soldiers stood up quickly and snapped their boots together. From the side of the building, an SS officer walked up and inspected their uniforms.

"Is that the chocolate guy?" Izzy whispered.

I shook my head out of relief, but decided to keep on my sunglasses in case he turned up.

The SS officer walked by the men who were playing checkers and stopped in front of them. He made a comment in German, which I assumed meant "at ease" because they sat back down to their game. The officer stood with his hand on his chin, awaiting their next move. He fixed his belt, turned to us, and lowered his hat as a greeting.

"Come, you can watch me beat my lieutenant," the officer said with confidence. He pulled his shirt down and fixed his belt buckle as he pushed aside the soldier who walked away to join the lady sitting on the porch. Izzy and I walked closer. Instead of stopping by the officer, Izzy continued farther into the camp when he eyed a tank.

"Is that a *Sonderkraftfahzeug* 250?" Izzy asked after turning around to face the officer.

He stopped playing and looked toward Izzy. "251 actually." He got up from his game and walked over to the vehicle. "That's the first time anyone has asked me that. You didn't fight during the war, did you? You look too young."

"No, I didn't."

"But your German is perfect. Are you from there?" he asked with enthusiasm.

"No, I'm not," Izzy lied.

"What's with the interrogation? He said he wasn't there." I blurted out, feeling I had to come to Izzy's rescue.

"My apologies, it's just that—"

"It's okay. About the half-track. Is it yours?" Izzy asked.

"No, unfortunately. But it's a beauty," he said while running his hand along the side.

"Really nice," Izzy added. "Whoever restored it did a great job. I've forgotten, how many guys can fit in here?"

"Twelve." It was a voice I recognized, but before I could turn around, I felt a hand on my shoulder. Greg and the boys had caught up, and I started to believe they took pleasure in sneaking up on me.

"Actually ten soldiers and two crew," Jack added.

"Izzy, are you finished looking at that Sonderschnitzer, or whatever it's called?" I asked.

"*Sonderkraftfahzeug*," the reenactor said, correcting me.

"Whatever. Guys, let's go," I demanded.

"*Auf Wiedersehen*. Enjoy the rest of your day," the soldier said and returned to his game of checkers.

We left their camp, and I put my sunglasses on top of my head.

"What was that about?" Jeremy asked.

"Yeah, Mom, you were pretty rude to that guy."

Jack was right about me being rude. Reading the file about Mitch put me in a foul mood. How could I work for someone like that and not let it bother me?

"Mom needs to chill," Jeremy whispered to Greg.

"I heard that; is that your favorite expression now?" I said and walked toward the food kiosks. "If anyone wants to join me, I'm getting a double cheeseburger. And fries and a really large soda. And a brownie. Never mind, I take that back. Think I've had enough chocolate."

Chapter 29

Back at our hotel room, Greg sat on the bed pulling up his socks. This time for the dance, I came prepared with a polka-dot dress and navy suede shoes purchased at one of those vintage-inspired fashion stores. Years ago at work, we checked out the same store to prepare for a pitch to a hat company. We didn't win the business but loved spending time imagining our coworkers wearing fashions from this era.

"I don't want you to say anything to Sam about your client," Greg said abruptly.

"Really? How can I market this guy's company?" I said while fastening my shoes.

"I agree, it's very upsetting. But have you thought it through? It could jeopardize your job. And I'm concerned if he finds out you know about his past."

"It's the principle. How can you not see that?"

Greg made it perfectly clear that he didn't want me to get more involved. He was worried. But he didn't have to market products and help make a profit for a guy who was an anti-Semite. Greg was a civil engineer, spending his days making sure buildings were up to code. His job didn't come without stress, but he didn't have to worry about losing clients or working weekends to win new ones, the usual affair that made it all worthwhile because I believed in our clients and their businesses.

"You can't blame me for worrying," Greg said and came over to fix the tie on my dress. "Let's forget about it for now. You look gorgeous."

"You're just saying that so you can get into my pants," I grinned and picked up the room key.

He kissed my neck. "You mean your dress. Do you want to stay in the room instead? Have a quickie while the kids are at the pool?"

"Tempting. But Izzy's meeting us in the lobby, remember?"

Greg held his arm out, and we walked into the hallway and waited for the elevator.

"I wonder if he has any dance moves left?"

The elevator door opened and Izzy was inside. "Well look at you!" he said as we joined him.

"Thanks," Greg replied.

"I'm talking about the lady. But you don't look half-bad yourself."

Soon, Izzy's vision would be filled with more fishnets and skirts that shimmied from side to side. We parked the car on the field and could hear the band when we stepped out. Part of me wished we had one of those old cars so that we could drive to the dance in full costume.

The three of us walked along the pathway and the dirt kicked up and made its way to the front of my open-toed shoes. A few pieces of gravel found their way inside, and we had to stop several times along the way so that I could lift my foot and wiggle it to get rid of the pebbles. When we passed a patch of grass, we took a shortcut that my feet longed for.

They had fewer chairs than last year and more room for dancing. Several older couples were sitting and watching the younger ones dance, and though I was half their age, I had already eyed a place to sit during breaks.

"Izzy, do you want to grab those few seats?"

"For me? I'm here to dance," he said while walking toward a group of women standing by the dance floor. "While the legs are still working and the heart's still pumping."

Izzy approached the group and chatted a few minutes, got a few laughs, then extended his arm. He chose a petite young woman with honey-colored hair, the one in fishnets and a light pink dress with a sweetheart neckline. Izzy looked nothing like my dad, but he danced the same way, putting his arms up to his shoulders, waving his hands to the beat. When I was younger, we spent hours in our den with my dad spinning his records. My sister would ask him to play disco hits over and over, and we'd dance while my mom watched.

"Thinking about your dad?" Greg asked after taking my hand.

"How'd you know?"

"Just a hunch. I miss him too."

We walked out to the dance floor and passed Izzy. Light on his feet and quick at turns, he impressed his dance partner who was a good forty years younger. I imagined Diane and Izzy dancing in their youth, spending hours on the dance floor during their first date.

"We haven't practiced at all," I said as we walked to the middle of the floor.

Greg took my hands, waiting for the right moment in the song to start. "You're too self-conscious."

"I'm counting in my head so I don't mess up the steps."

Greg raised his voice over the music. "You'll probably never see any of these people again. Just relax."

"You sound like my gynecologist."

Greg spun me around, and it made me feel like a little girl twirling on the shag carpet in our living room when my dad played his favorite tunes. The dance floor got crowded, and a few times we bumped into the couple next to us. It always took me a minute to find my way back to the beat. The other couple seemed to keep going—nothing stopped them—and I could tell they danced a lot together.

The musicians were dressed alike, with beige double-breasted suits, navy ties, and matching hats. Some snapped their fingers while others sat waiting for their part. After they played a few more songs, we stopped to catch our breath and walked off the floor. Izzy also walked off, only to ask another girl from the same group to dance. Here he was, thirty years older than the two of us, and he showed no signs of quitting. His contagious smile caught hold of the next girl, and they took to the floor like a bunch of teenagers at a high school dance-off.

This departed era was, at least once a year, remembered through dance, music, cars, and unfortunately war, a part we wouldn't be able to forget. But it was nice to see these make-believe soldiers have a reprieve from it all by dancing the night away. As we stood watching, someone tapped me on my shoulder.

Mitch, dressed in his black uniform with red swastika armband, stood behind me. "Stephanie, hi, surprised to see you here," he said. "Didn't know you were a fan of reenactments," he added, taking off his hat and pushing his hair to the side. Since the last time we met, he'd grown in a pencil-thin mustache and left his glasses at home.

"I'm not really. Our son wanted to come. But it's interesting."

Greg put his hand out and introduced himself. I glanced down at Mitch's pants, which were tucked into black shiny boots that came up to his knees, then looked up to the wide leather belt fixed tightly at his waist. I could tell he put a lot of effort into his depiction, one he seemed to pull off with perfection. He left his German accent, which he performed so well last year, at home or on the battlefield. From behind, someone called his name.

"Sorry, gotta go. Every year we drink beer and sing war songs at our bunk," he said.

As he walked off, I called out. "Mitch." I hesitated for a moment but walked toward him. It seemed like a perfect time as any to ask. We weren't in the office. We weren't in the middle of a presentation. We were on my version of a battlefield, and I was dying to hear his answer. "Just curious. Why do you go as an SS officer?"

"I like the uniforms. And Germany had a great army. Couldn't be defeated for the longest time. Why are you asking?"

I was about to answer his question, a little concerned about what I'd started and unsure about the outcome. Best-case scenario: he'd get upset and take his business elsewhere. Worst-case: he'd get upset, take his business elsewhere, and Sam would hold me responsible for losing the account.

"I think it's hurtful for a lot of people to see," I finally said.

He stepped toward me, a little too close for comfort. "Are you Jewish?"

"No. But does it matter?"

He looked at Greg then back at me. "I think we can all agree that war is controversial. But you can't look at it from one side. You have to study all sides to understand the past."

After we stared at each other for a few seconds, he added, "Like I said, the uniforms are cool."

Mitch walked off and called out before getting into the vehicle. "I'll see you at the office next week. Looking forward to the presentation."

I couldn't give him the benefit of the doubt. I wouldn't. I couldn't think, *Oh, he was just a young kid, a college kid doing stupid things*. I couldn't think that, not after seeing the file Izzy gave me. Now, more than ever, I wanted nothing to do with Mitch. But how would I convince Sam who wanted to sell his business? Getting rid of billings wouldn't be good for him or an offer. And how would he explain it to a potential buyer?

Izzy joined us, and we watched Mitch drive off with the other German soldiers. "Let me guess. The chocolate guy?"

"More like the asshole guy," I said while trying to decide how to tell Sam.

Chapter 30

July in the DC area wasn't for sissies. The traffic was a bit more bearable, but the horrible humidity made up for it. Work usually crept slowly, but this year it seemed the clients were postponing vacations and spending the last part of their fiscal budgets on marketing. We got the few new projects and thankfully held off letting the freelancers go like we did the year before.

I sipped on my second cup of coffee but didn't need the extra jolt of caffeine—my nerves were already bad enough knowing the AshLynne Chocolate presentation would soon begin. It meant I'd see Mitch again.

A few coworkers straightened their cubes, putting boxes underneath their desks and sliding papers into trashcans. Sveta pulled up the shades in the hallway to let in more sunlight because, as she put it so many times, she got sad if it was too dark. And, if she got sad, she'd turn to way too many tasty croissants, which would turn her life into drawstring pants, baggy shirts, and a cranky attitude to accompany the expandable wardrobe and waistband.

We worked hard to prepare for the AshLynne Chocolate branding campaign—logo design, website, billboards in airports, grocery store displays. It was all coming together, and even with Mitch on my mind, I still hadn't gotten up the courage to refuse to work on the account. My reputation was on the line—if I didn't deliver. If he liked the ideas, we'd get moving on production right after Labor Day, and by then I'd have to decide whether it was the right time to tell Sam, who was all business all the time. I brought my computer to the conference room and hooked everything up. Mitch wasn't expected for an hour, but I wanted to make sure everything worked and have time to run through the presentation at least twice.

"I knew you'd be here. Like always, always prepared," Sam said as he came in and shut the door behind him.

Sam walked around the room looking at the awards on the wall. "Remember that one?" he said and pointed. "That was an all-nighter or two. Client was making last-minute changes at midnight."

"How could I forget? It took me three months to get rid of the dark circles above the dark circles."

He continued to look through the projects and stopped in front of the shelf that held the awards. He seemed to linger longer than usual.

"Sam, what's going on?" I asked.

"I did it."

"Did what?"

"Made a deal to sell." He looked at me with a half-smile that resembled part regret, part what-the-hell-do-I-do-now? In all the years I'd worked for Sam, I never saw a look of regret or a pensive stare, all at the same time.

"Wait a second, I thought you declined the offer?"

"I did. But there was another, and they agreed to everything. And you'll get a percentage of the billings."

"Wow, thank you so much. You mentioned that, but I never really expected it."

"Can I give you some advice? Even if you don't want to hear it? Don't ever turn away business. You have to be profitable. It's a responsibility to those employees out there."

I got up my nerve and whispered, "What if I told you Mitch got busted back in—"

"I know, I know," Sam interrupted. "Back in college. But they couldn't prove anything so the charges were dropped."

"You knew about it? And you don't care?"

"Like I said, they couldn't prove anything. I don't even friggin' like chocolate, but it doesn't matter. I won't turn business away. Period. I have an obligation to bring in business and lose as little as possible. Stephanie, if you don't think you can handle it, then you should reconsider this new gig. Because there are things you won't want to do sometimes. But you do them. And you can't lose sleep over it."

I opened my computer and started looking at the files we would soon present to Mitch. I couldn't believe it. Sam knew all along, and it didn't phase him. There was an obligation, a responsibility to the people on staff, or at least he tried to convince himself. But how could I simply forget Mitch's history? Sam looked around the conference room, paying special attention to our older ads hanging on the wall, some from more than ten years ago when he started the business.

"Don't say anything about me leaving. I need to find the right time to tell everyone."

"When's it happening?" I asked.

"Early September."

"Wow, that was fast."

"Not really. I've been here thirteen years."

I chuckled and looked up from my computer. "I hear you. The years fly by."

"Steph, you'll do great. Probably better without my whiny ass hanging around. Remember, it's business. Don't get caught up in the lives of the clients. Do you really know, or want to know, what all our clients do outside work?"

It was a losing battle with Sam, and it really didn't matter anyways with him leaving. Now we'd contend with a new owner—a new boss and new beliefs. I hooked the cable to the back of my computer and pulled down the screen to project the images we'd present. The team did a great job on the campaign, making chocolate look so irresistible that Sam, who said he didn't even like chocolate, would be a firm believer.

Sam picked up his phone from the table and came around to look at the ads on my laptop. "Those look great. You should be proud of yourself."

"I still have hiring in my new role, right?"

"Why, you want to bring someone on board?"

"I want to promote Sveta. We can't afford to lose her."

Sam smiled and winked as he left the conference room. "We'll talk more after the presentation, okay?"

It would probably be the last time I'd see him do both—smile and wink—at the same time, and I knew I'd miss it.

***

Mitch arrived on time for the presentation. He was dressed in khakis and a blue button-down and had grown out stubble since the reenactment. We shook hands, and he took a seat at the table.

Lindsey and Brian, our writer-and-designer dynamic duo, took the lead in the meeting. I'd had my day and numerous presentations—the rest of the creative team needed to shine and get more experience presenting to clients.

I was there as a backup when any questions flew by that they couldn't answer, such as why we decided to use a forty-something woman in the ad rather than a younger one. I'd talk about the research and surveys we received. Or why we used collapsible bars on the homepage of the website. I'd talk about the user experience and how it was best to allow the user to control the content.

The cue was easy—Brian or Lindsey would look at me when they didn't know how to answer the question, and I'd take over. But we were prepared. We were always prepared. We never faltered in meetings, mostly because we lived and breathed the work and loved everything we presented. We always showed three options, and in case they didn't like our favorite, we had another one or two that were a little more conservative to appease a client. It was right in our back pocket, neatly organized in our computer's folder on the drive.

At the end of the presentation, Mitch said, "I love everything you showed us. We need to talk ad placement and when we want to roll things out."

Kevin, the marketing director, pulled out a folder and laid a few documents on the table. "I've already spoken to food marts and some airport convenience stores. We're looking at mid-November to put up some displays for our holiday packaging. We really need to have those ready by at least the end of October."

"That shouldn't be a problem," I said. "If we get approvals within the next week, we'll be good to go with production right after Labor Day. That's plenty of time." I paused. "As long as we have all the specs and get those approvals."

"Kevin will get you everything by next week. Right?" Mitch said while nodding back at Kevin.

"Yes, not a problem," Kevin said after pulling out his smartphone and adding a calendar reminder. He knew there was no room for error.

"Great, so we're all set," Sam said and got up. "Good work, everyone."

"Yeah, really great," Mitch added.

Sam approached Mitch and Kevin. "Do you guys have a minute? I want to talk to you briefly in my office, then maybe we can have lunch?"

"Sure, sounds great. We'll leave our stuff and come back for it."

"No problem. I'll be in here packing up anyways," I said as I got up.

"So, no notebook-stealing ninjas will get through?" Kevin joked.

"Nope, and my white belt in karate will come in handy if they do."

Lindsey and the rest of the team left the conference room. I unplugged the cords and got up to lift the screen. Behind it stood a framed ad for Kivah Moving & Storage, the first client we worked with at the agency. Sam was really hands-on back then, to the point that it drove people crazy. There was a pretty high turnover rate those first two years.

Often, Sam stood behind designers and directed the entire time. Move that line down. Change that blue to purple. I don't like her hair. Find another picture. And on and on. But since I'd worked with him for so many years, I could tell him to back off and give us some space. Nobody else felt comfortable doing it. But he didn't mean any harm. The agency was his baby, and it was in the nursing stages.

I looked around the room at the other ads and awards on the shelves. I had a piece in all of them and spent many nights away from my family to make them shine. Did I really want to continue doing this? Did I really want to take on this new role with more worry, more riding on my shoulders? What if the new owner had a different style and expected the same from me?

My phone pinged and right before picking it up, I remembered we had an office rule: all phones get turned off or set to vibrate during meetings. It had to be either Mitch's or Kevin's. It would be wrong for me to check. It would be very wrong. Of course it would, if somebody noticed. I leaned over the table and stopped to shuffle some papers as a few colleagues approached. They continued walking, and the phone pinged a second time.

Just got this, check your email for more pics.

Below the text was a photo of a white coffee mug with an SS emblem. My heart started racing. I sat down on the opposite side of the table and started doodling as a distraction. But it didn't help. Sam believed that what clients do on their free time shouldn't make a difference, because he had an obligation to keep the business running and people employed. But how could I pretend this was just about selling chocolate? How could I turn a blind eye? But, I didn't think it through—could the phone have been Kevin's?

I was about to get up and take another look but Sam's bellowing laughter got closer. He always laughed hard—and thank goodness—or I'd be scrambling to come up with a good excuse.

"How we doing in here? Keeping an eye on my stuff?" Kevin asked when they returned.

I wrapped the cord of my laptop and pulled the mouse out of the side. "No ninjas got in, so we're in the clear."

Mitch picked up his phone, the same one that received the text. He looked at the screen, squinted as if he'd forgotten his glasses. "My wife's always sending me photos of meals I'm missing while away. She loves cooking."

"Nice! Can I see?" I asked.

"I would, but she's kind of scantily clad. That's part of the fun."

I piled papers on top of my laptop and headed toward the conference-room door. "Good to see you, Mitch. Kevin, I'll check the email you sent and let you know if I have any questions."

I walked back to my cube feeling like I just confronted an ex-boyfriend who cheated and was covering his tracks. There could have been only one reason why he lied about the picture. Pretending to be a Nazi wasn't because he thought the uniforms were cool. And his past wasn't a faded, rebellious phase of his youth.

Chapter 31

At Western Warriors, Jack stood next to Greg, adjusting his uniform, pulling down the front and snapping his belt tightly so the knot stayed secure. How had time passed so quickly? I remembered when Jack came to his first class. He didn't know how to tie his belt and would stand in front letting me make the knot. After a year, he figured out how to tie it himself, and anytime I tried to help he'd say, "Mom, I can do it."

For the past few years, he'd learned how to chop, do tornado kicks, and perfect his routines. Today, he would stand in front of Master Reynolds and four other instructors to receive his black belt. He bit his lower lip and lifted the ends of his belt, a tell-all sign he was nervous.

"Damn, Steph. Why didn't you tell me how cute Master Reynolds was? I would have come to taekwondo sooner," Sveta whispered, while we waited for the other kids and parents to arrive.

"I told you a hundred times."

"Your neck must ache from all the gazing."

"You crack me up."

"What cracks you up?" Greg said from a few seats away.

"Nothing, just girl talk."

Master Reynolds carried chairs to the front then lined the black belts on a table. Proud parents, grandparents, siblings, and friends looked on. Izzy came up from Stevensonville, and

Jeremy, still home on summer break, made time to break away from texting to cheer on his not-so-little-anymore brother.

"Brown belts, come to the front," demanded one of the instructors. Master Reynolds and the other instructors took their seats behind the table.

"Yes, sir," they answered in unison. Greg had a big grin on his face, and Izzy gave a fierce-looking expression and overly animated chop.

After a quick run around the mat, the kids dropped to the floor for push-ups. Then, they sprinted to the wall and lifted their legs one at a time for a good stretch.

"Maybe I should take up taekwondo, looks like good exercise," Sveta said.

"You know he's a little too young for you, right?"

She laughed out loud as one of the parents shot us a look. "Knock it off or we'll get sent to the principal's office," she joked.

Master Reynolds called up each kid individually to perform and recite a speech in front of the spectators who were flashing their cameras as if an actor had stepped onto the red carpet, in this case a red mat.

Each kid had to prepare a speech, and when I reminded Jack the night before, he dashed upstairs to his room and slammed his door. A few minutes later, he ran downstairs, asked who was coming to his graduation, then ran back up to his room and slammed his door again. Slamming, as he always described it, was him rushing to close a door. It had no emotional attachment to it whatsoever. When I often told him to stop, he'd say, "I didn't slam the door. I closed it as I was running into my room." Jeremy used to say the same thing, and I always wondered if Jack picked it up along the way.

Ben was up next. He and Jack started taekwondo at the same time and spent these last years together in class. To celebrate the occasion, I invited the families to come over after graduation for a pizza party, something simple and easy. Ben thanked his mom, grandparents, and his instructors. Short, sweet, and to the point—the perfect speech.

"Jack Britain."

"Yes, sir," Jack responded and jumped to face the judges in the center of the mat.

"Too bad he doesn't do that at home," I said to Greg.

"Yeah, good luck with that," he replied with a wink.

Master Reynolds continued, "Jack Britain, you are here today to receive your black belt. You will perform your forms and techniques, but before that, please tell us about your journey and why taekwondo is important to you."

Jack pulled a folded piece of paper from the inside of his uniform, and some of the parents giggled when he dropped it then caught it in midair.

"Good reflexes," Master Reynolds said.

Jack unfolded the paper and cleared his throat. "When I was eight, I came to a birthday party here. It was a lot of fun. That was a few years ago. I would like to thank my old instructor, Master Kim, who moved away this year. I would also like to thank Master Reynolds for helping me become a black belt. It has been hard at times to learn the forms and concentrate on the techniques. I'd like to thank my parents, especially my dad who talked me out of quitting when I couldn't learn all the red belt forms. He told me to practice every day, even just for five minutes. He also videotaped me so I could see the mistakes and improve. Thanks to my brother Jeremy for being my brother and Svetlana for being here today. Thanks to Izzy, my mom's friend who came to watch me. Taekwondo has taught me to be flexible, have discipline, and be self-confident. I'm glad I took it, and I'm glad I reached my goal of becoming a black belt."

Jack folded his paper, and everyone clapped. He ran to the side and laid the paper down then ran back to the center of the mat. He performed all his moves, kicking over his head, flexing his martial arts muscles, all while trying to keep a serious face. Jack always said he was going for the face of a fighter, but it never made him look any tougher, only cuter.

Master Reynolds asked all the students, parents, and spectators to stand and congratulate the new black belts. He called out each student's name, and as they came running up to the front, Master Reynolds removed their brown belts and put on black ones in their place.

Jack ran off the mat holding his certificate. He turned his new belt around so that we could see the stitching. "Look—my name."

"Give me five," Izzy said. "Now you can star in your very own martial arts movie."

Jack put his hand up, and Izzy struck it as if sending a volleyball over the net.

"Good job, awesome speech," Greg said while also high-fiving him because we all knew hugs were out of the question.

"Dude, it's about time. Just kidding," Jeremy said.

Jack ran to the mat and posed with his classmates and instructors. We took a few shots, then Jack came over for photos with us. I called out to the other classmates to meet us back at our house. This was a big achievement, a goal Jack had worked toward for many years, and he followed through with it. That meant some celebrating.

Greg took the boys, and Sveta and Izzy rode with me. Soon summer would be over, and our leaves would change and fall. I imagined the beautiful views from Izzy's house, how he and Diane spent time on their front porch watching the seasons change, and the birds and deer come and go. He rarely talked about Diane, but when he did, there would be a pause between sentences before he continued. It was as if he'd taken a fist to the stomach, and there was no breath left. Sometimes when he looked out the window and didn't talk much, I wondered if he was thinking of Diane. And when he made all his silly jokes, was it his way of masking the pain?

I stopped at a light and turned to him. He was staring out the window.

"Everything okay?" I asked.

"Copasetic. Why?"

"I don't know. You've been pretty quiet."

"My mind is wandering."

"Do you want to talk about it?"

"I got a call from the Holocaust Museum. They want to interview me but not sure I want to."

As much as I wanted him to go through with it, I couldn't imagine what it would be like, and I couldn't push him either.

"Don't you think they have enough stories by now?" he asked.

"There will never be enough stories," Sveta said.

A car behind me honked, and I drove off, not realizing I'd been stopped for so long.

"They want me to do it before I croak."

"Aww, please don't say that. That makes me sad. You were really great when you spoke in Jack's class."

"That's because you were both there. If I agree, would you guys come?"

"Of course. We'd be there in a second."

Izzy sighed and took a deep breath. He was quiet for several minutes. "They'd have to come to Stevensonville. No way I can step in the museum."

"I hear ya," I said, wanting to tell him about my grandfather and how he couldn't make it into the museum twenty years earlier. Many times I'd planned to tell Izzy, changing my mind at the last minute, not wanting to make it about me and distracting from Izzy's own tragic youth.

Izzy continued, "Hey, do you want to hear a dirty joke?" he asked, completely changing the subject.

"Yeah, sure."

"A pig got stuck in the mud."

"Cute, but not very Kosher," Sveta said.

It was the silliest joke, one that distracted me enough to miss my turn, and maybe the same one that helped Izzy hide the pain of losing Diane and his parents all those years ago.

Chapter 32

The drive to Stevensonville was even more beautiful than the last, and when the highway curved, mountains perched in front of us, with fog casting a shadow around their peaks. With Jack stretched out in the back, it almost felt as if I were on a road trip by myself. He wore his headphones and escaped into his games and music.

I turned on my '80s playlists and let it keep me company on the way to Izzy's house. Each song reminded me of college. My roommate showing me her album covers. The day I met Greg. Getting high in the campus parking lot with the windows rolled up. Swapping mixed tapes with a girl on my dorm floor.

By the time we arrived at Izzy's, a couple of cars already sat in the driveway. Dylan had gone home for a visit, so I figured they belonged to the staff from the Holocaust Museum.

"I had on my favorite striped shirt, but they told me it wouldn't look good in the video," Izzy said as he greeted us. "So I have to wear something boring."

"Mr. Fischer, you don't want them to focus on your shirt when they should be focusing on your face," the woman said as she pushed her glasses up and came over to introduce herself.

"I'm Nicole. You must be Stephanie and Jack." She continued after we shook hands, "Jack, Izzy told me he wouldn't do the interview without you, so you must be pretty special."

Jack smiled nervously. I almost expected him to hide behind my leg like he did when he was four.

She continued, "Don't worry, I have all the questions written down. You'll need to sit next to me. We'll face Izzy, but we won't be in the camera. Just Izzy."

"And my boring shirt."

"And your handsome face," the videographer said.

"I knew I liked you for a reason," Izzy added.

Nicole smiled and fixed her scarf. She probably got a lot of flirts like Izzy, interviewing men in their seventies and eighties. I still felt the same as I did a year ago when we met—what wasn't there to like about a guy in his seventies who enjoyed life and made silly jokes?

"Okay, are we ready? Izzy, we're going to get you set up first, test the video, make sure the lighting and sound are good. So, take a seat, and if all is good, we'll get started."

Jack stood next to me, and I pulled him closer and tried to put my arm around him.

"Mom," he whispered. "Stop."

"Stop what?" I whispered back. "Why are we whispering?"

We both giggled, and when Nicole turned to us, I felt like we were being reprimanded for talking in class. The videographer rearranged Izzy's mic on his shirt, fixed a piece of his hair that fell over his brow, and asked him to sit a little more centered in the chair.

"Okay, we're good to go. Jack, come sit by me. You can ask the first few questions, and then we'll switch. I've highlighted in yellow the ones you should ask. Just speak slowly, loudly, and clearly. Wait for Izzy to respond completely before going to the next question."

Jack took the sheet of paper from Nicole, and the videographer put a mic on Jack's shirt.

"What is your full name?"

"Isadore Fischer. But people call me Izzy."

"What is your date of birth, and where were you born?"

"July 12, 1936, in Staufen, Germany."

His answer took me back to the day I found his mother's letter and how I discovered he shared the same birthday as my father. What could have been the chance to find something so remarkable? The barrel's sign said, "Love Letters From The War." Hanna's letter was nothing close to a love letter, unless you considered the love for a son so strong that you'd do whatever you could to save him, then yes, it was the most authentic love letter ever written.

Jack asked a few more questions then passed the sheet back to Nicole who continued with hers. They went back and forth, and I could tell she gave Jack the easier questions, the ones that didn't require a follow-up. He never noticed and that was perfect. Izzy seemed a little nervous, but he agreed it was important for future generations—then it dawned on me. Izzy didn't have a future generation. He had no kids or siblings. Why did he really need to suffer through telling his story again? But there were many sole survivors of the Holocaust who had brothers and sisters and aunts and uncles who didn't survive. And these survivors were interviewed where they talked about these horrific moments in their lives.

Izzy got choked up every now and again, so I left the room for a few moments to give them some space. I tiptoed to the back of the house, through the dining room toward the kitchen, stopping on the way to look at the pictures on the wall and side table. Diane and Izzy in all their travels. Sitting under a palm tree in Miami. Standing in Times Square looking up at a marquee. Eating baguettes in front of the Eiffel Tower. They sure enjoyed traveling. Did Izzy stop and stare at these photos like I did? Did he reminisce about their times together as I'd reminisced about my college days on the trip down?

After grabbing a glass from the cabinet, I opened the fridge for something to drink and took out the juice. Izzy had stacked several magazines and bills on the table. One of the envelopes caught my eye, from an oncology center near

Baltimore. Was there something wrong with Izzy? Or could it have been a bill from Diane that was still being paid off? Those times he'd visited us, or called to meet for lunch, saying he was in the area for an appointment—had he been going there?

But was it my business to ask? We were close, but a person's health issues are a different story. How could I say, "I happened to notice this on the table when I was snooping in your kitchen"? I could never say that. But at the same time, Izzy didn't have any family. Did he choose not to say anything because he didn't want to be a burden?

The doorbell rang, and I rushed to the front door.

"One large cheese, one veggie?" the delivery guy said, and when he ripped open the top from his pizza carrier, the sound echoed.

"Nice house, by the way," he added.

"Thanks. Just a minute, I'll be right back."

I closed the door and walked to the living room.

"We hardly had anything to eat. I remember my mother fishing out the carrot from her soup," Izzy said then looked up at me. "The pizza's here?" he asked, rubbing his hands together.

"Pause the tape," Nicole said to the videographer. "We'll have to do that question again because we can't have 'the pizza's here' in your answer."

"Yeah, they might think they served you pizza there," Jack said.

Izzy smiled and messed Jack's hair. "I wish. Can we take a break?"

"But we just got started," Nicole said. "We have a lot to cover."

"We have all day. I can't work on an empty stomach." Izzy took off the mic and went to the front door to pay the pizza guy.

"Is he always like this?" Nicole asked.

"Like what?"

"Like someone who knows exactly what he wants."

"It's refreshing, isn't it?" I added and left the room to help carry the pizza boxes to the kitchen.

As we gathered in the dining room while Jack fetched the crew some drinks, I could only think about the envelope. Izzy didn't show any signs of being ill. Maybe I was overreacting. Maybe it was a routine procedure and everything was fine. Or, maybe it was nothing at all, just some direct mail asking for donations.

Chapter 33

The following weekend, I slipped on my shoes and went downstairs. It was our date night. Every other Saturday, we went out now that we decided Jack was old enough to stay by himself. Our time was well deserved, and Jack didn't mind staying home without me nagging him to get off the sofa and do something more productive.

Since dancing at the reenactment, I realized how much practice we needed, so we recently traded in the movies for dance lessons. Greg balked at first then reluctantly agreed after I proved that the slow dancing we all did in ninth grade wouldn't cut it.

"You worry too much," Greg told me on our way to the dance club when I brought up the envelope at Izzy's. It could be anything he said, and even if it were bad news, it was the kind that was out of my control. Nothing I could do would change the situation. Greg asked me not to say anything. If Izzy wanted me to know, he'd tell me. But I wanted to know if he was okay. For now, I'd keep it to myself.

When we arrived, the club was packed with many eager dancers ready for lessons. We all stood in a circle as we watched the instructor and his partner show the bachata, a dance that involved some side-to-side steps with a little grinding. Anytime we tried the grinding part, I blushed. Something felt awkward about a couple of forty-year-olds, married for almost twenty years, grinding on the dance floor in front of others. But, when I looked around and saw a mix of people and ages—with many of them older—I stopped being so self-conscious.

"Just relax," Greg added.

"Okay, Doctor Britain," I teased.

"You two, over there. Keep it clean," said Eduardo, our instructor, as he pointed to the couple across the way. "We don't want anyone getting pregnant."

A different couple next to us, who looked about sixty, were great at the steps, but they wouldn't get close enough to grind. Either they were strangers who switched partners during class or were on their first date. Eduardo tried his best to loosen them up.

Fast-forward twenty years and that would be Greg and me. We'd also be pushing sixty—hell, we'd be almost halfway through that decade. Who knew where the kids would be, if they'd be married, with their own kids, or still single. Who knew what jobs they'd have. Would they be enjoying their careers? Would they remember their childhood, their grandparents, our family pets? Would they be happy?

The light from the club shined on the woman. Crows' feet and expression lines were marked and frozen, even when her smile disappeared. Life, whether good or bad, was etched on her face.

As Greg spun me and we repeated the bachata steps, I wondered more about the older women. Were they here to learn how to dance better, like me, or were they lonely and didn't want to be home with their TVs as companions? Had this become my mother's life, longing for companionship after my father died? I should have been more understanding about her traipsing across the globe. Maybe she didn't want to be alone. I couldn't relate. At the moment, my life wasn't etched on my face like on my mom's, like on half the women here on the dance floor.

Greg spun me around once again and dipped me low to the ground. My dress brushed against the floor.

"Our instructor's got nothing on me." He pulled me up slowly and could tell, even though I was half-smiling, that something bothered me.

"What's wrong?"

He stopped dancing and pushed my hair behind my ear as he does when I'm upset. It always made me feel better, but this time, the tears came. I put my head down and walked to a chair.

"Steph, what's wrong? Something with Jack or Jeremy?"

I shook my head.

"Something with work?"

I shook my head again. AshLynne Chocolate had been on my mind a lot, but it wasn't at that moment.

"The couple next to us made me think about my parents."

"Those two? Your parents made a much better-looking couple. Your dad was pretty hot, actually."

I hit him on the knee.

"Ouch. Have you been working out with Master Reynolds?"

"Yeah, right."

"You don't think I've noticed all the moms drooling over him?"

"I don't."

He lifted one eyebrow and planted a look he uses when he doesn't quite believe me. "It sucks your dad died. It sucks so much. I miss him, too."

"I've been too hard on my mom. I was … no, never mind. It's stupid," I said and waved off the idea.

"Just tell me."

"I was trying to protect my dad, pretending he was still around and she was off gallivanting." I felt the tickle in my nose as I held back tears. "He's gone, and I know it. I should have been more understanding with her."

"Your mom has always been a free spirit. I didn't expect her to sit at home. What was she supposed to do? Grieve her life away? She's still young."

"Young-ish," I added. "She's turning sixty-six in a couple of weeks."

"You should plan a visit and celebrate her birthday. You haven't been there in a while. Spend some time with her, just the two of you."

Maybe Greg was right. I should visit her, without the family. Just the two of us. With my sister being a few years younger and at home longer, I couldn't remember being in my childhood home often with only my mom.

By the time we got back on the dance floor, Eduardo had added a few new steps to the bachata sequence. We had a little catching up to do, but Greg kept spinning and dipping me instead of following Eduardo's routine.

"You two cuties," Eduardo called out and pointed at us. "I'm going to bring you a bag of chips. You know why?"

Greg shrugged. Eduardo whispered in his partner's ear then did some spins and dips similar to ours but much better. "Because you've got salsa moves going on over there, and you need some chips to go with it. Save those moves for the nine o'clock class." He looked at his watch. "That's in fifteen minutes. Stick to the bachata. Like this." He put his finger in the air, which was a cue to the DJ to restart the song. "I assure you. These bachata moves are a way to her bedroom—I mean her heart," he said with a grin. "And ladies, I want to see some hips moving. Imagine you're having sex with celebrity hottie, Sean Estrel. A one-night stand or a summer fling, totally up to you."

While we continued with the bachata, I tried to imagine Greg as Estrel just for fun. "That Eduardo's pretty strict," I said.

"Not really. Being Sean Estrel comes easy."

"I bet."

We counted to three to keep the steps, messing up a few times before getting it right.

"So, you really think I should visit my mom?"

"I do, I mean Estrel does."

"Well, if Estrel's insisting, I don't want to disappoint. I'll go in a couple of weeks."

Chapter 34

I couldn't wait to escape the sleepy North Carolina town where I grew up. The small-town feel wasn't for the eighteen-year-old me who dreamed of getting out after attending a New York City field trip in tenth grade. A big city, wherever it was, called for me, when most of my friends were staying in North Carolina to attend schools in Raleigh and Charlotte. Sure, some of those cities were much bigger than where I lived, but nothing compared to Baltimore. So, in the summer of 1986, I took off up I-95 with my clothes thrown in the back and the windows down listening to my favorite '80s mixtapes.

But a lot changes when you get older and you've lived in a congested area for so long. You start missing the slower pace, the smiling faces, the waves from neighbors, the ease of finding a parking space. Oh, how I underestimated easy-to-find parking.

Driving back home this time, I had different memories—my first kiss, hanging out with friends at the beach, the carefree life of a teenager. Our house wasn't the expensive, right-on-the-beach type. We were a few miles away set along Cooper Creek. You'd need a car to get to the beach, or if you were a daredevil, you could ride your bike on the two-lane highway and hope for the best. Ours wasn't technically considered a beach home with the best location, but it was still the hangout house, mostly because my parents let us raid the fridge and make a mess, and they wouldn't make a big deal out of it. Looking back, they were probably keen on having us home to keep an eye on my sister and me.

The year after I graduated high school, my parents built a screened porch on the back where they could sit and enjoy the creek and wildlife without being eaten alive by mosquitoes. Then after my sister left for college, they took up a few more renovation projects, turning their avocado kitchen into a modern one, and after that, they chipped away the pink and green tiles in the bathrooms in exchange for granite and stone. Luckily they had many years to enjoy the new rooms together.

By the time I turned down my mom's street, it was late afternoon. Her neighborhood wasn't quite what I'd call a neighborhood really. It had two streets—one that ran along the creek and ended with a cul-de-sac and another shaped like an inverted U that wrapped around and connected to ours. Even so, families with lots of kids filled these two streets and not much had changed in the twenty-five or so years since I'd left, which meant that I'd have to drive super slowly.

Kids ran around chasing each other with their dogs close behind. Whether there was a leash law or not, nobody obeyed it. Tweens rode their bikes up and down, some getting off and dropping them to run between houses, most likely to throw rocks in the creek like us when we were young.

I passed a couple of kids, and as I slowed down almost to a stop, I saw them poking a dead frog with a stick. Our next-door neighbor had three boys, and they did the same, even sometimes swinging dead snakes above their heads before throwing them as the girls ran screaming. Some things never changed. This small-town feel was growing on me. If you drove around our Maryland neighborhood, you'd hardly see a kid outside playing.

It was refreshing to step back in time, back to my child-hood. Most of the houses looked the same, with an exception of a few additions sprinkled on the block. Mrs. Mallory, now in her late fifties, sat on her front porch. She waved as I parked. Her kids, who I used to babysit, were ten years younger than me. Mrs. Mallory smiled as she looked back at the baby in her arms.

"Stephanie, so good to see you."

"Did you have a baby while I was away?"

She laughed as she fixed his cap. "Those days are over. I'm a grandma now. Kimberly finally got married. But Samantha, bless her heart, is still single in that roach-infested New York apartment that's the size of a matchbox. Not sure when she'll settle down. How can anyone meet someone in a city that big?"

"She will, don't worry." I pulled a little on her grandson's toes.

"Your mamma ran out, but she'll be back soon. Gone to pick up some groceries."

I grinned and remembered what I didn't like about small-town living, the part where everybody knows where you're going, where you've been, and practically what you've bought at the store.

"Sit with me until Katherine comes back. You can tell me all about your life up north."

As soon as I sat down, my mom pulled around the corner and into her driveway. One renovation they never tackled was turning the carport into a garage. Some of the neighbors had made the addition, but my mom always said she'd fill it up with useless junk like the rest of the block. She popped the trunk and lifted out the grocery bags.

"Hey, Mom," I called.

She turned to the left then right.

"Across the street, at the Mallory house." This time I stood up.

"Steph, you made great timing! I didn't expect you for another hour." She crossed the street, not bothering to look either way. Dressed in a full skirt with a floral pink print and lipstick that matched, my mom always looked put together. She never left the house in sweatpants and only on occasion wore jeans. When she went grocery shopping, she even wore her matching pearl necklace and earrings. "You never know who you'll bump into," she'd always say.

We hugged for a long time, and she rubbed my back before letting go. "Look how time flies. Anne's a grandma now. Remember when y'all babysat her kids?"

"Of course," I continued in a whisper. "Much easier than the Downing boys. I had to chase them all the time, and they were knee deep in the creek or covered in mud."

We stared at Mrs. Mallory's grandson for a few more minutes then said our goodbyes as we crossed back, grabbing the bag from my car and the groceries from the driveway. My mom never locked her car or house door when we were younger, and she still kept the tradition.

"You're always so nervous about burglars."

"And you're too trusting of people," I said as I double-checked that the door was locked.

"I have nothing exciting to steal. They can have whatever they want." She headed into the kitchen then called out, "Oh, the toilet is leaking in the hall bathroom. Andy's stopping by around five to fix it. Go on and use mine when you need it."

I went to my room and put my luggage on the bed. The pink walls were now taupe, and my old lavender comforter was now a navy plaid. My mother put a new robe and slippers in the mostly empty closet and some hair accessories on the dresser. A necklace with my name scripted in gold, the one my parents gave me for my tenth birthday that went missing for years, rested on the nightstand.

It took a little getting used to the quiet in the house. I still expected to hear my father call out from the den where he'd watch his favorite football and basketball games. He was loud when they scored, and even when they didn't. He'd always invite the neighbors over because he had a house full of girls who couldn't care two bits about sports.

I walked to the window and looked out back. The creek always brought all kinds of wildlife. Today, ducklings followed their mom across a patch of grass to get to the other side. The yellow kayak my father loved still sat by the dock. We spent many weekends on that kayak. Mom was never a big fan and always used the excuse that all four of us would never fit.

She came into the room and handed me a pair of sunglasses. "Do you miss the view?"

"That's one thing I'll always miss."

"Let me show you something," she said, and we walked to her bedroom.

The back wall, which had a window the last time I visited, now had a sliding glass door that led to a screened porch.

"Something I've always wanted. A porch off the bedroom."

She opened the sliding glass door, and we stepped down onto a slate floor. Her coffee cup still sat on the side table, and I could picture her lounging here enjoying the view, listening to the birds and doing crossword puzzles.

She sighed and looked around. "Your dad would have loved it. Sometimes I picture him sitting with me, then I think, 'Katherine what in the world are you doing? He's gone to another place with a better view.'"

"You really believe that?"

"Of course. It helps me get through the tough times."

"How are you? Truly?"

"Couldn't be better," she said after a deep breath, an almost weighted sigh, before fluffing the pillow on the patio chair.

"You sure?"

"Steph, you worry too much. I'm fine, really."

She didn't turn around. Instead, she walked toward the door, trying to get out of the room without looking up.

"You must be starving after that long drive. I made some sweet tea, brewed it outside the way you like it."

"Thanks, Mom. I'll be right there."

Since my bathroom needed fixing, I used the one in my mom's room. I had a bad habit of using the bathroom with the door open ever since I was a little girl. And not just ajar; it was completely open unless I was out in public. But, being in my mom's house was like being in my own.

As I was deciding whether to enjoy my sweet tea and BLT on the porch or in the kitchen, I noticed a hat lying underneath my mom's bed. My dad never wore hats, not even baseball caps. He had a full head of wavy hair and liked to show it off. Before heading to the kitchen where I could hear my mom singing her favorite tunes, I picked up the hat and recognized it right away. It was the baseball cap Izzy wore the first time we met at Krista's.

Chapter 35

Anyone could have owned that cap. Anyone. But we were in the South, and not the Charlestonian South where you'd find numerous transplanted northerners. I'd seen some Charlestonians proudly wear their favorite sports gear without thinking twice. But not here. We had the occasional families from Richmond, which was pretty much it, other than the locals who lived here full-time or North Carolinians with second homes. And, in my small town, they'd never root for a northern team, not even a college one.

I took a closer look and knew for sure it could only have been Izzy's. The last time he wore it, he'd added a couple of pins. One said "Say Yes To Donuts". The other was "Ask Me About My Pet Pig," and I always laughed at the reactions he'd get.

Sure we were adults, but talking to my mom about sex was off-limits. And we were talking Izzy here, not some stranger, which made me want to avoid the topic like a plague's plague. I held the cap and looked out the patio window, about to put it back under the bed when my mom startled me.

"Steph, what kind of bread do you want for your BLT? I've got white and wheat."

I didn't respond.

"Why are you standing there like a statue? Nanna used to say, 'Stand still too long and a bird will come poop on you.'"

I turned around with the cap still in my hand. She held onto the door knob, searching for words.

"Mom, spare me the details. I don't want to know."

"Don't worry, it's nothing exciting. Izzy visited me a couple of times. But we didn't have sex," she said in a calm and collected way, as if she had nothing to hide.

"Then why was this under the bed?"

"I did sleep with Izzy. We shared a bed. With our clothes on. We talked, laughed. It was great to have company." She paused. "You have no idea what it's like. We don't want to sit and talk to the walls. Why do you think I traveled so much after your dad died? He was the love of my life."

She hesitated and snapped her fingers. "Like that, he was gone. We talked about all the trips we were going to plan, all the long walks on the beach we'd take once he retired. Your dad and I had plans." She picked at her sandwich, and as her voice started to crack, she continued. "We had plans." She got up to pour more tea into our cups then pulled some muffins from the oven.

"I'm sorry," I said.

"I'm sorry for you, too, for losing your father. And for the boys not having their grandfather around. What do people say nowadays? It is what it is. It's out of my control. But sitting around staring at the walls ... I couldn't do it. That's why I started traveling and giving it a shot with George. And why I invited Izzy. He's a friend and nothing more."

"Why didn't you tell me?"

"I don't know. You're worried about me. You're worried about him driving. I thought you'd give us a hard time."

"Well, he did have that accident."

"Steph, sometimes you treat us like children. We're adults—independent, fun-loving adults. You don't have to worry about us. Let us live."

What could I say? My mother was more than right. I often treated her like a kid, but I also acted like one. I didn't understand what it was like to lose a husband, to share a life with someone for so long then be left alone in a house and the life you built together. I'd been hard on my mom for not spending more time with us in Maryland. I thought she wasn't interested in being a grandmother, but it turned out she just wanted to live her life. Just live. And that meant the travel she and my dad never got the chance to take. It meant staying busy so that she wouldn't stare at the walls wondering what she'd be doing next.

"If you didn't want to spend time alone, why didn't you stay with us after Dad died? It would have been great having you around."

"No offense, darlin'. I love you and the boys so much. But you're always on the go. When you're not at work, you're taking the kids here and there. It's the life of a parent now. And it's your life. I want my own. But enough of that. I have my moments and miss your dad, but I'm grateful. I have my health and my little house near the beach. Can't complain."

She continued, "Listen, don't mention this to Izzy. He'd be awfully embarrassed."

"Not a peep. I bet he's looking all over for that cap. He wears it all the time."

"Don't worry, I'll tell him. But I'll wait a little while—don't want him to think you found it."

"By the way, how does he seem? Does he seem okay?" I asked.

"Perfectly fine to me. Why?"

I paused before answering. I'd planned to tell her about the oncology center's envelope. But knowing my mom, she'd ask him right away, and I didn't want to worry her or make Izzy uncomfortable.

"Oh nothing. Just asking."

My mom could never sit for long. She started packing away the bread and muffins that sat on the stove then transferred the sweet tea to a pitcher before putting it in the fridge. She was always doing something in the kitchen or in her garden. When we were younger, she enjoyed reading her books, but it never lasted more than twenty or thirty minutes. She'd look at her watch and rush around to get her chores done.

"He was here last weekend. Seemed like the same ole Izzy, full of jokes and a hearty appetite. He loved my beef stew. I made it without carrots."

It turned out my mom was a good listener, remembering how Izzy told us at Thanksgiving he was allergic to carrots. Had he told her the truth, that it really wasn't an allergy but a bittersweet memory of his mother fishing the vegetable from her soup? He hardly talked about his past, so he probably didn't bring it up. Izzy was a live-in-the-moment kind of guy. I admired that way of thinking and wished I could be more like that.

Later in the day, we packed up a bunch of my dad's clothing for donations. Mom hadn't tackled it yet, and she asked for my help. We filled the first few bags, all neatly stacked like a folded accordion. As one hour turned into two, we grew tired and started throwing stuff in bags. At the back of my dad's closet, I came across a few fleece jackets and decided to keep some for Greg. I also asked my mom if I could take a few of his albums, especially the ones we enjoyed many years ago. Seeing the covers reminded me of how my dad checked the albums for dust then put them on the record player before turning back to me, snapping his fingers to the music.

My mom went to the next cabinet and took out an old record player and put it by my pile. A box with "old photos" written on top was in the same cabinet. I took out the box and started going through it, finding pictures of my sister, parents, and grandparents, and vacations we took over the years. I pulled some out, setting them aside, and rummaged through the box looking for more photos of my parents when they were young. I came across an envelope and inside were photos I'd only seen once before, the ones my grandfather took during the war.

"I didn't know you had these."

She leaned over for a look then sat next to me.

"You've seen those?"

"I kind of stumbled on them."

"Kind of stumbled?"

"They were in granddad's drawer. Can't remember, I was probably looking for gum. I was about to put them back when he caught me."

"Why didn't you ever mention it?" my mom asked.

"Not sure. Why didn't you?"

"I didn't know about it until he moved into assisted living. He gave them to me, made me promise never to throw them away. I figured he never wanted to talk about it, that's why he never brought it up before."

"What about the time we went to the Holocaust Museum? Didn't he tell you why we were going?"

"Only that his division was being honored, but no other details until he gave me the photos. How could anyone forget what happened when you look at these?" she said.

And that's what we did. We looked at them and sat in silence, not knowing what else to say. After a few minutes, my mom got up to grab a pen and wrote "1945, liberation of Dachau, photos taken by Sam Alden, father of Katherine Taylor, grandfather of Stephanie Britain" on the front of the envelope. I did the math in my head. Sixty-seven years had passed. Discovering these photos again made me think of Mitch, anti-Semitism still going strong sixty-seven years after the war ended.

"Come on, let's make a run to the thrift store," she said and extended her arm to help me off the floor.

We put the bags in her car and pulled out of the driveway. She had kept the same car for the past ten years, and when I told her it was time to upgrade, she said it worked fine and would drive it forever. "Darlin', it's like a tortoise," she added with a grin. "It'll never die."

With my mom at the wheel, it gave me a chance to look at the houses in our neighborhood. I asked her to go around the block a few times. Along the way, she gave me news on the neighbors, who still lived there, which kids got married, and what families moved away. After all, she and Mrs. Mallory were two of the few who remained on our street for more than thirty years. When I teased that she knew everyone and had all the gossip, she said, "Of course, I'm practically the town mayor."

She turned out of the neighborhood and onto the two-lane highway that led to the shopping plaza. It had been more than two years, and we were now just getting rid of my dad's clothing. There'd never be a good time to give away his personal belongings and detach ourselves from them. My mom's closet, organized and full for years, now had an empty space, like a grieving heart that makes room as memories fade to help us move on.

Chapter 36

The summer break passed by quickly, and I was not looking forward to Jeremy leaving. This time, for his sophomore year, we wouldn't drive him back to school. With my mom having good luck with her car, we bought Jeremy a 2007 model with low mileage—or at least as low as you could get with a six-year-old version. We made a trip to the grocery store and loaded his trunk before he headed back up to Pennsylvania. I waved goodbye as he drove off and couldn't believe my kid would be turning twenty. The last of the teenage years. It made me wish time stood still for a moment although, to be honest, the frugal part of me looked forward to car insurance going down a bit.

By the time I reached the office, Jenny, our production manager, had the printer on speakerphone to rush-deliver an AshLynne Chocolate poster for an event they had planned for the following week. The company app looked great, and Sveta was troubleshooting some last-minute coding. Things were on track with the branding campaign, and at that point, I oversaw the creative budget. There was nothing else I could do about the account, for now. Sam brought the business in, and as he reminded me, he never let it get personal when he had a business to run and people to employ.

"*Boja moi*," Sveta said while looking at her screen.

"Another crappy deadline?" I asked.

"Yeah, more changes on the recipe database, but the account manager won't budge on the deadline."

Sam didn't like conflict, especially when it involved different opinions about deadlines and client promises. He stayed out of those conversations and made me handle them. But what would the new owner be like? I complained about Sam, but who knew? It could be so much worse.

"I'll talk to her. And by the way," I walked into her cube so that I could whisper, "things are going to change if Sam retires."

Sam still hadn't told the staff about his deal. September was right around the corner and he had started to pack, using the lame excuse of getting rid of clutter when people asked. He was waiting for the right moment and asked me to sit tight for a few more days.

Sveta swiveled in her chair away from the computer. "Actually, I've been meaning to talk to you about that. I've got some news."

"Please don't tell me you're leaving."

"No way, we're a team, remember? Let's get some coffee and talk to Sam."

We walked to the kitchen then to Sam's office. "I'll join you in a minute," she said as I knocked.

Empty boxes sat along the floor and magazines from his shelf were thrown all over his desk. Books took up space by the wall and came up to my knees. He turned around and wiped the sweat from his forehead.

"Do you want any of those?" he asked, pointing to the pile.

"If only I had the time to read."

"I was going to keep them, but changed my mind. Just don't have the room. And the boxes would get shoved into some closet anyways, and I'd forget about them."

He put his feet on the only empty part of the desk and leaned back in his chair. "Turns out the person who bought the business doesn't want to bring on any more staff. She wants you to be the chief creative officer and officially second-in-command. What do you think?"

"Really? I didn't expect that."

"Don't worry. You'll have some help," he said right before Sveta walked in and closed the door behind her.

I looked over at her as silence filled the room.

"You haven't put two and two together yet, have you?" Sam added.

"Put what together?" I got up, and if I could, I would have stared at both of them at the same time.

"Svetlana's your new boss."

"What do you mean my new—What the heck?" It finally dawned on me. "Why didn't you tell me?"

"Do you want me to give you two a minute?" Sam asked.

"No," Sveta said. "But where can I sit? It's messier than Brezhnev's eyebrows."

"There were so many times I wanted to tell you," she added. "But, I thought you'd try to talk me out of it."

Sam laughed. "Yeah, I've been talked out of a business venture or two."

"Why would I do that? It's totally awesome, the best news!" I said then gave her a big hug.

While Sam started telling us a story about his crazy business ideas, most he never acted on, it became a blur. Where did Sveta get the money from? She never wanted for anything. But she never lived extravagantly either.

With Sveta's blessing, I'd champion all the work, market all the brands, and be behind our employees, like before but with more authority and the new title behind my name. Having been in their position, I'd finally give them the amount of time needed on projects. There wouldn't be late nights so that we could meet ridiculous deadlines. We would give ourselves the right amount of time from the beginning, as it should have been all along, and our staff would be happier and more rested.

"Are you upset I didn't tell you?"

"No," I fibbed. "You're right. I probably would have tried to talk you out of it."

"Stephanie," Sam added, "To be honest, Svetlana had reservations because she didn't want to take over the business if you were interested. That's one of the reasons why I asked you about it."

Now it all made sense when Sam told me the right offer came in. "What I told Sam is true. I'd worry too much."

Sveta looked out the window then around the room. "You can have this office. I've got my eye on the one next door. No offense, but I don't like corner offices. Too many windows, and the one thing I can't stand is glare on the computer screen."

In two weeks, this would be my office. I never imagined Sveta would buy the business and involve me so much in running it. I already worked hard, but there would be more at stake. We had a great staff of account executives, writers, art directors, and project managers. Sam never showed me the books, but we were doing okay. Whenever we lost an account, sooner or later, we'd win a new one or two. And our current clients wouldn't care, since we'd been dealing with them all this time, and it would be a smooth transition. But what about Mitch's account? Now I'd have to convince Sveta, who had a lot at stake and was a friend. I had to be careful not to take advantage of that.

***

Sveta chugged down her dirty martini. It didn't take long for her to get tipsy and confess she was nervous about taking over the business.

"I really hope you're not mad that I didn't tell you. But it took a while to make a deal, and it would have sucked if I told you, and it fell through," Sveta said as we sat at the bar down the street from our office.

"You have some balls, but you'll do great. I'm so excited for you."

"I guess you could say I'm making up for my shitty childhood," she added, something she never told me before.

"What do you mean?"

The bartender brought over our appetizer, and Sveta handed me one of the plates.

"There's a lot I haven't told you. My little brother, actually he's not little anymore, gave me most of the money and helped me buy the business."

Sveta talked about her brother before, but not much about her life in Russia. Whenever I asked, she'd always say she was an American now, and the past was the past.

"I didn't know he was rich," I said.

"He wasn't always. And, I never wanted to talk about it. I don't know, I was always waiting for the other shoe to drop." She held up her martini to toast mine and as quickly as her arm rose, her tears fell. It was the first time I'd ever seen her cry.

"Oh shit, what did I say?"

She wiped the tears with her napkin. "I'm so proud of him. After all he's been through."

Sveta ordered her second martini. She said it was a good time to tell me about her past. Younger by sixteen years, Misha was four years old when his father left one day and never came back. Their mother broke down, couldn't keep a job, and instead drank all day and night. While in college, Sveta found a job to support the family and take care of Misha. She got him ready for school, put food on the table, helped with homework, and did everything their parents should have done. "When our mother was awake, she was drunk and either screaming at us or having sex with strangers. When she slept, she snored so loud dogs would bark nonstop while the neighbors screamed at them to shut up. I'm so embarrassed to say this, but I prayed every night for a year she'd choke on her vomit."

Sveta pushed her martini glass away, realizing she'd had too much, and looked at me with her bloodshot eyes. "You know that saying, you should be careful what you wish for? When I was twenty-two and Misha was six, we had to bury our mother. At the time, and honestly until tonight, I'd never cried over the loss of my mother. I couldn't believe she abandoned her kids like that, but my father had done the same many years before. All was fine for a while, until Misha was fourteen. Then all went to shit."

One day, she got a call from the school's administrator who told Sveta they hadn't seen Misha in a week. She left work early and went home where she found him drunk on the sofa and his friend going through drawers looking for money. After what Sveta went through with their mom, there was no way she'd tolerate it. She begged one of her friends to swap apartments so that Misha could get out of the neighborhood, attend a better school, and get away from the bad influence.

"That was nice of your friends."

"It was my last resort. During that time, you couldn't get another apartment easily, like you can here. And I was married by then and Dimitry was seven. No way I was going to put up with it and jeopardize my own kid's life, no way."

"So then what happened? How did he become successful?"

"Well, more shit hit the fan, as you say. He got drafted in '95, which was the worst time ever because he was sent off to fight in the Chechen War. It was horrible, and there was no way for us to stay in touch. A few months later, I got a letter that he'd been injured. I had to call in all my favors to get him transferred to a Moscow hospital so he could be closer to me."

"But, the good part is," Sveta continued, "the story has a happy ending. While he was in the hospital, he was bored. So on my visits, I taught him some programming. Turns out, he had a knack for it. He got better, got his computer engineering degree, and started a company that developed security software. He sold his shares two years ago."

"For oodles of money, I hope," I added.

"I never asked, but obviously enough to help me buy Sam's company and still have plenty left. I wanted to say no, I could have, but what the hell? He's doing well and wants to share his good fortune with me."

I took my phone out to check the time. Sveta was smarter than anyone I'd met. She was a little tipsy, but I knew she'd still be direct and levelheaded. There would be no better time to ask. "Speaking of business, I wanted to ask your opinion," I said. "Would you work on an account that you didn't believe in?"

"What do you mean? Like furs? You're talking to a Russian who'd gladly wear one in the dead of winter, and has."

"Not exactly. The first time I saw Mitch, it wasn't at the office when we presented for the bid."

She raised her eyebrows, waiting for juicy details. I sighed, took a sip of wine, and told her how I saw him at the reenactment twice and found out about the articles and his arrest in college.

Sveta listened closely without interrupting. She finished the rest of her martini and signaled for the check. "I have to agree with Sam that it's never a good idea to throw away business. But, Mitch, how can he be ..." She paused. "I can't even say it."

"A neo-Nazi."

"You forgot *chmo*."

"*Chmo*? What's *chmo*?"

"Douchebag."

She pulled out her credit card and handed it to the bartender. "Steph, it makes me sick to think we have a client like that. But, and I'm saying but, so hear me out. It was twenty years ago. Maybe we need some proof that's more recent."

"Between you and me, I did a little snooping and read one of his texts," I admitted.

"And?"

I told Sveta about the message and how there might be more of the same in his email. We got up and put on our jackets. We waved goodbye to the bartender and walked down the street to our parking lot. Sveta knew me well and knew when I was worried.

"Be patient," she said. "We have to think this through."

I unlocked the car and threw my bag on the passenger seat.

"In the meantime," Sveta added and winked, "start thinking about how you're going to rearrange your new office."

Chapter 37

Sveta stopped by the following weekend so we could celebrate her new business venture. This time, she brought Evan and enjoyed her grandma-time, giving his parents a much-deserved break.

Evan followed in Jack's footsteps and started at Western Warriors right after Jack got his black belt. All it took was seeing Jack in his uniform kicking and jumping in the air one day at our house. "I wanna black belt, too," Evan called out the very next day. The white belt classes, held on Friday evenings and Saturdays, didn't offer much flexibility, but Evan didn't seem to care. All week, every day, he'd ask, "Is it Friday yet?" Then, when that day came, he was even more excited knowing he'd have taekwondo back-to-back. But this time, he didn't seem to mind. Evan ran off to play, and Ginger ran right after him.

"You look good," I said as Sveta handed me the wine bottle. Over the past month, she'd started to trim down.

"What are you talking about? I look tired."

I opened up the wine and passed her a glass. "No way, you're like a hot young grandma."

She laughed. "That's a first. Been doing water aerobics, like your mom," she said as she danced a few steps across the kitchen.

"Getting in shape for Master Reynolds?" I joked.

"Maybe. But I wouldn't want to ruin the fantasy. Who knows what would happen if he took off that uniform. He might lose his superpowers."

"Or be holding it all together with a guy girdle."

She snapped her fingers. "Now that's a money-making idea. We just need a good name and then cha-ching, cha-ching."

When Sveta mentioned water aerobics, I thought of my recent visit to Mom's and finding Izzy's hat. It wasn't my business, and I wanted to believe my mom when she said they were just friends. The older I got, the more I felt companionship was underrated, that sheer companionship and nothing else breathed life into the lonely. When she was off gallivanting with her male friends in Florida and South Carolina, was it also for companionship or was there more? It wasn't my business, and even though Jack and I were planning a visit to Izzy's in a few weeks, I'd never bring it up.

"Let's call my mom and tell her your news."

"That I'm having a fling with Master Reynolds?"

"That, and you buying the business."

I walked to the hallway and grabbed my purse, fishing out my phone from the bottom. "It's a bottomless pit, this thing."

"Who knows, you might find a treasure in there."

"Yeah right. Crumbs from granola bars and a few old candies."

"Did you say candy? Tip it over and let me at it."

Sveta held my bag upside down, and to no surprise, several candies, one without a wrapper, fell out. She blew the dust off before popping it in her mouth.

"Gross," I said. "That's even worse than the five-second rule." I put my phone on speaker. It rang twice before my mom picked up.

"Hi, Katherine."

"Svetlana, is that you? It's my lucky day."

She spoke loudly, and we could hear a lot of noise in the background.

"Where are you, at a rock concert?"

"Heavens no. I'm at the movies seeing *Detective Fire*. Loved the book. We'll have to wait and see how the movie lives up."

"What do you mean, *we'll?*" I grabbed a pencil and wrote the word "date" with a question mark. Sveta lifted her brows a few times and smiled.

My mom paused for a moment then added, "What did you say? It's loud here."

Sveta winked. We knew she could probably hear us fine but was avoiding the question. She said her movie was about to start and would call back. As we said our goodbyes and before I could tell her Sveta's news, the front door opened.

"Yoo-hoo, I'm home," Greg said.

"I don't know why my mom doesn't want to talk about her personal life."

"Because she's your mom," Greg said as he leaned in for a kiss.

"Where's my kiss?" Sveta asked.

"Watch it," I said. "I might have to report you to the boss for harassment."

I sipped on my wine, thinking about the mysterious person with my mom. Could it have been Mr. Edsyl, my high school teacher? Maybe Izzy? Or just a friend like Mrs. Mallory from across the street. It really didn't matter. What mattered was why she didn't want to tell me.

Chapter 38

Over the years, I'd only lied a handful of times. Once, I denied spelling out the words "punk rock" with black tape across my high school's cafeteria. My best friend, Debbie, wanted to spray-paint it, but I was scared that if we got caught, we'd be charged with vandalism. So instead, we used tape, and it took a hundred times longer—not only because we had to calculate the amount of tape, but because we argued about whether it should say "punk rock" or "punk rock rules."

We decided on "punk rock" since it would cut down on time and tape. Besides, we knew making an "s" would be challenging, and the artist in me knew it would look bad. Debbie was the lookout and tape-tearer while I, having pretty good art skills and no fear of heights, stuck it on the building.

As we finished the last letter, Mr. Wilson, the janitor, caught us in the act. He was pissed that he would be the one cleaning up our mess, so he told the principal in the morning, who wound up saying, "You're lucky you didn't spray paint it because you'd be charged with vandalism." Since there weren't any cameras, and it was Mr. Wilson's word against ours, Principal Stucker couldn't do anything. He warned us, and anytime we felt we were being watched by him, Debbie would say we had a case of Stucker Syndrome.

There were a few other times I'd lied or fibbed throughout my life. Once when my parents asked me about my grades freshman year of college. *They're fine*, I said, even when I was failing one class and getting a D in another. So when Jack told me his grades were fine at the beginning of his second quarter, turned out he'd been struggling in history, strangely enough from a poorly written paper about Izzy. Jack asked for my help, with questions I couldn't answer, so I suggested a weekend visit to Stevensonville.

As we pulled up to his house, Izzy sat on the porch reading a newspaper. He waved, stood up, and walked down the front stairs.

"Here, let me help you with your bags," he demanded.

"I got it," Jack answered and grabbed the bags from the trunk.

"Must be all that taekwondo." Izzy lifted a leg then chopped to the left then the right.

"Remembering your old moves?" Jack asked.

Izzy closed the car door and started walking toward the stairs. "Yep, I'm keeping my new ones a secret for my line of exercise videos."

We walked up the stairs and put our bags down in the foyer. Dylan was in the kitchen, shirtless, with his hair disheveled, shorts riding low, and plaid boxers peeking through, like Jeremy looked on weekends home from college. Dylan poked his head in the fridge.

"Hey, Izzy, where's the Chinese?"

"Sorry, kiddo. Ate it for breakfast."

Dylan turned around, scratched his head, and put both hands on the counter.

"All of it?"

Izzy passed by the fridge before reaching into the cabinet to pull out the coffee beans. "I think there's some egg drop soup left. Check the side door. Sorry—I got hungry after my workout. You should come with me in the morning," he yelled over the sound of the coffee grinder.

"Go where?" I said, then repeated it after Izzy gestured he couldn't hear me.

"To aerobics."

I was about to say, *You're doing aerobics, too?* but caught myself. Was it because of my mom? Was my mom secretly working for a fitness association, or touting it like she did with tennis all those years until her new fitness obsession came along.

I lifted my foot and showed Izzy my boots. "Not in these."

"Not a problem. You can go barefoot. It's dancing and exercise all in one. You'll be sweating like nobody's business by the time you're through."

Jack picked up my bag, and we walked to the spare bedroom. He threw mine on the bed and continued down the hall to the other room. I fluffed the pillow and sat down, ready to text Sveta about Izzy's visit to my mom's and the workout coincidence, but I knew she'd tell me to mind my own business, that Mom was all grown up and could handle herself. Besides, who wouldn't want to be around Izzy? College students wanted to spend time with him. Even my thirteen-year-old son liked hanging around.

I looked out the window, as I'd done at my mom's house. Instead of a calm creek, this side of Izzy's house had a mountain view. Cows and dogs replaced the crickets and geese I heard at my mom's a few weeks ago. Izzy knocked and came into the room. He lifted the blinds on the other window and looked out. "Let me know if the neighbor's dogs bother you. Last week, I threw them some salami, and it shut them up for hours."

"We'll be fine. If not, I have some bacon in my purse."

Dylan and Jack were already playing video games when we walked into the kitchen. Over coffee, Izzy told me how Dylan planned to move out at the end of the semester after living with him for two and a half years. Izzy would miss him, but he already had another roommate lined up, one who also played video games and would battle him during a thirty-minute war fest.

After he finished another game, Jack joined us in the kitchen. Izzy made him a peanut butter and jelly sandwich, cutting off the crust not because that's how Jack liked it, but because Izzy said it tasted better that way. Being in the kitchen reminded me of the envelope from the oncology center. I didn't see any mail on the counter, but the house looked a little more straightened up since the last time.

"So, big guy," Izzy said after handing Jack the plate. "Your mom tells me you have some questions."

Jack went to the front door to get his backpack. He opened it on the kitchen table, dumped out its contents in search of his paper. The theme was fortitude, and he chose to write about his experience meeting Izzy and about Izzy's life. The grade C minus was marked in red at the top with a note that said: "Not enough detail. Where's your research? You can rewrite to bring up your grade."

"I really don't care about the grade. I wanna know more about what it's like growing up Jewish. Did you get bullied?"

"I didn't get bullied because …" Izzy came closer and said in a low voice, "I'd kick their ass if they tried."

Jack smiled. "So you were in fights?"

Izzy got a glass. He held up both orange and cranberry juice containers and asked Jack to choose. Jack pointed to orange, and Izzy poured some into the glass.

"I was in two fights when I was younger. One in junior high and one in high school. But not because I was Jewish. It was because I was skinny. Skinny as a stripped-down toothpick." He pulled up a bar stool and sat across from us. "You know why I was in only one fight in each school?"

Jack shrugged and took a bite of his sandwich.

"Because I fought back. You might be scared shitless, but you have to fight back, or they'll keep bullying you."

"I don't know about that," I said.

"Mom, you have to stick up for yourself."

"Look, it's just my opinion, and you should definitely listen to your mom," Izzy said. "But you have to be strong. Always avoid fights, but if the same person keeps picking on you, you have to fight back—if they start it. Never start a fight, that's the number one rule."

"That's what Dad tells me all the time."

Izzy made sure Jack understood he wasn't bullied for being Jewish, but he didn't want to make light of the subject either because he knew kids were bullied for all sorts of reasons, some for their religious beliefs. He then shared stories of growing up and his first crush, who attended his Hebrew school, and how he went every Sunday to see her.

"Okay, let's forget about Boston for a minute. We need to impress your teacher with more details. But it won't come from my life, really," Izzy said. He opened a drawer, took out a pencil, and wrote *Kristallnacht* on Jack's notebook. "Go to the library and get a book on *Kristallnacht*. You could incorporate that into your paper. I think it would help your grade, and you'll learn a little something. *Kristallnacht* means 'crystal night,' and it represents the broken glass all over the streets."

"From what?" Jack asked.

"Stores owned by Jews in Europe had their windows smashed. Their homes were vandalized, and synagogues burned."

"Why didn't they do anything about it?"

Izzy smiled. "You asked the million-dollar question."

Jack look confused.

"That question has been asked so often, and nobody has a good answer. I'm assuming you mean, why didn't they fight back? Many did fight and there have been a few really good movies and books about it. But others lived in denial, thinking it wouldn't happen. Imagine you and your family living in a country for centuries, having citizenship, being a part of society. You might not think it would happen either. And then there were those who'd already fled to other countries, but it became more difficult. What they don't bring up in history class is that you couldn't just leave. A country had to take you in and by 1941, it was forbidden to leave."

"I didn't know that," I added. "I should read more, too."

Izzy picked up Jack's paper and read through the four pages. "This isn't bad. If she wants you to weave in more about me, talk about what I remember from the concentration camps. When you get home, ask your mom for the journal. There's not much there, but it's a start." Izzy went to the living room, opened a drawer, and pulled out a CD that contained his interview with the museum. "And take this. You'll probably be bored to tears. It's the full taping, even the part where I say, 'Pizza's here.' Remember that?"

"Yeah, that lady from the museum was pretty pissed," Jack said.

"So enough about school, who's up for *Undone*?"

"Me," both Jack and Dylan said at the same time.

"Sorry, guys, we only have two controllers," Izzy said, "so, it's me and Jack."

"That's cool," Dylan said and grabbed a bag of chips from the pantry.

"Stephanie, why don't you get some rest. We'll leave bright and early for our aerobics class."

Izzy sat down and picked up the controller. Jack parked next to him and crossed his legs. "And I won't take no for an answer. I know you like to dance because I saw you cutting a rug at the reenactment."

Chapter 39

The aerobics class was held in a strip mall at a small fitness studio on the other side of town. We pulled into the parking lot, and the sign Shape Your Booty, made me wish I'd come up with a cool name like that for the fitness club we marketed at my first advertising job.

Izzy parked his SUV and reached for his bag from the backseat. We entered the studio, and two young women at the front desk greeted Izzy with a big smile. There was a white board by the front with the day's schedule. Yoga at seven. Aerobics at eight-thirty. Weight-training at noon and three. And another aerobics class in the early evening. Obviously, Shape Your Booty had many ways to shape it.

"We could've come to the five o'clock class instead," I said and yawned as we walked to a bench.

"Early fitness bird gets the worm. Don't you know?"

Izzy opened his bag and pulled out two towels and handed me one. He got out a few terry-cloth bands, one for his head and two for his wrists. "All I need is a tennis racquet," he said. "But if I don't wear these, I'd probably slip from all my sweat that falls to the floor."

The room started to fill, and every woman in the class was gorgeous and in great shape, wearing fitted tops and yoga pants.

"Hi, Deena," Izzy said and stood up to wave.

"Hey, Izzy, glad you could make it."

"Stephanie, let's get a good spot in front so we can follow all the steps."

Now I knew why Izzy wanted to come to the morning class. It had more to do with the instructor than with exercise. Deena walked to the table and attached her phone to the speakers. Held in a high ponytail, Deena's brown hair with blonde highlights brushed against her collarbone as she bent down. Black short-shorts barely covered her bottom, and a light pink tank top uncovered cleavage that peaked out from her sports bra when she tied her shoe. I turned around once more to see how many people would be watching my ridiculous moves.

Deena tapped a few buttons on her display, and the music started. She walked to the middle of the floor and started moving her hips. "Good morning, everyone! Let's start with our warm-up." Deena took a few steps to the left then right and repeated it many times before adding her arms to the mix. The song was a mash-up of several pop hits, most that I recognized and often sang in the shower. Before long, Deena took us through turns and dips that, like Izzy said, had us all sweating for the rest of the hour. At the end of the class as we cooled down, I looked over at Izzy, who was drenched from the top of his headband down to his wrists. His T-shirt stuck to his body like a wet towel on a lawn chair needing a good wringing out.

Deena, who looked even better all sweaty, thanked the class for coming, walked over to turn off the music, and grabbed a towel to wipe off her face.

"That was fun."

Izzy didn't hear me at first. I changed tactics. "Deena's a great instructor."

He turned to me. "Sure is. She teaches other classes, but they're not my thing, sitting on a bike pedaling to no-wheresville. Phew, that was fun, huh?"

Izzy said goodbye to everyone, and we showered, changed, and drove back to pick up Jack for brunch. No matter where the road took you in Stevensonville, a beautiful view popped up at every corner, every slice of this laid-back lifestyle. Something about being in the mountains and being elevated made me relax. It was the same feeling that came over me driving down the street of my childhood home in North Carolina. Or maybe it was being in the South, the feeling of a small-town pace, those smiling faces, the politeness of strangers, all the advantages I didn't care about in my youth.

Growing up, I couldn't wait to escape the small town, the town I now appreciated. At the time, those smiling faces and polite strangers meant nothing to me. My prepubescent self played with matches, sat on the floor eating sugary cereals, and pedaled around aimlessly without a care. It was an easy youth, one I took for granted, especially compared to Izzy who was robbed of his.

"I have a confession," Izzy said out of the blue as he turned down his street. He stopped in front of the mailboxes. "I went to visit your mother a couple times in North Carolina. She was worried you'd be upset and asked me not to say anything. So this is between you and me."

I looked out the window and watched one of Izzy's neighbors cutting the grass. I could have fibbed again, like I had to Principal Stucker. Or to my parents about my grades. I could have. But what would it have gained any of us?

"To be fair, I found your cap when I was there. She asked me not to say anything."

"That cap is a dead giveaway. Listen, Katherine and I are just friends."

"That's what my mom said. It's really not my business anyways."

"I went to see her because, that time she was upset at your house, she confided in me." He paused for a moment to collect his thoughts. "She misses your father and still loves him very much. I was trying to help get her mind off it. I went there as a friend."

I wanted to believe him and my mom. But at this point, did it really matter if they liked each other in that way? Greg made me realize that not only had my father been gone for more than two years, my mom was a free spirit. She needed to live her life and not worry about what people thought, even what her daughter thought. "Could I ask you a question?"

"Anything," Izzy answered.

"Were you there recently when she went to see a movie? She was about to see *Detective Fire*."

"No way. The book scared the you-know-what out of me. I only like romantic comedies."

Izzy stepped out of the car to check the mail. He leaned down and put his arm in the box, pulling out catalogs and envelopes. He handed the pile over and asked me to put it in the door's side pocket.

"Izzy, thank you."

"For what?"

"For being a friend to my mom."

"I should thank her. She's a pistol and always makes me laugh," he said as we pulled away from the mailboxes and started up to his house.

I really did believe him, and it matched my mom's story that he'd been there a couple of times. But it still made me wonder. If he didn't go with her to the movies, who was with her, and why wouldn't she tell us?

Chapter 40

Since Sam's retirement, it seemed like everyone enjoyed the changes, even the small ones. Sveta and I already had a few meetings with the account executives, letting them know no deadlines would be promised to clients without my approval first. Sveta also decided that on Fridays she'd let the staff go at two so that they could get a nice start on the weekend. On Mondays, I'd treat everyone to coffee and bagels because, well, we all knew how Monday mornings could be. We expected good, hard work but wanted them to feel appreciated.

All seemed to be going well since Sveta bought the business. As usual, we made a great team. The first surprising turn of events was the return of PatchTree Ancestry. They said they got more financing, but it was too coincidental they contacted us right after Sam left. We were also preparing to meet with a seafood restaurant near Charleston and a North Carolina jewelry chain, which my mom got us as leads.

I was making my rounds, checking out the work, when Sveta called me into her office. She motioned me over to her computer and showed me an email from Kevin, the marketing director for AshLynne Chocolate.

Hi Svetlana.

Hope all is well. It was great having a drink with you a few weeks ago. Congrats again on buying the business. Don't forget I'll be in DC this afternoon for a fundraiser. Thought you might want to join me. Maybe make some new business connections? Let me know.

"Please don't tell me you have a thing for him."

"Are you serious? He's not even my type." She swiveled around. "I think I should go. Maybe I can get him drunk and gather some more intelligence on Mitch."

"What are you? Some covert agent?"

"If I were, I wouldn't be able to tell you, would I?"

Sveta left early to get ready, and I stayed to hold down the fort. But I also kept my promise to everyone at the office about late nights. The staff would never have to see another one. They could actually be home at a decent hour to enjoy the rest of their day, whether it was helping their kids with homework, having a meal with their family, or a hanging out with friends. I'd given up those all-nighters many years ago, when Jack was born, and didn't see a need for them, if projects were managed the right way.

Even though the business wasn't mine, my new role added more responsibility. But I still decided that on the family front, nothing would change. I'd still leave the office at a decent time and be there for all the activities. Mondays and Thursdays for taekwondo. Every third Tuesday for parent meetings.

It never failed that I lost track of time, and Jack would text me reminders. Now that he was working on his second-degree black belt, going to class was more serious than ever. By the time I got home, Jack was waiting by the front door, already dressed in his uniform with his black belt tied perfectly, as if it were cat whiskers to help him balance as he stood on one foot.

"Master Reynolds will be beside himself. Not only are we going to be on time, we're going to be early," I said as he climbed in the front and opened a package of pastries.

"Nice dinner."

He smiled and took two huge bites, and when the first one disappeared, he got out the second pastry. Now and then, I felt guilty about not making home-cooked meals. Sometimes I wished my mom would come up, like my friend's Polish grandmother who spent time in their kitchen cooking away. Her kitchen always smelled so good. Every week when I did my online shopping, I dreamed of piling the cart with all the ingredients to make soups and stews. But after realizing how much work it would take, I'd ascend the virtual aisles for already prepared meals.

When we got to Western Warriors, the kids were cooling down from the previous class. Master Reynolds stood front and center going through his routine while all the moms were going through theirs—watching him. Some of them pretended to look at their phones, but they always angled their heads to look up. Who knew if Master Reynolds noticed, but it really didn't matter. The moms enjoyed the view, and the kids got plenty of exercise. It was the perfect combination.

I started my shopping, as I normally did on Thursdays, in between checking work emails. My phone pinged with a text. This time it was from Sveta.

Can u meet me at the office?

Sveta texted me only one other time to meet her at the office, so it must have been important.

I'm at taekwondo. What's it about?

This isn't texting material.

Ok. See u in 90 min.

Later in the evening, I drove back to the office and parked next to Sveta's sedan and a few other cars, one of which never seemed to move. The person was either a workaholic, or dead and nobody came to claim the car. Neither one sounded great, and the way my mind worked, I imagined the worst. The building was locked, and I forgot the key to get into the office. I'd taken it off my chain a few months earlier and left it in my glove compartment. I walked back and dug around papers, a tire gauge, and some lip gloss.

A light glowed from Sveta's office, and the door was ajar. As I got closer, I could hear music. She cursed in Russian, and I figured she was coding some challenging project or responding to a ridiculous deadline request that somehow got around us. I poked my head in and was about to ask her what couldn't wait until the morning.

"Hey, you'll be proud of me," Sveta said. She fanned out a handful of cards and waved them.

"What's that?"

"Business cards. While Kevin was getting drunk, he was telling a bunch of guys how we could help them with marketing."

"Why do we want their business cards? Especially if there's a connection to Mitch."

"Lighten up, my *vetrushka*." She told me to pull up a chair. She looked through the cards and read their names and companies to me. Then she started her search, first looking for anything controversial that popped up. Then she researched each company name with the term "companies with neo-Nazi ties." Nothing popped up either.

"Open up a blank document then go back on each company's site," I said. "Cut and paste the names from the business cards, all the CEO names, and their board of directors. Or I can do it."

"Keep going with that. You might be on to something," she said. Sveta's phone rang, and we both jumped. It was Rob checking on her. He really liked Sveta and wasn't used to her working late since she'd cut back on her hours over the past year. But, since having bought the business, she started putting in more time, and he didn't seem to like it. He always worried about her working too much, so she told him she'd be home within an hour.

"Hey, isn't there an app where you can match up business connections of people and companies? I remember doing some research on that when we worked on a recent pitch."

"Let me look in my notes." She opened up the folder on her desktop and skimmed the document. She scrolled down and read through it. Sveta snapped her fingers and sat up more in her chair. "Found it! *Meelaya*, you're brilliant. I'll download it on my personal device."

Sveta opened up her desk drawer and pulled out her laptop. She powered it up and typed in the app's name.

"Ooh, it has good reviews and four and a half stars."

Sveta read the description aloud: A business application that works overtime, letting you find all your business contacts and figure out how they're connected. Get a leg up with one simple search, or enter up to five names to find the connections you need. Similar to other networking sites but one that lets you mind your own business—and grow it.

"Okay, now what?" I asked.

"Let's enter five names and see if the dots connect," she said and turned her computer toward me. "Here, you choose which ones."

I looked at the list for a moment and picked five. Sveta entered the names and waited for the information to load.

"No matches," Sveta said.

"It's okay. Let's try some from the boards."

Sveta cut and pasted one name from each of the companies and kept going down the list.

"Hey, you're a programming goddess. Isn't there some code you can create to randomly pick combinations of names?"

Sveta sat back in her chair. She looked up at the ceiling, which she always did when someone asked her about some formulaic approach or programming question that took a little longer to decipher. "I could do that, but it would take a while. We could set up some formulas in a worksheet. That would go much faster. Then, we can cut and paste them into the app."

I let her start her magic and walked to the kitchen. I pulled out a container from yesterday's leftovers, warmed it up in the microwave, and grabbed two forks. Sveta worked on it for a good thirty minutes, as I skimmed through several magazines.

"Woo-hoo, we've got a match," Sveta yelled. "Look here. They're all on the board of some organization called the Central Oberst Society. Interesting. I don't know if it's relevant, but *oberst* in German means 'colonel,' and it can also mean 'supreme,' kind of like top dog."

"Or supremacy?" I asked.

She pointed again. "And our good friend Mitch is one of them."

She minimized the worksheet and opened up a browser, typing in the society's name. As we waited a few seconds for the page to load, I expected the website to be dark and chaotic with a lot of ranting and commentary. Instead it was clean, with a taupe background and just two lines of text. The name, Central Oberst Society, floated in the middle of the page in all caps with the statement "Keeping Our Vision and Values Alive Since 1993" underneath it, both in a cobalt blue.

We wanted to find out more about their mission or projects, but the site had only one section, a Contact Us page, with an email and a post-office address in Delaware. Sveta looked at her watch. "Before I go, let me show you one more thing." She typed away then turned the screen toward me.

It didn't register at first. Then I realized we were looking at Mitch's emails. "What the hell? How'd you get in?"

"Doesn't matter. He'll never know, and I've already down-loaded what we're looking at," Sveta said before opening a document with a list of article links.

We clicked on each article, getting a closer look at the themes. One article rallied support against immigrants from Latin America. A few shared how anti-Semitism was on the rise throughout Europe with Jewish families leaving in droves. And an opinion piece blaming the collapse of the housing market on Jews.

Sveta closed the articles and opened a folder where she had downloaded some photos. The same guy, who looked about thirty with short black hair and blue eyes, was in every shot. In a few images, he showed off an SS tattoo on his shoulder. In another, he wore a black t-shirt and held a coffee mug pretending to make a toast. I'd seen that mug before, the mug with German writing below an SS emblem, the same symbol emblazoned on his shoulder. It was the coffee mug from the text on Mitch's phone. If I weren't so horrified, the art director in me would have suggested a better font instead of the script in all caps that was impossible to read. I stared at the mug trying to decipher the words then looked at the guy's face, his jagged smile and blue eyes pierced right through me.

"That's some freaky shit, who in their right mind would get an SS tattoo?" I said and got up from the chair.

"I know it wasn't all up-and-up for me to hack in."

"Ya think?"

"Here's the thing. Mitch hasn't written any articles since college, from what I can tell, that's if he's using his real name. And he's kind of hush-hush about his views, just talking about it within his circle."

"So it's okay that he's an introverted neo-Nazi?" I smirked.

"Oh, hell no. What I mean is I don't think he'd ever admit to his personal views, even if we called him out. It would hurt his business too much. Think about it. Who would want to buy his chocolate if word got out that he was anti-Semitic?"

As much as I wanted Mitch gone, Sveta was right. If we confronted him, he'd probably deny it and figure out we were snooping, which made me nervous. Greg didn't want me to confront him either. Still, I couldn't imagine working one more day with Mitch, and Greg knew it.

"Let's pretend for a minute he was gone. Could you afford *not* to have his business?" I asked.

"Sure, we'd be fine. But kicking them to the curb isn't an option, since we don't want to confront him. I'm open to ideas."

I walked over to straighten the awards that lined Sveta's shelf and looked out the window at the office buildings across the street.

"What if we come up with a way for Mitch to leave and take his business elsewhere—on his own accord."

"Not sure how we'd do that."

"Why?" I asked.

"Because he loves your work too much."

Chapter 41

I didn't sleep much that night, tossing and turning often, thinking about how we could get AshLynne Chocolate to leave. Mitch didn't seem like the type to walk away without a good reason. Sveta was right. He liked our work and considered throwing us more after their quarterly numbers came in, if all looked good. I tried my best to conceal my dark circles and ordered a double espresso at the café, a rarity and something I'd done during those all-nighters so long ago.

Jessica came up the hall as I hung my coat behind the door. "I tried to call you. Is your phone off? Some lawyer named David Wexley called, says it's urgent."

The name hadn't registered at first. For a moment, I tried to recollect how I knew a David Wexley. But then it clicked. Jessica tore off the page from her notepad where she wrote down his number, and I rushed to my desk. Wexley answered on the first ring.

"Is Izzy okay?" I asked in a panic.

"Is this Stephanie Britain?"

"Yes." My heart was pounding.

"Ms. Britain, are you in a good place where we can talk? You're not driving are you?"

"No, I'm not driving! What's wrong? Is Izzy okay?"

"I'm so very sorry. Izzy passed away yesterday."

I dropped to the chair and kept asking him the same question. *What happened?* But it was a blur, as I sat there, my body shaking. There was a knock and Sveta came in. She didn't say a word. Instead she put her hand on my shoulder and took the receiver. After speaking to Wexley, she called Greg because I couldn't get in a word without crying. I turned in the chair and caught a glimpse of my reflection. My eyes and nose were bright red, as if I'd been standing out in the cold waiting for a very late bus.

"I don't know how much I should tell you," Sveta said after making the calls. She grabbed the box of tissues and pulled one out to wipe the tears off my cheek.

Why didn't I ask him about the envelope I'd found? Why didn't I show I cared about his health?

"I'm fine. Just tell me."

"He had a heart attack."

"A heart attack? At home?"

"The lawyer said he collapsed at a fitness center."

"Jesus, I knew he shouldn't have gone!"

After a few moments of catching my breath, I told Sveta about aerobics, how Izzy made it his routine, sweating like crazy and going because of Deena, the instructor. Sveta said at least Izzy saw a beautiful woman before he died. She was trying to cheer me up, but of course, I broke down again because it reminded me of the time Bailey ran out of the house to chase after Cookie.

"What else did Wexley say?"

"He wants you to come to Stevensonville."

I left work and waited in the kitchen for Jack to come home from school. It wasn't that long ago when I had to tell him about my dad's passing. Jack was nine at the time. It was a Sunday morning, and we couldn't wait any longer to tell him. Greg and I knocked gently on his door and when we entered his room, he was already awake, still in his bed playing with his toy cars.

Jack looked up, and maybe it was the expression on our faces but right away, he asked what was wrong. After I told him about my dad, he curled up in a ball and threw the covers over his head, like Jeremy did when Cookie died. Jack cried hard that day, and Ginger came running in and pushed her muzzle against the pillow. Yet again, I would be the bearer of bad news, this time Ginger would comfort us both.

Chapter 42

As soon as Jack came through the door, I called out for him. He came to the kitchen and dropped his backpack on the floor.

"Mom, what's wrong?"

My red nose and bloodshot eyes were a dead giveaway.

"Is it Izzy?" he asked, and when I nodded and wept, he came over to hug me. It was the first time my son had hugged me in a long, long time. We cried together then finished off a family-sized container of chocolate ice cream, while crying between bites as I told him what happened.

"Hey," I said as he offered me the last spoonful. "Why did you think it was Izzy and not Grandma?"

"Because we just texted."

"You and Grandma text?" I said, all surprised.

He nodded.

"How often?"

"Every day. I guess she wants to make sure I get home okay. And she makes me text back."

"Really? Why didn't you ever tell me?"

He shrugged then got up and grabbed the whipped cream from the fridge. He tilted his head back and shot a huge amount into his mouth. After a few seconds, it began to drip onto the floor. Normally I'd tell him to stop being so silly, but that day, he could make all the mess he wanted.

I reached for a tissue from the silver box my mom gave me during one of her visits. When Izzy visited her, did they sit on her new porch, drink sweet tea, and chat about their younger days? Did they talk about their spouses and how they missed them? Did they share regrets, if they had any?

"Don't mind me," I said to Jack as I wiped my tears. "I'll be a mess for a while."

To make me laugh, he made a bunch of silly faces then showed me funny pet videos to pass the time. It worked beautifully, and I laughed between the tears until Greg got home.

***

With Greg at the wheel the next morning, I stared at the cars on the road as we made our way to Stevensonville. All the crying the day before made my vision blurry and eyes bloodshot. They'd clear up only to last until the next cry, which came every few minutes. Nothing seemed to do the trick.

Greg kept his hand on my leg. He'd been through this twice with me now, three years ago with my dad. I was emotionally drained from losing him, but then I didn't have the task of being the executor. I knew it was a big job, and along with work, my hands were more than full. How would I pull it all off? How would I pull myself together after another loss? Millions of people had done the same. I just didn't know how.

We pulled onto Wexley's street after searching for his practice. It was so secluded that the GPS didn't pick it up. Twists and turns, not only to stay on the road but to miss a couple of deer, had Greg gripping the wheel tightly.

As we went up the driveway, I could see why David Wexley worked out of his home. Set on top of a mountain, the two-story Victorian had a light gray façade, red slate roof, and a wide porch that wrapped around to the right. A dark green sign with "Wexley, Attorney at Law" in white writing hung outside on the front railing. An orange tabby slept on the steps next to a flowerpot, and as soon as we closed the car door, she woke up. The cat stretched then pranced around and rubbed up against a post.

A woman opened the door as Greg reached for the bell. "Hello, you must be Mr. and Mrs. Britain. I'm Laura Wexley, Dave's wife. Come on in."

The foyer had beautiful dark molding and a decorative runner that kept the cherrywood floors warm and protected. Laura walked us to Dave's office. He was on the phone and gestured for us to sit down.

Laura whispered, "Y'all must be tired from the drive down. How about a sandwich and some lemonade?"

We smiled and nodded before thanking her. Mr. Wexley held up his finger and mouthed, "one minute," as he listened to the caller. Dave was a lot younger than I imagined, although after knowing Izzy, it didn't surprise me since he enjoyed spending time with younger people. Dave looked about forty, could spare to lose a few pounds, and was dressed casually in jeans with a cardigan sweater over a striped, button-down shirt.

Laura came back with a tray and set it on the coffee table. "I threw in a few cookies, didn't think you'd mind." She walked out and closed the door behind her.

Dave finished his call and came around his desk to shake our hands. "I'm so sorry about Izzy. It was such a shock to me." He paused. "Man, what a loss. What a great, great guy."

I didn't say anything for fear that I'd start bawling again, so I nodded and picked up my glass of lemonade.

"This part of my job is never easy, but it has to be done. Have you seen the will?"

I shook my head, and he pulled out a folder. "Izzy asked me to keep the original. He wanted you to be able to access it right away. The good news is that it should be fairly easy. He kept it simple. There are only a few individuals listed in the will—you, Janet Goodman, Ellen McKinley, and Dylan Jacoby.

I have their contact info once we get started on the paper-work."

"Izzy left me some notes," he continued and looked down at his pad. "Janet and Ellen are sisters, daughters of a childhood friend named Rebekkah. And you know Dylan, his roommate. Izzy left him some money to help with student loans."

"That's really nice. So, what do I need to do as the execu-tor? It's all new to me."

"There's a lot of paperwork, but I'll handle all that," Wexley said. "You need to sign some things, and we'll get started. Oh, one more thing. Izzy did a quick video that accompanies the will, basically saying he was of sound mind when he made it."

"Why would he do that?"

"Some people do that in case anyone wants to contest. But I don't see that happening. The three aren't relatives, and I'm pretty sure they'll be happy they're getting something."

"What do you mean 'getting something'? Aren't they splitting the estate?"

He looked up at me. "You didn't know? Dylan, Janet, and Ellen each get a sizeable amount, two organizations get donations. You get the rest."

"His house?" Greg asked, surprised.

Dave turned back to the front page of the will and leaned forward to show us the text. "I hope you like Stevensonville. Izzy left you a beautiful property."

Greg took my hand. Izzy was a little dopy from the pain-killers when he told me I was like a daughter to him, but I guess he really meant it.

"Can you tell me which organizations are getting dona-tions?" I asked.

Wexley picked up the will and skimmed through it, turning to the second page.

"The Commonwealth Commission on Holocaust Remembrance and Brooklyn Way Middle School."

"That's Jack's school," Greg said. "Wow."

"Oh, there's one more thing." He reached into a locked drawer and pulled out a small envelope. "Izzy has a safety deposit box. He gave me the second key. Normally you'd have to wait until you get assigned executor by the court to access it, like transferring the house deed, but he didn't want you to wait, so he made it POD."

"What's POD?" I asked.

"Payable on death. He put it on his accounts too, so if something happened to him and you needed to pay bills, you could access the money. I recommend we wait on that. But while you're here, you can go through the box."

He took a bite of the sandwich Laura left on his desk and looked at his watch. "And I suggest you go now. Tomorrow is Saturday, and you know we're talking banking hours." He handed me his card. "Call me if you have any problems. I've known the branch manager for as long as a giraffe's neck. Actually, I'll call Sharon right now and let her know you're on your way."

Chapter 43

By the time we reached the bank, Sharon was waiting for us. She gave us a hug and was visibly upset about Izzy's passing. He'd been a customer for a long time, and they loved him like we all did. We sat at her desk and reminisced. She shared great stories of how he'd come in and sit in her office and tell silly jokes.

Sharon opened a drawer, pulled out a record book, and asked me to sign the card for the box. She checked the signature against my photo ID before asking us to follow her to the back. She put both keys in and turned them in the box. I lifted it out as we walked to a private room.

"Y'all take your time. Call for me when you're done," Sharon said before walking to the teller.

Greg locked the door behind us and rubbed my back. I opened the box and pulled a few items out. To my surprise, there really wasn't that much, although I had no idea what people kept in their boxes.

On the top was an envelope with my name on it. I set it aside and looked through the rest. Photos of Izzy and Diane on their travels. More photos of Izzy as a teenager, a picture of a house, and one more of Rebekkah. Each photo had a description and year written on the back, making me want to do the same with all my photos when I got home. There was a large yellow envelope that contained his naturalization certificate from when he became a United States citizen and the deed to his house. The letter his mother wrote that I'd found sat on the bottom of the box, along with a copy of the original. I put everything in a bag except for the envelope that had my name on it.

"Can you open it?" I asked Greg.

"Are you sure?"

"I'm nervous."

Greg ripped the envelope and took out a piece of paper. He showed me a letter, and I asked him to read it to me.

Dear Stephanie,

No matter how many times I tried, I could never call you Steph like everyone else. Although to me, you look like an Irene, but that's beside the point. I told you once when I was in the hospital that you were like a daughter to me. I was a little loopy from the medication but I promise—I meant every word.

Greg paused and showed me a smiley face Izzy inserted. Then he continued.

I love these little smiley faces you can put in your documents now. Dylan taught me how to do it.

I wasn't planning on leaving you a note, but I wanted to explain. Remember my little car accident while texting? You know, the one where you said I was acting like a teenager, which by the way, was a compliment, so thank you! The hospital had to do some scans and it turned out that I had more than a few bruises here and there. They discovered a sizeable tumor. They sent me to a specialist and when she started talking about tests and more scans, treatment options, and prognosis, I just said, thanks, I'll be in touch, and then threw all their paperwork in the trash on the way out. Are you kidding me? A 76-year-old guy going through all that? For what? To live maybe another year, two, or five if I'm one of the lucky ones? They told me I wouldn't have long if I did nothing, so I had to get everything in order. I didn't tell you because I didn't want you to try to talk me into it, into something I didn't want to do, or even worse, for you to feel guilty that you couldn't convince me. Honestly, I never thought I'd live this long anyways, being orphaned at six and "living" through the war without my parents. But by some miracle I did, all while making my way to the U.S., going to college, meeting my beautiful Diane, and becoming a professor. What a great life I've had.

I'll never forget how you went out of your way to find me. I'll never forget your beautiful family, especially Jack. I don't know when you'll get this letter, but I've had time to think about this client of yours. I know you can't stand the thought of doing business with him and, of all people, I completely understand. But no matter what you decide, he will still be anti-Semitic even if you get rid of him. I'm not keen on giving advice, so that's all I'm going to say. I know you'll make the right decision—for you. And you know how I know? Because you're creative and unbelievably smart and savvy. Maybe use those traits to help guide you.

If you ever get the chance, take a trip to France on my dime and visit Meribel Street where I lived during the war. That's one thing—the only thing—I regret not getting around to doing. I have a photo in this box of the house. As you know by now, you are listed as my executor, and Dave Wexley, who's a great guy, will help you. Another recommendation—go to Krista's and enjoy some lemon meringue pie. I went there recently and had two pieces of the good kind, not the no-sugar, no-fun version. Might as well splurge. Nobody's checking my sugar levels where I'm going.

On a final note, Stephanie, please enjoy your life and make time for some fun. Before you know it, you'll be 80 and wondering why you didn't dance more with Greg. You're a beautiful, thoughtful woman, and I'm so glad I had the opportunity to know you and your family.

Love,
Izzy

"Wait a second," Greg said. "Didn't they say he died of a heart attack? But he talks about cancer in the letter. So he didn't want to go through all those procedures, but even if he did, he would have probably died anyways. So sad."

I leaned against the table in disbelief. "Life is so complicated. And then it's not."

Greg folded the letter and put it back into the envelope. "I know this isn't going to help, and I know everyone always says it, but I'm glad he didn't suffer. Izzy didn't need to suffer." He came in close and held me. "He was definitely right about something."

"My client?"

"No, the dancing."

It was the first time I'd laughed all day. Izzy was right. We should dance more. And we should definitely laugh more. One day, I'd honor him and take a trip to Meribel Street where he hid by blending in. He also knew how much the chocolate account bothered me. Izzy didn't want to come across as giving advice but did his words ring true? That I should rely on my creativity, the skill used in my career for all these years and for so many clients, to help guide me? If this were true, more than anything, I'd need to figure out how.

Chapter 44

When I stopped at Izzy's house before heading back home, I found a large, opened envelope on the dining room table from my mom. His baseball cap, the one he'd left at her house, sat next to the envelope with a note that said, *wear in good health*. I figured she had no clue he was sick, which was typical for Izzy, typical not to let anyone feel sad or get burdened by him. We brought the cap back with us, knowing it belonged with my mom, not accidentally dropped under the bed or packed up in a box sitting in a closet somewhere.

Knowing Izzy, he wouldn't want us crying for long. He'd want us to laugh and enjoy life like he did. So a few weeks later, we threw a party at our house in his honor. It wasn't a surprise that a whole slew of out-of-towners showed up. A dozen college kids and his roommate, Dylan. A couple of waitresses from his favorite restaurant, along with Krista and her famous pies. And my mom, who made the long trip because she wouldn't want to miss what she called a tribute to a remarkable man.

Greg made sure they all had a drink in one hand and snacks in the other. Then we stood back and watched. All of them, except for my mom, knew Izzy longer than me, and they saw him more frequently. Would their grief be stronger than mine? Would Krista think of Izzy every time she made her lemon meringue pies? Would Dylan think of him when he played video games? And would they forget about him as time went by? Would they forget what he looked like? What his voice sounded like? How his contagious laughter bellowed out and filled a room?

I supposed that day would come. Like it did with the loss of my dad. I'd forgotten traits of his in the three short years since he passed. And more than his traits. Important dates. I wept the day he died yet forgot his birthday the following year, mad at myself when I realized I let it slip by, just like that. Some say it's part of healing, when you start forgetting moments and milestones of the dearly departed. I say it's simply the distractions of life.

Those similar, faded memories would eventually come with Izzy. But until then, everyone would remember his stories, funny jokes, and great joy for life. Dylan and his friends even hoped to be even half as cool when they got to Izzy's age.

Across the living room, my mom sat on the sofa watching the kids. She chugged down her wine and called Dylan over to fill it back up, hoping to fill the void with a cheap bottle of Pinot Gris.

"Hey there, you look hungry." I sat down and handed her a plate of appetizers.

"Steph, I'm not hungry at all."

"Okay, but your wine needs some company. And we don't want the bed to spin."

She laughed, put the glass down, and took the plate. "Okay, Mother," she teased, "if you insist."

Dylan's girlfriend switched the music to her playlist, and they all began dancing.

"Greg," my mom called out, "push the table to the wall so there's more room."

We both leaned back on the sofa and slid down a bit to get comfortable. Ginger came around the corner with her tail wagging, looking for uneaten food. When she eyed me, she put her head down and stepped back. I was the strict one in the house, and Ginger knew she couldn't break me. I never gave her scraps, and even in her old age, I wasn't about to make an exception. Every once in a while I'd catch the boys throwing food on the floor, and I'd pretend not to notice. If Jeremy were here, Ginger would follow him around getting crumbs so effortlessly.

"Steph," my mom said, "the last time I saw Izzy he told me about your client."

"Which one?"

"The chocolate guy."

"Yeah?"

She turned sideways to face me. "I know you don't like advice."

I looked down, expecting to get a lecture or unwanted advice like parents love to dish out.

"I know Izzy worried about you doing something drastic, but I think it's good to have strong principles. It makes you a better person, maybe even a better businessperson."

Her encouragement took me for a loop. I didn't expect that from her, at all. I thought for sure she'd be more conservative about the business or disagree with me just to disagree. Maybe we were more alike than I imagined.

"Thanks, Mom." I paused. "Can I ask you something?"

"Of course, but pour me some more wine, will ya?"

I got up and brought the bottle over, pouring the rest into both of our glasses.

"Remember last month when Sveta and I called you? You were about to see *Detective Fire*. You said, 'We'll have to see if the movie is as good as the book.'"

"Well don't we?"

"Don't we what?"

"Hope the movie is as good as the book."

"That's not what I meant."

"Well, sugar, get to the point. You and your beating around the bush."

"You said 'we'll,' like you were with someone. Who was with you?"

She took a sip of her wine. Then another. "You won't laugh?" She winked and gently tapped my nose like she did when I was little, like I always do now with Evan. We looked at each other for a minute, sitting silently, waiting for her to answer. She looked over at Ginger who started to bark when she heard the bell.

"Sorry we're late," Sveta said, arriving with wine in one arm and Rob on the other. He was about ten years younger and the quiet type who idolized her.

"Rob reminds me of that actor, what's his name?" my mom said. "The manly looking one, overflowing with muscles, with the great British accent."

"That narrows it down a lot."

"It's on the tip of my tongue. Heavens, I hate when that happens. Anyways," she whispered. "Rob's sexy, don't you think?"

"Mom, you've had enough wine."

"Look at you! Why can't I talk about men without you getting embarrassed?"

"Because you're my mom? Because I think of you and Dad together? I know, it sounds stupid."

"It's okay. I'm glad you still think of us like that. He was the love of my life."

We sat for a moment sipping on our wine, watching Sveta and Rob as they talked to the college students and filled their plates with snacks.

"Mom, you didn't answer my question about the movie."

"Don't laugh," she said. "But I made it all up to pretend to be with someone."

"What for?"

"So I wouldn't feel embarrassed about going to the movies by myself on a Friday night. So you wouldn't feel sorry for me. I've made progress. I can officially go to the movies and eat out by myself now."

I put my arm around her and my head on her shoulder. "I'd never feel sorry for you. I'm proud of you. It sounds like you're doing okay."

"I'm doing more than okay. And I know one thing's for sure."

"What's that?"

"You need to loosen up." She sat up and called out over the music. "Sveta, bring some of that wine over here for Steph. It's time to get Izzy's party started now that you're here."

"Woo-hoo, Izzy, did you hear that? This one's for you," Sveta said and put her hand up, shaking it in the air as she danced across the floor with Rob, almost spilling the wine along the way.

Chapter 45

Thanks to taking my mom's advice to drink more wine, I had a hangover from Izzy's party. I should have cut myself off, but Sveta kept filling my glass. After telling my mom we didn't want her bed to spin, mine was the one out of control. On Sunday, we cleaned and mopped the beer and wine that had stuck to the kitchen floor and, along the way, munched on snacks left out on the counter from the night before.

Monday came too soon, but at least my headache had retreated and the bed no longer turned. Before heading to the office, I stopped by the café and picked up coffee and bagels for the crew like I did every Monday morning. It was late-November, and even though the weather in Maryland was always unpredictable during this time, it was one of the coldest days.

As I drove up to the office, the parking lot was closed for construction so I turned around and parked in front of the building. After pulling on my hat, I stayed in my car for a few minutes to enjoy the view of the park across the street. A young mother sat watching her toddler who was skipping and picking up rocks. Their dog stood next to the stroller, and his tail wagged when the little girl bent down to pet him. I smiled, not only at the sheer joy of watching this family, but from thinking back to when Jeremy was a toddler. Going to the park with our dog Bailey was always one of our favorite activities.

A tap on my window startled me. I waved, got out of the car, and went to the passenger side to pick up the boxed coffee and bagels.

"I'm going to call you Stalker Stephanie from now on," Sveta said after I locked up. "Do you always watch kids at the park?"

"All the time. Call America's Most Maniacal before I get away."

"Did you survive the party?" she asked as we made our way to the lobby.

"Barely, no thanks to you and that bottle of wine."

"Well, we had to toast to Izzy."

"Twenty times?"

"Why not? He lived large, so we had to party large."

Between helping Sveta run the business, taking care of my family, and dealing with Izzy's estate, I needed a vacation. Luckily, Wexley handled a lot of it for me, but I still had to contact the utility companies to change accounts into my name, put a change of address for the mail to come to me, pay final bills, and talk to Wexley on a weekly basis so that nothing fell through the cracks.

When I got to the office and booted up my computer, I read an email from Mitch confirming his visit the following week. He wanted to come down and talk about new business. *Great.* If it were any other account, I'd be thrilled about the added billings. But he was the last person I ever wanted to hear from again. A notice came up reminding me of lunch with the executive director of the Commonwealth Commission on Holocaust Remembrance, the organization that received a donation from Izzy's estate. She wanted to thank me personally for handling Izzy's affairs and share how they would use his donation to fund programs in schools.

At noon, I walked across the street to the Irish pub and grabbed a table by the window. No matter what time you came to the pub, it was busy. They had great food and service and were conveniently located—already prepared for success without the added expense of advertising. The artist in me, though, took one look at the menu and made a mental note to chat with the owner about a redesign.

The circular door spun, and a woman with red, wavy hair approached the hostess on the phone. She put down the receiver, and the two of them walked toward my table.

"Stephanie?"

I got up and shook her hand.

"So nice to meet you. I'm Irene."

She took a seat, and though we looked nothing alike, we had the same wavy, auburn hair that fell to our shoulders. She ordered a sweet tea and had to settle for club soda when they told her they only had unsweetened.

"I grew up in the South, and it took me a long time to get used to not having sweet tea. It's definitely not the same," I said.

"It's fine, really. It's probably better that I don't have all that sugar."

"Let's leave it for dessert," I said.

Irene thanked me again for taking care of Izzy's affairs quickly and said that the commission was beyond grateful for the donation. Irene then asked me to tell her how the two of us met. I told her about his mom's letter, how I searched for him—although with the Internet these days, searching for people was so much easier.

We joked about looking up all kinds of information in an encyclopedia and how it would take hours to do a research paper in high school. We were about the same age and related to stories about neighborhood kids who went door-to-door to make extra money by selling encyclopedias until they no longer wanted to carry all the heavy samples around. So, instead, they got jobs at fast-food restaurants or as summer lifeguards.

The waiter brought our sandwiches, and in between bites, we talked more about our childhood, where we went to college, and how we met our husbands. We swapped stories about our religious upbringings and how she and her brothers played hooky all the time when they attended Hebrew school. I was jealous, I told her, because so many times I wanted to skip Sunday school, but my parents took turns teaching our Bible class, so I never had that chance.

"Stephanie, there's another reason why I wanted to meet you. I feel I can tell you now, I mean now that a little time has passed."

My heart started racing. "Tell me what? I hope everything's okay."

"Everything's fine. I'm not sure how much Izzy shared with you, but did you know he sent us a check every month? It was always for the same amount, two-hundred-and-fifty dollars. He was very particular in how he wanted it used. We set up these traveling exhibits, and he wanted the money to fund those. They went all over the country. It was a huge part of our educational program."

It didn't surprise me that Izzy helped the organization. I took another bite of my sandwich while she continued.

"But about four months ago, he sent us fifteen-hundred dollars, six times the amount he normally sent. It was as if he knew something was going to happen. I wanted to call him to see if he'd made a mistake, but I never did. At the time, I felt uncomfortable. But I'd like to give it back to the estate."

"No, please, absolutely not. He sent it to you, so it's what he wanted. There's no way I'd take the money back."

"Do you know why he'd send this larger donation? Did he know he was ill?"

Even though she shared the information about the payments, I didn't want to share anything about his health, the envelope, or the letter he left for me explaining his circumstances. I wanted her to remember the Izzy she'd known all these years, happy and healthy. "He seemed fine to me," I wound up saying. "I saw him a few weeks before he passed. He was really happy go lucky."

We weren't surprised that Izzy left a donation for the commission. Just because he didn't want to talk about his past didn't mean he didn't want other people to learn about what happened. Just because he wanted to move on didn't mean he didn't want other people to stop for a moment and remember.

She continued, "We'd love to honor Izzy during our twentieth anniversary. His generous donations allowed us to educate so many people. And we'd like you and your family to come."

"That would be wonderful. We'd love that."

Irene bent down and took a folder from her bag. She opened it and pulled out brochures, a calendar, and other marketing pieces. "We've started promoting the event, and we have some emails coming up next month I can forward, so you'll know what we're planning."

"Have you thought of some additional marketing for fundraising?"

"Not really, but that's a great idea."

A car's horn startled me, and I looked out the window. Traffic was stopped at a red light. As people crossed the street, they passed two homeless men who were no more than a few feet from each other. They sat on a ledge and each held a cardboard sign that said the same thing: "Lost Job, Need Money For Food."

"Irene, we choose a couple pro bono accounts to work on each year. I'd really like to help you come up with a fundraising campaign. At no charge."

She took a bite of her apple pie. "I can't let you do that. You've already done enough."

"I insist. Can I have these?" I said as I held a brochure. "And can you send me your logo and brand identity guidelines?"

She smiled and took a sip of her coffee. "Only if you let me buy lunch."

"Deal."

We said our goodbyes, and I crossed the street to go back to the office. On the way, I passed the homeless men who were still holding their signs. One of the signs seemed more beat up, and it looked like, because of it, the man had more money in his cup. It could have been my imagination, or it could have been pure marketing, that a more beat-up sign made people take notice, made more people feel sorry for him.

And then it hit me as the words from Izzy's letter rang out. If I wanted to get rid of AshLynne Chocolate, I had to think creatively and use this trait to help guide me. I had to send Mitch a strong message, one that was pure marketing. And one that would hit him right in the gut.

Chapter 46

Jenny, our amazing project manager, had a troubled look on her face. She always worried about deadlines, even though we never missed one, even after we changed the rule about not staying too late.

"Don't worry, Jenny. I put the Casa Koolers' ads on the drive yesterday, so they're ready for client approval."

"Good, thanks, I was about to ask." She walked off and turned around quickly. "Oh, Mitch from AshLynne Chocolate is waiting for you in the conference room."

"Thanks, I'll be right there."

I'd prepared all week for my meeting with Mitch. I was ready to send my message. But would he take the bait? Would his true colors show through? I continued down the hall to the kitchen where I put my lunch in the fridge then went to the conference room. Mitch stood by the back wall looking at some of our campaigns. He greeted me and shook my hand.

He turned back around and looked at the rest of our work. "You have the right combination. You're talented. But you also have determination. You need that to succeed in business."

I agreed. "That's true. Talent alone won't work. That's for sure."

He took out his pad and looked through his notes. "That's why I like working with you. Everything you've done has been great. Every ad, the website, banners. And you've met all our deadlines."

"Thanks, so how are things looking for next year?"

"In terms of throwing you some more work?"

"Well, that wouldn't hurt," I lied. But I lied for a greater good and part of the plan. He looked again at his notes and rambled on about the supermarket displays and a recipe book, asking if we had anyone on staff with book-design experience.

"I have some thoughts about marketing and promotions. I'm not sure if you're up to hearing more options."

He agreed that the company was open to any and all ideas. We walked down the hall and passed Sveta. "Hey, Sveta, why don't you join us. I was about to tell Mitch the new marketing ideas." She picked up her coffee cup and followed us into my office.

After my lunch last week with the commission, Irene overnighted me two posters, one of their traveling exhibit and another from their ten-year anniversary, with the title "Let's Not Forget the Faces" along with hundreds of portraits that formed a Star of David. The posters hung on my office wall and the marketing collateral sat spread out on the round table. When Mitch walked in, he noticed the posters right away.

Sveta took a few brochures from the table and handed them to Mitch. "I'm not sure if Sam ever told you, but he did pro bono work every year, and we're planning to keep the tradition. Basically we work on two projects, one that senior management chooses and another everyone in the office votes on. This year, the staff voted on the Stantin Animal Welfare League, and senior staff chose the Commonwealth Commission on Holocaust Remembrance. The commission is planning a gala and silent auction for their twentieth anniversary in January. I thought we could tie in your company as a sponsor." Sveta continued, "Perhaps you could donate some chocolate for their event? It would be great exposure for your brand, and it would be for a good cause, to continue educating people about the Holocaust, a part of history that needs to be remembered."

I stood up and took a sip of water then brought over my laptop. "They also raise funds for the aging Jewish population, which I think is great." I showed mocked-up posters created for the fundraiser, using AshLynne Chocolate as a major sponsor. "I hope you don't mind. I came up with some ideas," I said and passed him the laptop to take a look. "If you sponsor the event, your company's name will be seen by hundreds attending, plus you'll get media coverage not only in the area but throughout the country and other networks that pick it up." I got more excited, like I do when we're presenting a new business pitch. "From what I've heard, a former senator plans to commemorate them, although I'm not able to share the details until it's confirmed."

Mitch looked at the ideas for several minutes then set the laptop down. "Ladies, it's very admirable what you're doing. But we don't get involved with charitable events like this." He paused then got up to look at the posters. "We don't want to pick a group of people then not be able to help another." He turned around and with a serious look continued, "You understand, don't you? I'm sure you'll find another company to help...." He glanced at the poster again. "this organization."

"Are you sure? It's a way to remember the victims and help keep history alive," I added.

Sveta picked up the brochures and stood next to Mitch. They stared at each other for a long minute. I could tell she wanted to ask the real reason for deciding against it—and throw in a few Russian profanities while at it. Instead, she smiled. "No problem, we understand. We have other ideas for ongoing marketing efforts. No need to get stuck on this one. Let's talk them through."

Mitch listened for the next several minutes. He was distracted as he looked at his watch a few times during our conversation. He no longer appeared like the enthusiastic client who minutes ago complimented our work that hung on the conference-room wall. We shook hands again and walked him to the elevator. Sveta and I waved goodbye, and he said he'd be in touch.

"Do you think he bought it?" I whispered.

"Hard to tell. My heart was pounding faster than my first visit to the immigration office."

We walked back to my desk to talk about other business and a new pitch we had the following week. A few moments later the phone rang, and I noticed the Pennsylvania area code, thinking it was Jeremy on the other end, though he usually resorted to texting. "Hi sweetie, is everything okay?" I answered.

There was laughing on the other end at first. "Not sure if you meant to call me 'sweetie.' It's Mitch."

Shit! I mouthed to Sveta.

"Oh sorry, hi, do you mind if I put you on speakerphone?" I put the receiver down and pushed the button.

Sveta got up slowly and tiptoed to close the door behind us.

"Did you forget something? I'm happy to bring it down."

"No, I've got everything. All this time, for the life of me, I couldn't figure out where I'd seen you before. I ran into you at the reenactment that time, but we already knew each other. As I was walking to my car, it dawned on me."

I continued to listen, looking up every now and again at Sveta, not knowing what he was going to say next. "It was at the reenactment—but not the one where I saw you at the dance. It was the year before."

"Are you sure it was me?" I lied.

"Positive. Something you said today, about keeping history alive. That's when it clicked. You were asking me a lot of questions that day."

"Now I remember," I said, looking at Sveta and getting nervous. "I was curious."

"I get it, but it's a reenactment. We get together, sit around the campfire, sing battle songs. It's fun and something we look forward to every year, and it's *my* way of keeping history alive."

Sveta lifted both of her middle fingers and pointed them at the phone. Before speaking again, I recalled the words the SS reenactor stated in the Russian camp. I'd never forget those words and leaned closer to the phone. "I remember you or one of your buddies said, 'It's a part of history, and we shouldn't be denied to represent it.' But I'm not sure how I feel about that."

I didn't mention anything Izzy had found out about him. That wasn't part of the plan, and besides we weren't up for a fight.

There was silence on the other end. "Mitch, are you still there?"

"You don't have to agree with it. Like I've always said, war is controversial. And there are always two sides to every story, every war."

Sveta couldn't sit silently anymore. She leaned over to get closer to the phone. "Hi, Mitch, it's Sveta. Let me chime in, if you don't mind. After you left, Stephanie and I came up with other marketing ideas, hoping we can run them by you. I can put our notes together and shoot them over in an email."

At this point, Sveta was winging it. We hadn't spoken at all about his company, except when she told me that the business would be fine without it.

"Actually, Sveta, there's something else I wanted to talk about. Just got off the phone with Kevin, and he's advising me to bring the marketing in-house. Using consultants is getting expensive. And I have to agree."

Sveta rolled her eyes and played along. "Oh, I'm so confused. I thought you liked our work." Sveta said while continuing to flip him off. "And the analytics show good results, right?"

"I was always a proponent of doing everything needed to introduce our brand. Now I have to be fiscally responsible by watching our spending. Especially if my marketing director is recommending it. I'll have Kevin contact you to tie up the loose ends."

"Sorry to hear that. I'm glad we've been able to get you off to a great start," Sveta added.

"If you know any writers and designers looking for work, send them my way."

My jaw dropped.

Sveta shook her head and pretended to hang herself with her scarf. "Sure, no problem, I'll let you know if anyone's looking."

I pushed the "end call" button on the phone and put back the receiver to make sure the call was dropped.

"*Skatertyou darozhka.*"

"Let me guess. Large pig?"

"Nope," Sveta answered.

"Goat?"

"Believe it or not, I was simply saying good riddance."

Good riddance, for sure. I looked up at the light, the light that always helped keep my tears at bay. There was no way that guy was going to make me cry.

Deep in my heart, I knew he wouldn't stay, even if he loved our work. His hatred for our cause was way too deep. But he was a businessman, and when you're a smart businessman, like Sveta said, you walk away quietly so your business doesn't suffer. Using consultants was expensive. It was a sensible reason to leave, one that wouldn't be criticized.

Sveta got up and stood in front of the commission's poster that hung on the wall. "It's beautiful, isn't it?" she said.

I leaned on the back of the desk while staring at it. "Yep, so beautiful I'm not changing a thing."

Chapter 47

The Commonwealth Commission on Holocaust Remembrance rented a beautiful space for its anniversary gala, an old library converted to a social hall in the 1960s. Wood floors, window frames, and stair posts were brought back to life and to their original luster. This would be a beautiful place to get married, one of the guests said, as we walked to the credenza to find our table number. The posters, updated with the new dates, hung beautifully throughout the room, and Casa Koolers, our client who sponsored the event, lined gift bags along the back row for the guests.

The commission gave us a table for six. Greg, Jack, and my mom came along, and quite frankly, I couldn't have imagined speaking without them. We had two seats left at our table, and Jack invited his history teacher, Mrs. Beauregard, and her husband to join us.

I'd given so many presentations in my career that I should have been a pro at speaking anywhere. New business pitches never made me nervous for more than the first few seconds. Maybe because I was used to them, used to telling companies how we could do great work marketing their products and services. But this was different. This wasn't about work. This was personal.

Irene took the stage and gave a beautiful speech about the history of the commission and the projects they'd worked on for twenty years. She thanked everyone for all the donations and the volunteers for their dedication. Irene called the volunteers up on stage, and we gave them a standing ovation. *I have to follow that*, I thought, and my heart started to race. Then the memory of my father and grandfather comforted me. How I wished they had a chance to meet Izzy, to tell stories, to trade jokes, to talk about their shared birthdays.

After the room settled down, Irene approached the podium again. "Unfortunately, not too long ago, we lost a dear, dear friend, Isadore Fischer, who was not only a Holocaust survivor and hidden child during the war, but a huge supporter of the commission. In his honor, I'd like to call up Stephanie Britain, a friend of his, to say a few words."

Irene shook my hand as I walked on stage. Holocaust survivors, some in wheelchairs, others with canes resting on the tables, sat in the front row with their families. The survivors smiled at the young kids, like all proud grandparents do. I scanned the room and saw Mrs. Beauregard and her husband take their seats.

"I'm honored to be here and to offer my deepest respect to all the Holocaust survivors and their families who are with us tonight. I'm honored not only to remember Izzy, but to have called him my friend. For those who didn't know him, Isadore Fischer was born in Staufen, Germany, in 1936. As Irene mentioned, he was a hidden child during the war. An incredibly courageous woman named Berneen Powers saved him right before he was about to board a train with his parents to Auschwitz. When he talked about what happened, which was only a few times, I always thought it was a miracle he survived. For me, meeting him was just as much a miracle.

"It's still hard to believe I met him because I found his name in a letter written by his mother in 1941. Somehow this letter made its way from France, across the Atlantic Ocean to the East Coast of the United States, amazingly like Izzy did. And somehow this letter made its way into the hands of a

World War II relic collector who was selling them at a living-history event. Imagine, I picked this letter out of a barrel of hundreds of letters. Hundreds.

"Izzy was truly one of a kind, so full of life, and so funny. There were many questions I asked him, but my favorite was, 'Izzy, why do you tell so many silly jokes?' At first, I thought he'd say, 'Because laughter is the best medicine,' but then he surprised me. He said, 'Laughter is the only medicine.' I won't share his silly jokes, mostly because my delivery stinks, but also because it wouldn't be the same. Like when you try to make your grandmother's chicken soup or, in my case, my mom's sweet tea. When our loved ones make them, they're so good because they're made with love.

"Izzy's jokes were told with love, the love of storytelling and the love for life. Even though his life started out badly, he told me more than once that he had a blessed one. He didn't want to dwell on the past. He wanted to live in the present, move forward, and enjoy it, which he did with his beautiful wife, Diane, who is also no longer with us. So, in his honor, let's lift our glasses. To Izzy, an amazing man who lived life to its fullest. And to his parents who had the courage to hand over their beautiful six-year-old boy to a complete stranger in order to save him. To the Fischer family!"

Irene walked to the center of the stage and once again shook my hand. The room applauded as I walked back to our table.

"You were great," Greg said.

"How can you honor a great man in a two-minute speech? I'm not even sure if he'd want me to talk about his past."

"But you *should* talk about his past," Mrs. Beauregard said. "If you don't, who else will?"

"She's right, Mom."

Jack's teacher snapped her fingers. "You should come and talk to my students, like Izzy did last year. I still have a copy of his speech. You could use that or come up with your own. That would be such a nice way to honor him."

"I don't know. I'm not sure if he'd want me to dwell on it."

"You're not dwelling on it at all," she added. "A minute ago, you talked about his great sense of humor. And honestly, I bet if you told him you wanted to keep his memory alive, he'd be honored."

Maybe she was right. Maybe he would be okay with me meeting with students. I could talk about his experience during the war, but also tell the kids about his positive attitude and how he made a great life for himself. I pulled out my phone and opened the calendar. "When would be a good time to come?"

"Anytime, but it would be great if you could come in a few weeks when I begin the lesson on World War II. This year, I'll be incorporating a trip to the Holocaust Museum."

Jack asked. "How come we didn't get to go last year?"

"I heard we're getting more funding, so I requested it."

Greg leaned in and put his arm around me. "I guess the school already heard about the donation. What an awesome guy," he whispered.

I marked it on my calendar and wondered how I'd reach the audience, a room full of twelve-year-olds with wandering minds. Like Izzy, I'd start by making a few jokes to lighten up the mood, to bring cheer to the room and grab their attention before diving into the heart of the story. Who knew Izzy would teach me so much about presenting, something that had been part of my life and my livelihood for so many years.

Chapter 48

Two Years Later
May 2015

Since inheriting Izzy's house, we spent one weekend there every month as our getaway retreat. It was a great escape from the traffic and congestion of the DC suburbs. Greg and the boys wanted to take some of the trees down to have a better view of the river, but I was against the idea. I liked the privacy, the extra foliage that would block us from the neighbors across the way.

As much as I loved the house and getting away to Stevensonville, I wasn't sure if I wanted to keep it at first. It has been two years, and I still missed Izzy every time we went and would get upset thinking about him. Greg thought it would help to pack up some of Izzy's belongings, but I didn't want to change a thing. The photos of Diane still stood on the side table in the kitchen and hung on the wall leading to the bedrooms. The sofa in the living room, where he and Jack played *Undone*, remained with the same pillows and throw blankets. There was no reason to keep his clothing, though. I donated it all, except for his baseball cap, which my mom proudly displayed on the shelf in her foyer.

"I could get used to this," Greg said as we sat on the front porch on a late Saturday morning.

"So you want to say 'screw it all' and move here? What would you do?"

"Get a job at the university."

"You could teach civil engineering," I added.

"No way. I'd teach French like Izzy."

"You don't even know French," Jack said.

"Sure I do. Croissant. Escargot."

Jack rolled his eyes then bent down to pet Ginger's head. A couple of birds got her attention, and she opened one eye from her sleep. She was too frail to stand up and bark like she used to.

"Good girl," Jack said and petted her neck. She lifted her muzzle and placed it on his foot.

"All this talk about croissants is making me hungry," Greg added. "Let's go to Krista's?"

"Sure, why not." I got up to help Ginger in the house, grabbed my bag, and locked up.

The drive to Krista's with its winding roads always reminded me of the first time we met Izzy, how he pulled up to our car, and told us to follow him closely because of all the twists and turns. To help with the bittersweet memories, I'd load up on Krista's comfort food and Izzy's favorite lemon meringue pie.

We piled in the car and headed down the driveway. There were several neighbors in kayaks for their afternoon row. I looked back at the house as we drove away and watched the sun fall across the front stairs. Keeping up with the grass wouldn't be easy. Before long, it would be as high as little Evan, who not too long ago celebrated his eighth birthday. Or maybe it would grow as tall as Jack or even Jeremy. But certainly time, or rather the seasons, would tell.

"Hey, it's the Britain family," Krista said as we got to the hostess booth. "Just made some fresh pie for Jack."

"You knew I was coming?" he asked.

Krista pulled out a few menus from the stand. "Had a hunch." Krista added, winking at me, "Sorry, sweetheart, your usual table isn't available."

"It was Izzy's, not ours. Any table is fine by me."

"That, sweetheart, I can do." Krista walked us to the back as I smiled at the few men, the "regulars" as we used to call them, enjoying lunch while reading their newspapers without a care in the world.

By the time we finished lunch and drove back to the house, Sveta and Evan had arrived. Mom also came along for the milestone event and hitched a ride with Sveta. Jeremy's graduation ceremony was later in the afternoon, and no matter what we'd all be there to see it. After sophomore year, he switched to the University of Central Virginia, his first choice that rejected him when he applied in high school. After a couple years of Jeremy keeping up his grades, they found a spot for him in the engineering program.

Izzy's house was an hour from the campus and a perfect meeting point. We unlocked the front door and Evan ran up to hug Ginger. He stopped and looked before softly petting her back. She wagged her tail and licked his face. Evan had known Ginger for his entire life. I dreaded the day Ginger would no longer be with us, and I'd have to break the news. That kid, though, was smarter than any of us and would probably say something beyond his years, like she wanted to hang out with our first dog Bailey now.

"Guys, last chance to pee," I called out.

"Good heavens, darlin', a little discretion would be nice," my mom said.

"We're all family," I added before placing my bag on the hood.

As we piled into the SUV, Greg looked at me from the driver's seat and rubbed my arm, like he did the day we took Jeremy up to college his freshman year. If I looked too long, the tears would flow.

"Just think, Jack," I turned to face him. "In two short years you'll be off to college."

"I know, right? I'm planning to go to college in Sweden."

"Sweden? Why in heaven would you want to go there?" my mom asked.

"Because it's cool."

"It's cool here. At least in the winter," Evan said.

We all laughed. Evan, who wasn't so little anymore, was always right, so clever, so opinionated. He had everything figured out, like the time I dressed up as Ripsie for his birthday party.

"Hey," Greg called out. He wiggled the keys in his hand. "Want some practice?"

Jack, who turned sixteen recently, had his learner's permit. In a few months, he'd be able to get his license and drive on his own.

Jack jumped out of the car and went over to the driver's side. I opened the door, but Greg put his hand on mine to stop me. "Where do you think you're going?"

Greg moved to the backseat, and as we went down the driveway once again, as we had many times, I didn't gaze back at the house or trees that surrounded it. I looked over at Jack, who had both hands gripping the wheel.

When we hit a bump, the glove compartment opened. A tissue, probably the same one I used when we sent Jeremy off to college, wouldn't be needed. It was a happy moment, having my family together, aging together. When would there be another moment like this?

In the corner of the compartment, an old map of my hometown, a pencil with Ginger's bite marks, and a forgotten AshLynne Chocolate caught my eye. I grabbed the chewed-up pencil to show to Evan and put the uneaten truffle in a garbage bag resting near my leg.

Acknowledgements

Some authors say writing is a lonely profession. Watching the blinking cursor, staring out the window, waiting for the ideas to come. But, for me, writing has never been lonely. I've always had a dog or cat keeping my feet warm and my husband Evgeny close by asking, "Working on your book?"

It was Evgeny who, in 2013, encouraged me to get up, shake off previous publishing rejections, and start another book. From his support, *Among the Branded* was born and is now, my dear readers, in your hands. Thank you, Evgeny, for your endless love and support, and your belief in me and the words on these pages.

There are so many other people to thank:

Libby Tripp Cox, Marla Greif, Jennifer Schulman, and Jill Yager for reading early drafts, sometimes more than once. I've known you all for a very long time and thank my lucky stars for each of you.

My amazing editors Sharon Honeycutt and Nicole Tone for helping me whip this novel into shape.

My son Alek for his computer expertise and patience with correcting the "teenager" dialogue I read or texted to him.

My in-laws Mikhail and Galina for encouraging me to "go for it" and always asking when they could read my book.

Authors Edwin Fontánez, Laura Heffernan, and Allison Winn Scotch for giving me great advice along the way. Their guidance helped me realize there's no point in quitting when the going gets tough.

And my beloved parents. Although they're gone, they're with me in spirit.

About the Author

Linda Smolkin always wanted to be a writer—ever since she saw her first TV commercial and wondered how she could pen those clever ads. She got her degree in journalism and became a copywriter. She landed a job at an advertising agency, where she worked for several years before joining the nonprofit world. Linda lives in Virginia with her husband, son, and their 70-pound dog. *Among the Branded* is her debut novel.

Made in the USA
Middletown, DE
17 July 2017